"You can go in a minute," Boles told him. "This should only take a minute."

Max eyed the phantasmagoric farrago of indiscriminately interconnected electronics gear dubiously. "*What* should only take a minute?"

Boles glanced up briefly from his work. "Making contact with the world next to ours."

"Next to ours?" Max didn't bat an eye. He'd interviewed too many loony scientist/inventor types to be surprised by anything the affably chatty Boles had to say. "You mean, out in space?"

"No, no." Within the enclosed underground room both light and sound were magnified. "I mean *next to ours*. I am a great believer in the existence of parallel worlds, or paras, as I call them. Always have been. Over the past several years I have been constructing a device with which to prove my theories."

"Prove them, huh? Prove them how?" Max gazed yearningly at the doorway.

"By making actual contact with one. With this . . ."

By Alan Dean Foster
Published by Ballantine Books:

The Icerigger Trilogy
   ICERIGGER
   MISSION TO MOULOKIN
   THE DELUGE DRIVERS

The Adventures of Flinx of the Commonwealth
   FOR LOVE OF MOTHER-NOT
   THE TAR-AIYM KRANG
   ORPHAN STAR
   THE END OF THE MATTER
   BLOODHYPE
   FLINX IN FLUX
   MID-FLINX
   THE HOWLING STONES

The Damned
   Book One: A CALL TO ARMS
   Book Two: THE FALSE MIRROR
   Book Three: THE SPOILS OF WAR

THE BLACK HOLE
CACHALOT
DARK STAR
THE METROGNOME and Other Stories
MIDWORLD
NOR CRYSTAL TEARS
SENTENCED TO PRISM
SPLINTER OF THE MIND'S EYE
STAR TREK® LOGS ONE-TEN
VOYAGE TO THE CITY OF THE DEAD
. . . WHO NEEDS ENEMIES?
WITH FRIENDS LIKE THESE . . .
MAD AMOS
PARALLELITIES

PARALLELITIES

ALAN DEAN FOSTER

A Del Rey® Book
THE BALLANTINE PUBLISHING GROUP • NEW YORK

This book contains an excerpt from a forthcoming novel by Alan Dean Foster. This excerpt has been set for this edition only and may not reflect the final content of the forthcoming edition.

A Del Rey® Book
Published by The Ballantine Publishing Group
Copyright © 1998 by Thranx, Inc.
Excerpt copyright © 1998 by Alan Dean Foster.

http://www.randomhouse.com

Library of Congress Catalog Card Number: 98-92742

ISBN 0-345-42461-1

Manufactured in the United States of America

First Edition: October 1998

10 9 8 7 6 5 4 3 2 1

PARALLELITIES

I t was one of those special late June days that the Greater Los Angeles Area Chamber of Commerce tries to bronze and preserve for all eternity—as well as for the sake of civic advertising. Semitropically hot but not suffocating, multicolumnar traffic on the freeways actually free of vehicular stasis by nine o'clock in the morning, no major sigalerts, and the limpid turquoise sky brandishing a lovely pink tint thanks to a wispier-than-usual permeation of smog.

Other than in his highly restricted capacity as a civic-minded citizen, Maxwell Parker could not have cared less about the current condition of the metastasizing megalopolis's vaunted but frequently arteriosclerotic freeway system. As one of those fortunate folk who could commute from home to office on the overstressed but still highly preferable surface streets, he was immune to such vehicular concerns. All he had to do was drive the few blocks from his apartment building up to Lincoln Boulevard, cross the Santa Monica Freeway, turn right on Wilshire, and mosey his leisurely way up to Bundy Drive, occasionally shaking his head in empathetic but distanced wonder at the traffic reports that periodically interrupted the morning news.

He would have preferred keeping the Aurora's stereo set to one of L.A.'s innumerable small specialty FM music stations, but starting the day by listening to one of the several all-news channels was one way of getting a jump on work. After all, the news was his business. Or rather, a certain fringe element of it was. Max worked, unabashedly, in the journalistic freak zone. His job was to make the news—not read about it.

Scrupulously avoiding eye contact with the haggard homeless hawkers of makework newspapers who crowded the median on Lincoln and haunted the street signals at the freeway overpass, he turned up Wilshire Boulevard. Maneuvering skillfully around a shambling, shaggy, vaguely anthropoid figure fervently hoping to force his energies upon the Aurora's already speckless windshield, Max crossed Bundy and ducked smoothly down into the *Investigator*'s underground parking lot.

As a prolific, inventive reporter whose current status vacillated between junior stringer and respected craftsman, his status was sufficiently ambivalent to qualify him for a comparatively convenient parking space, but on the lower level.

Not only did he not mind having his car consigned to the concrete abyss, he preferred it. The deeper in the multilevel labyrinth one parked, the cooler one's car stayed during hot weather, and the less it was subject to the unwanted attentions of visiting delivery vehicles.

The modest but modern glass-sided high-rise was home to other enterprises besides the paper, from the ubiquitous law offices that migrated constantly in search of more prestigious addresses, to fledgling film producers unable to afford locations close to the studios, Beverly Hills, or the better parts of the San Fernando Valley.

The top six floors and most of the parking spaces belonged to the corporation that owned Max Parker's employer, the *International Investigator*. A youthful but energetic competitor of other weekly tabloids like the *Star*, and the *World*, the *Investigator* had carved out a niche for itself by emphasizing the newly grotesque as opposed to the traditionally bizarre. Its computer-generated graphics were lively, its layout fresh, its prose florid, its weekly quota of insupportable but nonlitigious accusations slyly incendiary. It was a paper on the way up, its circulation steadily increasing, and always on the lookout for enthusiastic, moldable, and generally unprincipled young talent.

Max considered himself lucky. Still only in his late twenties, he had already succeeded in dumping whatever ethics and integrity he might have once possessed in return for scads of filthy lucre and a modicum of fame within the field. Unlike some of his less fortunate coworkers, he had been blissfully free of scruples for several years, dating his freedom from the morning he had taken his carefully collected bonuses and used them to move from the dump he had been sharing with a hopeless would-be screenwriter and a short-order cook into a prime one-bedroom Santa Monica beach apartment. By the end of the first week he knew in his heart that the location and setting were worth any number of abstract moral principles.

He smiled to himself as the aged but still serviceable elevator carried him upward. The owners didn't have to put more than the minimum back into their hugely profitable old building. Given its location, people would have lined up to rent the small but cozy apartments if they had come without electricity, telephone, or running water.

The California summer sun was out and the UCLA coeds would soon be emerging from hibernation, shedding their heavy winter coats in favor of freshly molted thong and net swimsuits. Though it was still midweek, he was already looking forward to the weekend.

"Hey, Max!" Phil Hong was a hyper would-be movie reviewer who lived beyond his means by cadging loans from the gullible and uninformed, his relatives as well as his coworkers. Around the office he was known, not always affectionately, as Phil No-dough. Executing a feint to the left while accelerating to his right, Max put a move on the eager younger writer that, if he had been dribbling a basketball in a college game, would certainly have made the Monday-night-after highlight film on any local station.

"Sorry Phil—I'm late for the morning bull session. Talk to you later, man." Leaving a slightly bedazzled Hong gaping foolishly in his wake, Max lengthened his stride. He paused only long enough to say good morning to Calliope Charming, manufacturing idle small talk sufficient to gain him a decent gander at her estimable cleavage before moving on.

The not-quite-the-top-floor-but-the-people-who-met-there-were-still-considered-of-moderate-importance-to-the-success-of-the-business conference room boasted a long window with a pleasant, if not sweeping, view of the Santa Monica Mountains. The stunted chaparral that clung forlornly to those smog-swept slopes was barely visible through the increasingly turgid brown atmosphere. As the sun rose higher in the sky, the atmosphere heated up and the ozone gremlins awoke to their noxious toil. What had begun as a Chamber of Commerce day was rapidly becoming little more than a fading morning memory.

The room contained a long conference table; chairs fashioned of shiny, fine-grain plastic; insistently throbbing air-conditioning; and small green garbage cans that were already half full. He greeted his colleagues cheerily, swapping unforced insults and convivial small talk with the ease of long practice, before sliding into a chair and removing his laptop from its satchel. Hatcher (oh blissfully apropos moniker for a tabloid scribe!), who concentrated on sports-related scandals and turpitude, used pen and paper. So did the excessively slim but unmodelish Penelope Nearing. Their concession to tradition impressed no one.

The raucous chatter terminated when Kryzewski lumbered in and took the chair at the head of the table. It was as if a raven had somehow bought a ticket to a convocation of crickets. Not only at the offices of the *Investigator* but within the greater tabloid universe as a whole, Moe Kryzewski commanded a good deal of respect as well as admiration. In the elegiac prose of an esteemed contemporary, it wasn't so much that the senior editor knew shit from Shinola as the fact that during his more than thirty years in the business he had been consistently able to sell the former as the latter.

Flipping open the laptop, Max fingered a few keys. It was middle-of-the-line, six months old, and would be outdated in another three. At that time he would have to buy a new one. Not because the one he now owned was insufficient for his needs. In point of fact, a two-year-old edition of the same machine would have been more than adequate for the work he did. But it was important to keep up appearances. In the tabloid business the appearance of the writer didn't matter nearly as much as the appearance of his laptop.

After insuring that the requisite files had been brought up to where he could get at them quickly, he looked out into the respectful silence. Eager, venal expressions transfixed the faces of his colleagues. He was confident his own was no less.

"Well, what have you lazy pricks and prickesses got for me this morning? There's a weekend edition to fill and we ain't got shit to put into it. Longstreet!" Kryzewski barked.

The reporter in question looked up from her palmtop. Her delicate fingers were small enough to manipulate the tiny keys, and to minimize mistakes she had filed her nails down short as a longshoreman's. Around the office she was known as "Longstocking," as in Pippi.

"It's been a slow week, Moe. My boy in Florida tells me some cracker's hauled a six-legged gator out of the 'glades."

The editor snorted. In the old days he would have been filling the room with cigar smoke: carbonized essence of Havana. But this was contemporary Los Angeles. In his day Moe Kryzewski had battled crooked union bosses, corrupt cops, angry politicians, and homicidal movie stars, but not even he could stand against the nicotine police.

"Photo op, no story," he commented curtly. "Got anything else?"

Longstreet pursed her lips. "L'Elegace's new summer line for the ladies features soft transparent plastic tops over Vassarely-styled printed skirts and culottes."

"Angling for a trip to Paris?" Kryzewski grinned. "Sorry, Charlie. If readers can see naked French tits in *People*, why should they want to read about it in the *Investigator*?"

Longstreet looked crushed, but not to the point of giving

up. "There's a rumor going around that one of L'Elegace's senior models is supposedly sleeping with Anais Delours."

Kryzewski perked up. "Isn't she the one who's married to
Phillipe Boison, the director? The guy who makes all those in-
terminably boring flicks about French adolescents growing up,
and all that crap?"

Longstreet nodded. "It's just gossip going around."

"Gossip my prostate! Get on it. When you've got the
story done let me know and I'll tell Travel to cut you a ticket.
To 'verify sources.' And you'd better do some work this time
instead of hanging out in Montmartre trying to pick up the
overage graduate students who drift over from the Sorbonne."

Longstreet mustered as much indignation as she could
manage. "I do not pick up college boys." Her mouth subsided
into a fey smile. "They pick me up."

"Whatever. Just pin a source or two to the board. I want it
by next week."

The session continued in that vein, the writers laying out
their respective story ideas, the majority of which were immediately shot down by Kryzewski. Too old, too thin, not involving
enough, insufficiently provocative, hard news, too expensive to
research, inadequate glamour, no buzz—Kryzewski could kill a
story with a cocked eye. Though everyone at the table was open
to all possibilities, each writer tended to specialize in one area,
from sports to entertainment, crime to consumer goods, politics
and politicians to miracles and popular music.

Having been dragged kicking and screaming through several science courses while he was at university, and having been injudicious enough to commit this fact to print in the form of a line in his résumé, Max had been assigned to the wonderful world of weird science by default. Faced with a fait accompli and no accomplices to pass it off on, he had chosen to accept the appointment and run with it—or at least hobble. The result had been some singularly notable stories whose popularity with the paper's readers had surprised and delighted everyone from himself on up.

In his skilled hands a report that started out as a straight piece on the CERN collider in Switzerland would end up informing readers not that a new subatomic particle had been discovered, but that gremlins had sabotaged the apparatus to prevent physicists from opening a door to Hell, or that bosons and mesons were really different species of elves moving at high speed, which was why humans could not see them unless they chose of their own accord to slow down—or could be trapped in the accelerator.

From a reporter's standpoint it was reassuring to be able to turn in stories knowing that nearly one hundred percent of those who read them understood absolutely nothing about their scientific underpinnings. Max preached bullshit to the ignorant, who were ever ready to accept the outrageous as gospel provided it was described in words of more than three syllables. Wasn't that, after all, what science was all about, and didn't folks know what was really going on in this country, and wasn't it his, Max Parker's, job to tell them the real truth? As opposed to the fake truth, which was usually embodied in unreadable, incomprehensible government reports?

When the piercing glare of the senior editor finally focused on him, he was ready. The screen of his laptop glowed with multitudinous absurdities, any one of which he was ready to promulgate as the absolute truth to a gullible public. The people wanted to know, and the *Investigator* was ready to tell them. So was Maxwell Parker.

"Evan Thibodeux of Avery Island, Louisiana, has caught a mermaid."

Kryzewski rolled his eyes. "Pictures?"

"Not yet." Max smiled confidently. "Binky Chavez, our photo stringer out of Houston, is going to check it out and get back to me some time tonight or tomorrow. If the photos are usable I figure it's worth at least half a page."

Kryzewski nodded approvingly. "We'll make 'em usable. That's what computer photo touch-up programs are for." He looked momentarily wistful. "Wish we'd had a couple of those around in the old days. Half a page, you got it. We haven't had a good mermaid story in years."

Farther down the table, Stu Applewood piped up. "Wonder if anybody's got a Cajun recipe for blackened mermaid?"

"Oy, that's good!" added Brick the Brit from his chair. "Maybe it's a black mermaid. Then we could run a recipe for blackened black mermaid."

"The Japanese would do her as sushi," put in Deva Singhwar. "The Japanese will eat anything."

"Full page, maybe." Kryzewski was clearly warming to the story's potential for exploitation. "Half for the story, half on how unscrupulous chefs around the world have been serving mermaid to unsuspecting customers for years, and passing it off as shark." The editor was almost enthusiastic, a rare state of being. Beneath the envious stares of his associates, Parker swelled with a sense of accomplishment. "What else you got for me, Max?"

Parker searched his "new" file. "Truck farmer in South Jersey claims to be able to grow tomatoes with the face of Jesus on them."

"Great." Dyan Jefferson had just had her tres chic rows done by a hairstylist recently immigrated from Windhoek, Namibia, who week after week brought forth for the edification of all who might gaze upon his favorite client yet another new and wondrous prodigy of coiffure. "People will be able to slather their dead cow burgers with holy ketchup instead of holy water."

Jefferson was a notoriously militant vegetarian. It exposed her to a certain amount of ridicule around the office, which she handled with aplomb. And the occasional a-punch.

Ignoring the chuckles and wisecracks, Kryzewski wrestled briefly with the proposal before giving it the thumbs-down. "Can't use it, Max. But don't throw it away, file it. Two weeks ago we had the face of Jesus in the oak tree in South Carolina, and the week before that it was the Polaroid from New Mexico. The *Star* just did a story about a crucifix in Guadeloupe weeping real tears, and there was something out of Italy about a month ago on blood liquefaction." He scratched at his chin. "It's too soon for your take. Christ's a little overexposed right now."

Max melodramatically pushed the Save button. "It's filed, Moe."

"Fine. What else you got?"

Parker considered the screen. "A local source I've used before told me yesterday that there's a Mary Collins in Toluca Lake who's convinced she's found a medium capable of contacting and conversing with her dead son." He looked up from the laptop. "Cost me, but I got her address. The medium's supposed to show this afternoon." He checked his watch. "Three o'clock."

Kryzewski nodded brusquely. "So what are you doing here? Get out to the Valley, find the place, and invite yourself in. I don't have to tell you how." He waved indifferently. "Position yourself as a distant cousin who's heard about the contact, as a psychic investigator—whatever the situation requires."

Max nodded. "Pictures?"

The editor shrugged. "Psychic sessions usually don't make for good photo ops. All mumbling and no action. But take a Minox along. If the light's not too bad you might get a good shot of the weepy mom."

"I'd rather interview the mermaid catcher."

Kryzewski was conciliatory. "Let's wait and see what we can do with the photos. Meanwhile, you can do something on Mom and the medium this afternoon. Oh, and I've got something for you." He scrolled his own laptop. "Receive."

Max turned the right end of his machine toward the head of the table. A moment later, the infrared information transfer was complete. He studied the new file.

"What's this?"

Kryzewski made a face. He was a master of the disgusted expression and utilized them with the profligacy of a true connoisseur. "You can read it later. It's a lead on some nut in North Malibu. But a nut with money. Monied nuts are always worth a column or two. From what I see the angle is right up your alley." Summarily dismissing Max, he turned back to Jefferson. "Now what have you been able to come up with on that Philippine 'spiritual surgeon' working out of Miami? That's right in our competitors' backyard. Be great to steal a nice, juicy story right out from under them."

Max tuned out much of the rest of the brainstorming session. As usual, Kryzewski was pleased with his work, and that was all that mattered. The approbation of his colleagues he could not care less about.

After making a cursory check of his desktop, fax, and in-file, he left the building and headed north. Taking the not-too-bad San Diego to the could-have-been-worse Ventura, he exited on Buena Vista Drive, having to prowl around a few back streets before he located the address that had been provided by his source.

The house was substantial, a sixties-era dichondra-fronted pseudo-ranch wood and brick sprawl in a nice old heavily treed neighborhood. It bespoke a solid upper-middle-class income—or a substantial inheritance. Parking on the street, he set the Aurora's alarm and made his way to the gate in the waist-high chain-link fence. It was unlocked. A winding path of cobbled stepping-stones led past neatly trimmed rosebushes and explosively beautiful rhododendrons flush with California sun and imported Sierra water. A late-model blue Lexus and an older black-and-silver Mercedes were parked in the driveway.

At his touch the bell chimed and the door reluctantly opened half a foot, to reveal a gold-hued safety chain and the uncertain face of a diminutive but not unattractive woman in her mid-forties.

"Yes—can I help you?"

"Mrs. Collins?" Max employed his most boyishly sympathetic voice: sincere, with a touch of helplessness. "Mrs. Mary Beatrice Collins?"

"That's me, yes." Her expression squinched to match her tone. "Do I know you?"

"No, ma'am. I'm a reporter for a magazine called the *Skeptical Enquirer*. Maybe you've heard of us?"

"I'm afraid not, Mr. . . . ?"

"Crowley, ma'am. Al Crowley. I hope you don't mind my just dropping in on you like this, but our sources have reported to us that you have actually managed to make contact with your unfortunately recently deceased loved one and . . ."

The door started to close. "Go away, please. I have company and . . ."

Max spoke quickly in hopes of keeping the door from closing. "Please, Mrs. Collins! Our magazine specializes in exposing the fraudulent and deceptive who prey on grieving individuals such as yourself. When something wonderful happens for real, as has apparently happened to you, we desperately want to share it with our readers." He tried to see past her, but the front curtains were closed and the room beyond the entry hall only dimly lit.

The door slowed, motherly incertitude playing across the face of the woman within. "You . . . you're not from one of those awful tabloid newspapers, the kind you see at all the supermarket checkout stands?"

Max was properly aghast. "Absolutely not, Mrs. Collins! The *Skeptical Enquirer* prides itself on the objectivity and fairness of its reports. I am here at the behest of another to do my best to validate whatever experience you believe you have been having. At," he hastened to add, "no charge. And of course nothing will appear in print without your express consent and signed permission."

"Well . . ." What she feared wrestled with what she had been told. "It might be nice to have an expert present. I don't see how it could hurt anything."

"Nothing whatsoever, Mrs. Collins. I promise only to observe and not to interfere with the proceedings in any way. Surely you can sympathize with the need to insure scientific accuracy in such matters, and to promote the truth of such a remarkable assertion?"

"Yes, yes." Whether convinced of the veracity of his claim or too tired to argue he could not say, but she conceded, and a hand reached up to unfasten the security chain. "Please come in, Mr. Crowley."

The house was upper-class San Fernando Valley, as old and comfortable as a favorite easy chair. Family portraits lined the hallway wall, and the furniture was relentlessly ranch contemporary. She led him through the living room, past the homey kitchen, and into a sunken den located at the back of the house. The drapes there had been closed tight and secured in the middle with clothespins to block out as much of the light as possible.

In the center of the room, facing a large fireplace of distressed brick, was a round oak table encircled by four matching chairs. It was original oak, Max saw as he stepped down into the room, and not one of those veneered and laminated mass-produced reproductions. A simple silver candlestick stood in the center of the table, the tall white taper it held flickering energetically. Its light was barely sufficient to cast shadows in the darkened room.

In a tall chair on the far side of the table, her back to the fireplace, sat a voluptuous woman who might have been thirty-five—or ten years older. Given the subdued light and aggravated makeup, it was hard to tell. She wore a simple silk dress emblazoned with flowers, an entire thrift store's supply of cheap copper and silver bangles, and a silk scarf over her long hair. Her eyes refocused from something off in the distance to acknowledge the arrival of hostess and guest. The start of recognition Max experienced on seeing her face when her eyes came up was instantly reciprocated.

Their fidgety, anxious host performed introductions. "Madame Tarashikov, this is Mr. Al Crowley, from the *Skeptical Enquirer* magazine. Mr. Crowley, Madame Tarashikov."

With great deliberation, Max walked over and lifted the woman's hand off the table, kissing the back of it firmly. "Madame Tarashikov, it's always a pleasure to meet a true master of the otherworldly."

The kindly Mrs. Collins was taken aback. "You—you know Madame Tarashikov?"

"I know of her. She has quite a reputation." What sort of reputation he was not about to say.

Madame Tarashikov, alias Ms. Billie Joe Heppleworth, originally of Topeka, Kansas, but late of Beverly Hills, California, and points equally transcendental, relaxed as soon as she saw that her visitor was not going to expose her. Greatly relieved, she turned solemnly to their hostess. Her accent was distinctively Midwestern. Midwestern East Europe.

"Ve should begin as zoon as possible, Mrs. Collins. I discern that the auguries are propitious, and ve dare not vaste time."

"Yes, yes, of course! I'll be right back." Their breathless hostess vanished in the direction of the kitchen.

As soon as she was out of the room, Max leaned forward in his chair. "So now you're a genuine, gosh-darn-for-real medium, hmmm? Okay, I keep an open mind and I'm always willing to be convinced. Let's hear you spell 'propitious.' "

Heppleworth-Tarashikov raised a hand to shush him. "Shut the fuck up, Maxwell! I've got a real thing going here." Straining to see past him, she glanced nervously toward the doorway that led to the rest of the house. "How'd you know I was here?"

"I didn't." He sat back in the hard wooden chair. "One of my sources just fed me this story about a dead kid's mom and a medium. I had no idea it was you until I walked into the room."

Madame H-T sighed resignedly. "All right, what do you want? How much? For a change, I can afford it." She jerked a finger in the direction of the distant, unseen kitchen. "The old broad's the best mark I've hit on in six months. Got real money. Her late husband left her plenty."

"So she's lost her husband and her son." Max was making

notes as they talked. He looked up from the pad and grinned thinly. "You really are an unscrupulous bitch, Billie."

She sniffed, unperturbed and unimpressed. "And who the fuck are you—Walter Cronkite? What do you want?"

"How about a date?" He leered openly at the tight dress.

"I'd rather cough up a kickback. Besides, I'm too experienced and too much for you, Max my boy. You wouldn't survive." But she returned his slippery smile. "It's the story you want, isn't it? Just leave it to me. I'll pour it on like molasses. You'll get a good one."

"You read my mind. How appropriate." Anxious footsteps signaled the return of their hostess, and he lowered his voice. "But I'd still like that date."

Her smile widened, her tone a blend of disgust and admiration. "The Fates do not foretell it in your future, you nasty little shit."

He chuckled. "Well, that's sure as hell proof of nothing."

They adopted an air of mock solemnity as Mrs. Collins returned.

The séance itself was very straightforward and convincing. The room was not adulterated with hackneyed howling, nor did the curtains blow forcefully inward, but at Tarashikov's invocation the single candlestick levitated impressively, hovering above the center of the table while bobbing slightly. Their thoroughly enthralled hostess uttered a squeal of delight when a deep male voice seemed to emanate from the vicinity of the flame.

There followed a five-minute question-and-answer-session during which Tarashikov prompted appropriate queries from the tearful Mrs. Collins while the flame supplied sufficiently nebulous answers. The blatant absence of definitude, so transparent to an uninvolved outsider, made no difference. By the end of the encounter, at which time Tarashikov pronounced the relevant spirits "exhausted," their hostess had her head in her hands and was bawling unashamedly, convinced she had just spent five minutes conversing with her recently deceased son. Max could not make out the figure on the check that Collins handed the medium, but from the half smile that made Tarashikov's face twitch he knew it must be more than adequate.

"And you, Mr. Crowley." Collins wiped the crust of dried tears from her cheeks with a cotton handkerchief. "What do you have to say about what you have just seen and heard? What will you write in your *Skeptical* magazine now?"

Glancing over at Tarashikov, he saw her watching him closely, trying hard not to appear too interested. It was a struggle, but he kept a straight face as he replied.

"A most impressive demonstration, Mrs. Collins. It certainly gives one something to think about. Why, if I were in your position I would take every opportunity to utilize the extraordinary talents of Ms. Tarashikov to the fullest. Cabalistic perception like hers doesn't come along very often. In fact, I'm not sure I've ever seen anything quite like it before." On the other side of the table, the comely medium smiled softly as she expertly snuffed the candle.

"You can be assured that I will. Skeptics!" Haughty, dignified, and flush with success, their hostess escorted both of them to the door.

"Same time next week then, Mrs. Collins?" Tarashikov's faux empathetic smile bordered on the artlessly predatory.

"Of course, Madame." Her face was shining, her enthusiasm unbounded. "To be able to hear my dear Eric again, after the accident . . ." Choked, she took the medium's free hand in both of hers and squeezed thankfully.

Tarashikov gently but firmly disengaged her fingers. "Rest assured that I am at your service, Mrs. Collins. And if I am not available because I am helping another poor soul in distress, please do not forget to fax me, or leave a message with my answering service."

A last parting handshake and they fled the house and its tearful but satisfied owner. Max escorted the medium to her parked car, enjoying the sway of her hips as they walked the short distance together.

"You need an answering service? I thought the spirits would take messages for you."

She snorted derisively. "Sometimes even the spirits refuse to work overtime. On such occasions a little technological supplementation may be called for." Grabbing his shoulder, she squeezed hard, the nails digging slightly into his flesh. "Thanks for backing me up in there."

He shrugged. "Hey, if it works out I might get a small continuing series out of this."

She leaned close and whispered. "You might also, as you said, get 'the opportunity to utilize the extraordinary talents of Ms. Tarashikov to the fullest.' "

He eyed her in surprise, then smiled broadly. "I've got a candlestick of my own you can manipulate. Speaking of which"—he indicated the one that was poking out of the oversized handbag she was carrying—"how'd you manage the levitation? That was well done. I didn't see any wires."

"There aren't any wires. I told you, there are times when a little technology is in order. Even a professional medium needs to keep abreast of the latest developments." Pulling out the candlestick, she upended it to show him where the base was screwed tight to the shaft.

"There's a small but powerful magnet inside and a bigger battery-powered electromagnet in my purse."

"Which was under the table," he filled in.

"Right. This ring," and she indicated one of the many bulky rings that decorated her long fingers, "holds the on-off switch. Makes it easy to raise and lower the candlestick. These new magnets are very precise. You can really keep control."

"That's fresh. How about the dead kid's voice?"

"Tiny speaker inside the top of the candlestick." They were approaching her fittingly sepulchral Mercedes and she nodded in its direction. "George, my assistant, is in the trunk. Don't worry—he's in there with air-conditioning and a cooler of cold drinks in addition to the base unit for the candlestick.

Staying in the trunk keeps him out of sight and forestalls any awkward questions from the mark . . . from the customer. We found out by accident that it also adds a nice reverb to the voice. George is very versatile. If the spirit I'm contacting is female, he does a nice falsetto." Her smile widened. "There are a lot of unemployed actors in this town. If George moves on to bigger and better things, I can always find a replacement."

"And the questions and answers are kept general enough to satisfy the suckers," he said.

"Please." She eyed him distastefully. "The bereaved supplicants. That's been standard operating procedure in the business for hundreds of years." She disengaged the Mercedes' alarm and opened the driver's-side door. The thick, heady aroma of new-car leather drifted out.

"And it doesn't bother you that you're preying on the susceptibilities of ordinary people who are drowning in their own misery?"

She all but laughed out loud. "That's pretty funny, coming from someone who works for the vampire rag you do. I've always felt that if they're stupid enough to fall for this old-fashioned traditional hokum, then if I don't take their money someone else will. Besides, I give great séance and my clients always feel better afterward. That's more than you can say for anyone unfortunate enough to be the subject of one of your scabrous stories. I like to think of what I do as therapy." She squeezed his hand. "Give me a call, Max. I owe you a session."

Favoring him with a last, appreciative smile, she turned and slipped behind the wheel.

He nodded agreeably. "You bet I will. I've got one hell of a spirit you can call up."

Waving a final farewell, he followed the Mercedes with his eyes as it backed out of the driveway and turned south. A glance at the sky showed that it was getting late. Time to head back home. As for the story itself, there was plenty of time to do that. He could type it up after dinner. It wouldn't take long, and he could add suitable embellishments in the morning, before heading out to follow up on Kryzewski's tip.

On the other hand, he mused as he walked back to his own car, if he could do the follow-up tonight it would save him a drive tomorrow. That would allow him to do both stories in the morning and then take the afternoon off. Not far beyond the front window of his apartment, the beach beckoned. The cool Pacific and the first scantily clad sand bunnies of the season were calling to him.

The true nutcases were often the most accessible, the most eager to discuss their obsessions. From the notes Kryzewski had supplied, this Barrington Boles character certainly sounded as if he qualified. If he could get in to see him tonight, Max thought, and get enough notes to put together a story, then he would not have to deal with him tomorrow.

He was already out in the Valley. If he could find a halfway quiet coffee shop he could rough out the Boy-Killed-in-Car-Crash-Speaks-to-Bereaved-Mom story while he was having dinner. Then shoot out to Malibu after rush hour and do the Boles interview, polish both in the morning, and take the rest of the day off. Maybe two, if the Boles lead turned out to be really worthwhile.

Feeling very good about himself, he slid into the Aurora, started the engine, and headed off in search of sustenance and silence.

II

Having previously written several dozen stories of the medium-contacts-dead-loved-one variety, he had no difficulty embroidering the encounter he had just witnessed to the point where it was sufficiently florid and outrageous to fit the needs of the *Investigator*. The plebeians who purchased the paper as they waited in line for their groceries to be scanned and totaled lapped up this sort of saccharine pabulum like mother's milk. It fed their need to believe in everything from maternal love to a kind and beneficent afterlife.

Disdaining fast food, he settled on a neighborhood coffee shop where the fries arrived cold but the hamburger wasn't half bad. He wolfed them down in between bites of the sprout-addled salad. Not everyone in Southern California, he reflected as he idly scanned the rest of the menu, was happy to subsist on tofu and sushi.

Satisfied with the preliminary draft of the story, he made sure it was saved to the laptop's hard drive before packing up, paying, leaving the absolute minimal tip that would not have the waitress chasing after him with a butcher knife, and returning to his car. It had been quite a while since he'd driven to Malibu the back way. Since he might be arriving at Boles's address in the dark, he wanted to be sure not to miss any of the right turnoffs.

Malibu Canyon Road wound its way through dry mountains spotted with pockets of chaparral forest and million-dollar homes, the latter expensive retreats from the insanity of the city. The venerable road connected the San Fernando Valley with the Pacific Coast Highway. Once there, he turned north, grateful for the lack of traffic, the Pacific on his left and an unblinking diadem of lights pointing the way to points north.

Boles's place lay atop a ridge well back of Trancas Beach, at the very end of a convoluted, unhappy stretch of one-lane road. Max had no trouble with the guard at the gatehouse where the road met the highway. He'd been dealing with such people for several years and had learned that where bullshit failed, folding currency usually succeeded. Besides, he carried legitimate press credentials that were easily checked and his demeanor was clearly different from that of the average Southern California maniacal fan or mad bomber.

The house was big (there were no small houses in this part of Southern California, unless one made allowance for separate servants' quarters) but by no means overbearing. A two-story contemporary Mediterranean, it faced the Pacific and looked down upon the more extravagant homes below. Its stuccoed turrets and red tile roof were subdued compared with the grandiose architectural fantasies that marched in million-dollar rows down the hillside toward the coastline. Soft light from within illuminated several windows. He pulled into the circular drive that fronted the main entrance and, without any directives to the contrary, parked.

A small, clean Toyota stood between him and the main house. Its engine idled uncertainly, stressed by the burden of the air-conditioner. The short, stout woman loading something into the trunk looked up as he walked over. She was Hispanic but not Mexican, he saw. Probably an economic refugee from Nicaragua or Honduras. L.A. had seen a jump in the number of immigrating Hondurans recently. Her English was surprisingly lightly accented.

"May I help you, sir? I am Azulita, Señor Boles's house-keeper. I was just leaving for the night." Wary and protective, dark black eyes sized him up.

Max looked past her, at the house. "Mr. Boles doesn't have a live-in?"

"No, sir." She walked around from the back of the car and opened the driver's-side door. "I asked him that myself, when I started to work for him. He says he likes to be alone at night." She glanced up at the house. "Myself, I am glad. I would not want to stay here at night."

"Really? Why not?" Max's mental recorder was already humming.

"Too many funny noises." She crossed herself.

"You don't say? What kind of funny noises?"

She slipped behind the wheel. "If you stay, maybe you will hear them for yourself. I have to go." She closed the door and reached for the key.

"Wait a minute!" He leaned close. "Do you think Mr. Boles will see me? I don't have an appointment."

She studied him silently for a moment, then smiled. "I don't see why not. He is a very friendly man, Señor Boles. He likes people. But people treat him badly, I think. I have heard him talking, and sometimes his visitors laugh at him." Her expression turned earnest. "You are not here to laugh at him, are you?"

"Hey, not me. I promise." *At least, I won't laugh at him in person*, he added silently. *Print's another matter*.

The old compact coughed a couple of times before settling into gear. He followed its progress as it hummed down the driveway and out onto the main access road, a small metallic blue beetle disappearing into the gathering night. Then he turned and walked over the interlocking red paving bricks and up the concrete stoop to the front door. It was a plain, ordinary house door, not one of the garish amalgams of rare wood and stained glass—designed to intimidate visitors—that were so commonly encountered in the Brahman environs of power-conscious Los Angeles, where even the styling and construction of a front door were often construed as a sign of status.

Similarly, the doorbell did not play Beethoven, tell jokes, or attempt an imitation of Big Ben on New Year's Eve. Its chime was ingenuously normal.

The man who opened the door was in his late fifties but remarkably fit. He wore Nikes, bright baggy multicolored weight lifter's sweatpants, and a wrinkled T-shirt two sizes too big with the legend Keetmanshoop Hotel on it above a black-and-white drawing of a gemsbok at rest. Cut fashionably short, his gray-blond hair gave him the look of a retired Marine. From a slim gold chain around his neck dangled a gold charm in the shape of a bar code. The watch on his right wrist was a hard plastic multifunction Casio; nice, but hardly a Rolex or Patek Phillipe. Thick gray chest hair shoved its way out of the V neck of the tee, and more hair bristled on his exposed arms. He was six feet or so, muscular from years of chucking iron in the gym. Probably Boles's bodyguard or senior manservant, Max decided.

"Good evening. I'm looking for Barrington Boles." Straining to see past the doorman, Max made out a normal-looking hallway. No skeletons hanging from the rafters, no cross-reflecting mirrors, no probing laser beams; just a few shelves lined with expensive but unpretentious objets d'art. Too bad. He'd been hoping for an immediate dose of weirdness.

The man promptly extended a hand. "Pleasure to meet you, young man."

While his brain struggled to catch up, Max's hand reacted instinctively and took the older man's. In keeping with the rest of the tanned physique, the grip was powerful, but re-strained. "You're Barrington Boles? I expected . . ."

The older man grinned as he cut him off. "Someone much older? Or a clone of Christopher Lloyd's Doc character from the *Back to the Future* movies? Somebody with wild eyes, frizzing hair, and a colorfully stained white lab coat?"

"Yeah, that would be about right," Max replied, deciding to take a chance. "Your standard clichéd garden-variety-issue mad scientist."

The welcoming hand withdrew. The skin on the back was wrinkled from long hours spent immersed in seawater. "Sorry to disappoint you. I'm neither mad, nor a scientist. And my taste in lab clothing runs more to shorts and tank tops." He beckoned as he stepped aside. "Won't you come in, Mr. . . . ?"

"Parker. Maxwell." As he entered, Boles shut the door behind them. Though it smelled of money, the house felt far more normal than Max had anticipated, based on what he'd been told. The initial edginess he tended to feel when entering the lair of the presumably deranged was rapidly slipping away.

"Nice to meet you, Max." Boles guided his visitor into a spacious den dominated by redwood burl furniture, the kind that tended to swallow you when you sat down in a couch or chair fashioned from the stuff. An entertainment center with large-screen TV was built into the wall off to the left, while cathedral-sized picture windows directly opposite provided a view of the now dark coast and the immeasurable blackness of ocean beyond. The other walls were lined with built-in book-shelves. All of these were filled, in some cases to overflowing. Dominating the Mexican tile floor were several large, elaborate Persian rugs of estimable vintage and, even to Max's untrained eye, considerable value, and a startling coffee table that consisted of a thick slab of glass mounted atop the shiny brown skull of an allosaurus. Max gestured as he sat down across from it.

"That's one of those cast-resin reproductions, isn't it?"

Displaying an utter lack of pretension, his host flopped into the chair opposite and shook his head, grinning proudly. "Nope. It's an original. From Colorado. Nice, isn't it?"

"An original, huh? Okay, I'm impressed." So that Boles could see what he was doing, he made a show of removing his recorder from his shirt pocket, but did not turn it on. "It's pretty late in the day for this sort of thing, and I'm sure your time is as precious to you as mine is to me, so I won't mince words with you, Mr. Boles."

"Please. Just call me Barry." His host's smile was as ingratiating as that of a head waiter at a trendy Japanese restaurant.

"Okay—Barry." Max refused to be drawn in or disarmed by his host's evident charm. It was much too soon in their relationship to take a liking to the man. "I'm a junior science reporter for the *L.A. Times* and I . . ."

"No you're not," Boles declared with his irrepressible good humor intact. It was the second time his host had interrupted him. "The *Times* would have called before sending somebody out. Besides, I've already had a couple of their people here. A writer and a photographer." The smile diminished slightly. "We didn't get along."

Max was not in the least nonplussed, switching conversational gears as easily as his Aurora. "I thought you might see through that. It's just that it sounds more impressive if you say you're from the *Times* instead of from the *Orange County Register*. Or the *Free Press*." His follow-up grin was only half forced. "Saying that you're the science columnist for the *Free Press* doesn't carry much weight at, say, JPL."

Boles crossed one leg over the other, cocked his head sideways, and rested chin and cheek against one hand as he studied his guest. "You're not from the *Register*, either. Or the *Free Press*, or the *Valley Times*, or the *San Bernadino Sun*, or any standard Southern California paper. I like you, Max, but don't try my patience or insult my intelligence or this meeting will be a short one. Now, who do you represent? Really?"

Max debated whether to confess he was a freelancer in search of a good story or a stringer for Reuters. The latter claim was sufficiently impressive and obscure enough to deceive most potential interviewees. But the longer he considered his subject the more he found himself thinking that there was more to Boles than there was to the usual fruitcake with a wild idea. The man had let him into his house without an appointment and had so far treated him in a fair and courteous manner. Why not try something different from the usual endless loop of subterfuges for a change and respond in kind? He took a deep breath.

"Barry, I'm a reporter for the *International Investigator*."

Boles nodded and looked satisfied. "There now, doesn't that feel better? You want to interview me, do you?"

"Very much so. Are you familiar with the *Investigator?*"

His host nodded once. "I've seen it around."

Max kept his tone casual. "And the thought of being reported in it doesn't bother you?"

Boles squirmed slightly, straightening in his chair. "Max, I've dealt with reporters from every legitimate newspaper and magazine in the country as well as a number from overseas. Not to mention writers for various documentary series, assorted sensationalist television shows, and a goodly number of respected and not-so-respected scientific journals. I doubt that you can treat me any worse than they have.

"Besides, your paper deals in exposure as opposed to truth, and exposure is what I need now. Given sufficient exposure, the truth will follow of its own accord. What I don't wish to be is ignored. It just so happens you have arrived at a propitious time. I'll see to it that you get your story, and you will reciprocate by providing me with national exposure. Handed that, people can make up their own minds." He nodded at the recorder. "By the way, I don't mind that you're recording this."

Max looked down at the compact device in mock surprise. "Oh, sorry. I guess I must have turned this on while we were talking." He smiled wanly. "Reflex action. I meant to ask you if it was all right."

Boles's grin returned. "No you didn't, but it's okay. I *want* our meeting recorded. Like everyone else on the planet I am at least passingly familiar with the tabloid style. I know that you probably intended from the start to embellish the consequences of this interview, but that doesn't bother me either. After what I have to show you, you'll find it won't be necessary."

Ignoring his host's observation, Max pressed on with a question. "I'm a little confused by something you said earlier. I was told by my source that you held some kind of radical scientific theories. But you say you're not a scientist."

"That's right. I don't have the patience for theoretical work. I'm more of an inventor. A scientist would care deeply *why* something works. I just care that it works."

"That what works?" Max's gaze kept straying to the vacant eye sockets of the fossilized theropod skull. It seemed to be staring back at him. Four-inch-long scimitar-like teeth wore dark stains. The colors of random mineralization, he told himself. Not blood. He found himself struggling to avoid looking at the coffee table. It persisted in looking back, across the floor as well as across the eons.

Boles rose abruptly from his chair, his own eyes bright and alert. "My new dragon board, for one thing. But you didn't come out here to go night surfing." He turned to his right and winked. "Come with me and I'll show you something. As I said, you've chosen a propitious time to pay a visit."

Max stood, holding the recorder out in front of him as he followed his enthusiastic host through a portal and down a hall lined with costly, beautifully framed signed and numbered prints of sea life and African big cats.

"So you think it's all right to share your secrets with me?"

Boles looked back over his shoulder. "You had enough imagination to get past the road guard without an appointment. Anyone without imagination isn't ready for what I'm about to show you."

They halted at the end of the hall and Max waited while Boles unlocked a door. A door, he noted, that had been fashioned from heavy steel. Recalling the maid's comment about strange noises, he hesitated. Boles talked and acted as straight as a county lifeguard. But then, Hannibal Lecter had been a practicing psychiatrist.

He wasn't reassured when the open doorway revealed stairs leading down into darkness. "A basement? You've got a basement? In Southern California?"

"It's an architectural anomaly I'm rather proud of." Boles started down. "Please close the door behind you."

Uh-huh. Max lingered at the top of the stairs. The hallway, the invitingly open den that now lay some distance behind him, and his car all beckoned. But there was no story in any of them. Any story lay ahead, and down. With a shrug he pulled the massive door shut behind him, surprised at how well balanced it was and how easily it moved. In his young career he'd already found himself in much worse places and confronted by far more candidly unstable types. He felt confident he could deal with any surprises Barrington Boles might spring.

Well, reasonably confident.

The basement was enormous, much more extensive than he had expected. Relieved to see that it was not done up in contemporary dungeon, he allowed his initial wariness to give way to something like reluctant astonishment. His feeling that he had made the right choice was enhanced, if not completely confirmed, by the numerous diplomas and awards, all seemingly genuine, that decorated the wall immediately on his right.

Brightly lit by ranks of overhead fluorescents built into the twenty-foot-high ceiling, the single room was immaculately clean, so much so that it reminded him of the production rooms he had once visited while touring the plant of a major microprocessor manufacturer. Every device, every instrument, was as spotless as if it had just been unpacked from the original shipping materials.

Everything appeared to be interconnected. Possessing the scientific sophistication of the average educated American, he recognized absolutely none of it. The impressive aggregation of gear was dominated by a fifteen-foot-tall arch in the center of the room. Fashioned of some silvery metal, it hung heavy with coils, cables, and a fuzz of fine filaments that would have done an alien spider proud.

Something snapped and he looked around sharply. Ignoring

his guest, Boles was busy at a half-moon-shaped console, flipping switches and thumbing buttons. In sections, the impressive interconnected confabulation began to come alive. There was a sufficient surfeit of colored lights to put to shame the best outdoor Christmas display in Beverly Hills. No nomadic bolts of lightning, though, and no explosive bursts of elegiac electricity. Quite frankly, Max had seen better special effects in half a dozen recent films. The requisite slobbering, hunchbacked assistant with the terse Slavic name was missing as well. And Barrington Boles's casual beach attire ruined any covert Gothic atmosphere completely.

"I'm sorry, Barry, but I have to tell you: You don't look the part at all." Max had to raise his voice slightly to make himself heard above the rising electronic thrum of the machinery.

Boles responded with a boyish, slightly lopsided grin. "Sorry. I spend most of my time in sweats and tees. I don't even own a white lab coat." He returned to his work.

Max wandered over to watch, but the energized instrumentation that filled the underground chamber was much more interesting than his host's methodical pushing of buttons and monitoring of readouts. Since he had not been ordered or instructed to do otherwise, he wandered freely, examining different bits and pieces of equipment, careful to touch nothing. It all looked brand-new and very expensive. He did not have a clue what it was for or what it was supposed to do, nor could he have offered even an educated guess, and the busy Boles was not being very forthcoming. Max did not think that the aged surfer was being evasive; he was clearly preoccupied.

The increasingly irritating whine leveled off while thousands of mini-lights and gauges continued to glow and blink. It was all very impressive and very pretty and, after thirty minutes of nonstop glowing and blinking with no explication, very boring. Max checked his watch. While he did not have a story, Boles had provided the foundation for one. Given the now validated existence of a glut of arcane scientific equipment in a sealed basement in the mountains, Max knew he could fill in the reportorial blanks between bites of a fast lunch. He had already decided that he would have to come up with something other than the clichéd hunchbacked assistant, though. A mysterious, attractive girl with dark hair, an Eastern European accent, and carefully concealed origins who ostensibly served as the maid, perhaps. Like a good double espresso, his imagination began to perk.

Why hang around and kill the evening in search of a story, when with the material he already had at hand he could invent one infinitely more interesting than anything he was likely to see? He smiled ingratiatingly at his busy host.

"Thanks for the demo," he told the would-be inventor as he started toward the doorway. "This is all very high-tech and I'm sure it can do some fascinating things—once you've got it up and running. But it's getting late and I don't want to impose." Half expecting Boles to try and intercept him, either physically or with an argument, he lengthened his stride.

"You're not imposing. You're going to expose me, remember?" Boles spoke without looking up from the arc of glowing console.

"Expose what?" Noting that his host showed no inclination to interfere with his departure, Max hesitated. He made a gesture that encompassed most of the huge room and its inventory of shiny, blinking, humming, apparently purposeless electronics. "A failed ride proposal for Disneyland? A Westinghouse science fair entry gone mad? What's all this supposed to be for, anyway?" He could not quite keep all the sarcasm out of his voice. "I'm assuming it's supposed to be for *something*."

Boles made no attempt to hide the pride he was feeling in his perceived achievement. "You will be privileged to witness the first fully scaled-up run-through of the system, Max. I really would rather that you were on the staff of *Nature* or *Scientific American*, but given some of the scuzzball would-be writer types that I've had to deal with these past several years, I suppose I'll have to settle for the *Investigator*."

"I'll settle for coffee and Danish. I'm really sorry, but I've got to go, Barry." He did not, but willing to play the game to the last move, he made a show of checking his watch.

"You can go in a minute," Boles told him. "This should only take a minute."

Max eyed the phantasmagoric farrago of indiscriminately interconnected electronics gear dubiously. "*What* should only take a minute?"

Boles glanced up briefly from his work. "Making contact with the world next to ours."

"Next to ours?" Max didn't bat an eye. He'd interviewed too many loony scientist/inventor types to be surprised by anything the affably chatty Boles had to say. "You mean, out in space?"

"No, no." Within the enclosed underground room both light and sound were magnified. "I mean *next to ours*. I am a great believer in the existence of parallel worlds, or paras, as I call them. Always have been. Over the past several years I have been constructing a device with which to prove my theories."

"Prove them, huh? Prove them how?" Max gazed yearningly at the doorway.

"By making actual contact with one. With this." He gestured proudly at the confabulation of disparate electronics.

The reporter's skepticism continued unabated. "There's more than one?"

"So theory insists. Hopefully we will be the first to find out."

Max struggled to suppress a smile. "Mind if I take pictures?"

"Not at all." The reporter's sarcasm lost on him, Boles returned to work at the console. "Documentation is what I'm after."

As he pulled the Minox from a pocket and checked to make sure there was a full roll of film on board, Max found himself liking his host more and more. Nuttier than a Texas fruitcake he might be, but he was a regular guy. A dangerous opinion for a reporter to hold, he knew. It might interfere with his objectivity—though this was not really a problem in Max's case, because he had none.

A really colorful explosion, now, when all this expensive gear blew sky high, would make for a great shot. Trouble was, he was likely to find himself in the middle of it. Therefore, despite a missed photo op, he found himself hoping that everything would remain intact. He made a mental note to contact Southern California Edison for a copy of Boles's monthly electric bill. It would give him a nice, absurd, appropriately mad-scientist statistic to slip into the story. One that could, for a change, be verified.

As Boles had not warned him to keep away from any particular piece of equipment, Max roamed among the lights and sounds, snapping shots of gear he did not recognize while wondering what each piece was for. Of one thing he had no doubt, and that was the cost of the futuristic setup Boles had put together. Everything looked new, state-of-the-art, and expensive. It was all very impressive, even if it didn't do anything more than just turn the basement into a kind of low-key nerd-styled disco.

A bright flash of vaguely violet light strobed the room and he found himself blinking at the pretty colored dots that had suddenly chosen to do the two-step boogie on his retinas. "What the hell was that?"

"Don't know," Boles called out to him. "Generated some intriguing readings, though."

Disneyland, Max decided silently. Or maybe Universal Studios. Boles was actually a clandestine consultant to the secret masters of contemporary consumer fantasy and he was working out the details of a new ride in his basement and Max was going to be the guinea pig for the first tryout. If so, his verdict was going to be unfavorable. As far as entertainment value went, the subterranean setup boasted plenty of color, but no action.

As he contemplated an entirely new take on the story he was going to write, the ceiling lights began to flicker and the pervasive electronic hum to fade. The occasional second or two of total darkness that resulted bothered him more than he would have cared to admit.

"Hey, what's wrong?"

"Nothing's wrong." The disappointment in Boles's voice was unmistakable. "I'm shutting the system down. It didn't work."

"Oh well. That's physics for you. Maybe next time."

"You're humoring me," Boles said flatly.

His host's genial personality notwithstanding, Max had had about enough. He had a life outside the basement, and he was ready to get on with it. "Don't you want to be humored? Or would you rather I went on and on about what a waste of time and money this is?"

Boles came around from behind the console. Though

older, he was a lot bigger and in much better shape than the reporter. He was also between his guest and the doorway. Max tensed slightly. It would not be the first time he'd had to dodge an irate interviewee. If it came to that, he calculated he was quicker on his feet than the tall inventor.

But there was no animosity in Boles's voice as he addressed his visitor. No overt animosity, anyway. "Is that what you're going to write in your article?"

Max hedged his reply; an occupational necessity in his line of work. "I don't know what's going to be in my articles until they're finished. I mean, trying to contact parallel worlds with some homemade basement gizmo, Barry—what did you think I'd write?"

His host sounded faintly wistful. "A respectful report detailing serious efforts to expand the scope of contemporary dimensional physics."

Max's expression turned apologetic. "Sorry, Barry. Wrong paper."

"I know, I know. Just be as kind as you can, will you? Despite appearances and what you may think, I'm partially dependent on a couple of outside sources for funding, and ridicule still hurts."

"Okay, I promise. No ridicule." A little laughter and some smug supercilious sniggering, maybe, but no ridicule. He liked Barrington Boles, in spite of the fact that the guy had inherited money. He was an okay bloke, as one of the reporters for the competing British tabloids might say, even if mentally he did list strongly to one side.

Wanting to end the interview on a more upbeat note, he switched to a subject devoid of controversy. "How's the surfing these days?" He smiled in what he hoped was an ingratiating manner. "I can deal with the concept of parallel waves if they're the watery kind."

"It's fair." Boles led him up the stairs and back through the eclectic but subdued den. The reporter breathed an inner sigh of relief when they reached the front door. Right up to the end, Boles had seemed stable enough—but you could never tell. Max had learned soon after starting out that it was important never to let your guard down in the presence of the truly wacky. "Although since I passed fifty, I tend to fall off the board a lot more."

Max allowed the other man to open the door for him. Heading out and not wishing to leave his kindly host wholly downcast, he volunteered what he hoped would be construed as a mildly backhanded compliment. "At least you're not doing cold fusion."

It was Boles's turn to laugh. "Not me. I'm into science, not fantasy." He stared out into the gathering darkness. Cool coastal fog was starting to creep onshore. "Can I offer you something to eat? My fridge serves as sort of an unofficial annex for the Pacific Rim Deli down in Malibu. How about a corned beef or pastrami on rye? Or I could nuke some brisket?"

"No thanks. I've got work to do at home and I'll heat something up there. Good luck proving your theories and finding your parallel worlds, Barry. Of all the, um, revolutionaries I've interviewed, you're one of the few I'd actually like to see succeed. Better a para world than a para normal."

"I expect that's para for the course." The inventor grinned as Max winced.

Half a story was better than none, he decided as he guided the Aurora down the winding access road toward the coast and the highway. It was too bad Boles was so damn normal. It muted Max's enthusiasm for the ferociously caustic piece he had planned to write. As for the pictures he'd taken, including those of his host, the touch-up guys in the photo department could spice them up as required. Electronic image manipulation had been a tremendous boon to the likes of the *Investigator*, where any story, no matter how imaginative or outrageous, could now be supported by photographic "evidence."

The gate guard did not look up from his TV as Max exited the walled compound and turned south onto the highway. It was a crisp, windless night, the fog was atmospheric rather than intrusive, and he was able to enjoy the drive down through Malibu and into the city. Once back up on the bluffs, he headed briefly south on Ocean until he could turn down Appian Way toward his building. The electric garage gate responded swiftly to his remote.

He was relieved to see that his parking space was empty.

Late-night visitors tended to appropriate unused stalls on the assumption that their owners were out for the evening, instead of parking in those spaces that had been reserved for them. He backed in effortlessly.

It had been a productive, if busy, day, and he was feeling very good about himself as he took the elevator to the top floor, exited, and strolled to the far end of the hall. His was the last apartment on the left, near the front of the building and facing the water. Fumbling in a pocket, he pulled out his key.

He did not need it. The door to his apartment was ever so slightly ajar. Muted light emerged from within.

It was too late for the manager to come calling, he thought furiously. Besides, the building's manager, an affable guy named Tim, was not in the habit of paying uninvited visits to tenants' apartments, much less hanging out in them for extended periods of time. The same held true for repairmen, and in any case, nothing in his place was broken. That left two possibilities; a thief, or one of the several women friends to whom he had extended the courtesy of a key. Living in a beachfront apartment in L.A. offered benefits beyond a view.

Who had his key, and who might have dropped in to surprise him? He struggled to remember. Leaving the door ajar might be a certain lady friend's way of teasing him in, in which case the longer he stood there toying mentally with possibilities the longer he was putting off nascent pleasures. Leaning close to the crack, he listened intently. No banging or bashing about piqued his interest, but neither did he hear the stereo softly pumping out Yanni or Barry White, either.

He considered alerting the manager or retreating to the garage to use the cellular phone in his car to call the police. If his visitor was feminine and less than immoderately dressed, however, the arrival of several cops clutching drawn pistols and nighttime attitudes was likely to dampen the mood somewhat. Dare he risk that? It certainly seemed the most likely explanation. After all, his was a security building.

Putting on his best smile, he pushed the door aside and entered. At the same time, a figure emerged from his bedroom to greet him. It was clad entirely in black. Not black lace, but black sneakers, socks, jeans, and long-sleeved overshirt. In silhouette it did not in any way remotely resemble the feminine form, and it was carrying the twenty-inch Trinitron that under normal circumstances reposed sleekly atop the dresser by the foot of his bed.

"Aw, shit!" Catching sight of Max, the man promptly set the TV down gently on the nearby coffee table. "Look, don't call the cops, man! I'm leaving quietly, see? I didn't take nothing else and I ain't taking nothing. Gimme a break, man! I've been hungry."

"Hungry, my ass!" The outraged reporter was emboldened by the fact that the would-be burglar displayed nothing in the way of a weapon. The intruder was also several inches shorter than the outraged tenant and slim to the point of emaciation.

"Aw, shit!" exclaimed a new voice unexpectedly.

Turning, Max saw a second man standing in the doorway behind him. He was exactly the same height and weight as the burglar, wore exactly the same clothes, spoke with precisely the same intonation and phrasing . . .

He was, in point of fact, an uncannily exact duplicate of the equally stupefied burglar presently standing slack-jawed in the middle of Max's den.

"Who the hell are you?" the newcomer inquired sharply the instant he caught sight of Max's unwanted visitor.

"Screw you, Jack!" The would-be television hoister's expression flattened like a punctured tire. "Son-of-a-bitch but you look a lot like me."

Ignoring a stunned Max, the newcomer marched into the room. "A *lot* like me? Shit, you look *just* like me!"

"Just like who?" A third visitor made his presence known as he wandered in from the hallway. He wore black sneakers, black socks, black jeans, and a black long-sleeved pullover shirt. All three men shared the same attitude, not to mention the same eyes, the same disreputably acquired notch in their right ears, the same beer stain on the hem of their shirts, and the same edgy irritation. They clustered together in the middle of the modest den alongside the coffee table and the nearly purloined Sony, and argued vociferously.

Max quietly closed the door, then turned and waved. "Hi. Remember me?"

Going silent simultaneously, they turned to look at him for the briefest of moments before returning to their arguing. This was complicated by the fact that they often had the same thought concurrently and attempted to give voice to it at exactly the same moment. The ensuing confusion created by identical-sounding overlapping voices only added to their exasperation.

I'm being burgled by triplets, Max thought wildly. *Triplets who don't seem to know each other.*

"Hey," declared the first intruder, "we can sort this out. After all, you guys sound like fellas I could get along with." He gestured in Max's direction. "But first we've got a job to do, and that doesn't include letting Mr. Homeowner here run around loose."

Max didn't resist. There were three of them and they were all probably crazy to boot. He let them tie him to one of the kitchen chairs and watched while they sat calmly in his den and argued energetically. One of them had the nerve to go to the refrigerator and help himself to three of Max's choicest cold brews. Their subsequent exclamations of delight indicated that, unsurprisingly, they all favored the same brand of beer. This mutual bonding gave him time to note that the similarities between the three extended far beyond the superficial. Even their hand gestures were so similar as to be indistinguishable.

After some thirty minutes of increasingly jovial cama-raderie, they rose and shook hands. The one who had been carrying the bedroom TV heaved it back up off the coffee ta-ble while his companions cleanly and efficiently disconnected his stereo and desk computer. In response to his frantic plead-ing they graciously left him his backup disks, whereupon after making a quick check of the hallway to insure that it was empty, they filed out the door and closed it behind them. His neighbors, he knew, would invariably tell the police they hadn't seen or heard a thing.

His restraints were tight but not painfully so. In less than an hour he managed to twist and wriggle free. Though far too late to do any good, the police responded with admirable speed.

He sat morosely in his den while a middle-aged officer with short blond hair and the first stirrings of middle-aged paunch dispensed professional empathy, asked questions, and took notes. Her partner made the obligatory sweep of the apartment, looking for nonexistent fingerprints (true pros that they were, the three thieves had never removed their black gloves) and other information that would prove useful. Nei-ther they nor Max held out much hope of seeing his property again, but they were at least sympathetic.

"I'm sorry we can't be more encouraging, Mr. Parker, but I've learned it's better to be straight with people than raise false hopes. We do solve many of these household burglaries, but not as many as we'd like." She put her pen and pad back in her shirt pocket.

He nodded listlessly. "I can imagine how many petty thefts you have to deal with every week," he muttered.

She looked down at him. "I won't lie and say they're a priority, Mr. Parker. This is Los Angeles, after all. At least they didn't get away with anything irreplaceable." Recognition brightened her expression. "Parker, Parker. Maxwell Parker? Don't you write for that newspaper, the *Investigator*?"

He offered a wan smile. "That's me."

"I remember reading your story on the Mexican Bermuda Triangle and how it was all tied in with those descendants of the Aztecs who are still living up in the mountains. You're a good writer."

"Thank you. That story took a lot of research." To be precise, ten minutes with a little-used library copy of DeSoto, he remembered.

"Yeah, I could tell. I read a lot, and you can always tell when a writer's done their homework or not." Frowning, she pulled the pad and pen back out and returned to her note-taking. "You're sure these three guys all looked alike?"

"I told you." He looked up tiredly from where he was seated. "They didn't just look alike. They were triplets. For all I know, all their talk about not knowing each other was part of some demented routine they use to disorient their victims. Or amuse themselves. There are a lot of frustrated stand-up comics in this town. Maybe these three hope that someday they'll be robbing someone in the entertainment business who'll hire them to appear at the Comedy Club." He eyed the vacant shelving where his stereo had previously reposed. "Wouldn't surprise me a bit. Instead of the Brothers Karamazov we'd have the Brothers Sutton."

"The brothers who?" The cop gave him a blank look.

"Forget it."

She scratched at the back of her blond crew cut and shrugged. "Triplets, huh? Well, that'll save space on the duty board. One artist's rendering will be enough." She grinned and turned toward the bedroom as her partner emerged. "Find anything, Remar?"

"Cigarette butts." The cop held out a palmful of crumbled debris. "Three of 'em. Same brand, all smoked down to the same length before being discarded."

"Well, that's it, then. We've got them now," Max muttered.

"There's no call for sarcasm, Mr. Parker." The female and senior half of the investigating team eyed him disapprovingly. "Don't knock the evidence before it's processed. You never know what's going to give the bad guys away. Neither do they, or they'd be more careful. The department recovers stolen property all the time. You might get lucky. Of course, you've used an electric engraving pen to mark all your valuables in an inconspicuous place with your driver's license or Social Security number or some other easily recognizable code."

"Uh, no," he confessed, his self-righteous sardonic condemnation of metropolitan police procedures instantly deflated.

The officers exchanged a knowing glance. "Citizens always do all they can to make our jobs easier."

"There were three of them!" Who was the victim here? he reminded himself. "Triplets! They ought to be easy to find."

"Only if they hang out together when they're not working." She put away her notebook. "We'll call you if we have any news or make any progress, Mr. Parker. Meanwhile, keep on writing. I'll look forward to more of your articles. Oh, and I suggest you contact your insurance company if you haven't already."

With a tip of her hat she followed her partner out the door, thoughtfully closing it softly behind her. Max was once more alone in his apartment, sans stereo, Sony, and computer. The emptiness he felt was not internal.

Sitting and brooding would get him only an ulcer, and he did not need to add to the aggravation he received daily in the course of his work. Taking the departed cop's sound advice, he called his insurance representative, explained what had happened, and detailed the thievery. The agent promised him a check to cover his losses within two days—minus his deductible, of course.

Muttering under his breath about the injustices life visited on the virtuous, he made ready for bed. It was the first time he had ever been burgled, and living in Los Angeles, he knew it would likely not be the last. Not as long as he lived in a nice place at the beach.

The beach. Silent recitation of the very word seemed to soothe him. He had notes enough for two stories in the can, both safely stored in the laptop computer locked in his car. He'd work on them in the morning and take the afternoon off. The weather was predicted fine, the sand shouldn't be crowded, and he would let the afternoon sun melt away his trauma. He went to bed feeling better than he had anticipated. What the hell, his deductible was reasonable and he'd been wanting to get a new stereo anyway.

Many of the city's residents kept an earthquake emergency kit handy in their homes. Drinking water, food bars, medical supplies, and so on. Max maintained an equally compact beach emergency kit: suntan lotion, towel, Walkman, and so on. Thus equipped, he exited the building the following afternoon, crossed Ocean Avenue, hotfooted it across the already baking asphalt parking lot, and trudged past the steel swings and monkey bars until he found a spot where the sand began to slope toward the water.

The ostinato pounding of the surf was already relaxing him as he spread out his towel, pinned one corner down with the compact chilled cooler, adjusted his shades, and took a seat. By the time he started slathering on the tanning lotion he was feeling no pain. He'd spent the morning polishing the story on

Mrs. Collins's medium and the conversation the two of them (leaving himself out of the equation) had had with her recently deceased offspring. Tonight or tomorrow he would bestow equal treatment on the amiably mad Barrington Boles and his colorful if impotent parallel-world machine. Two substantial stories in twice as many days would net him a nice paycheck in addition to Kryzewski's grudging compliments.

Meanwhile he could spend the rest of a truly fine day lying back and watching the gulls, pelicans, joggers, and surfers. The rewards of the righteous, he told himself without a hint of false modesty.

When the bounty presented itself, or rather herself, he knew for a certainty that God was Just.

She was not simply pretty. Los Angeles was overrun with pretty girls. No, the visitant was drop-dead gorgeous, a fully-matured member of the migratory species instantly identifiable to those who did their socio-scientific homework as *Starletus californicus*. As matters developed, it was not his irresistible good looks that had drawn her to him, nor his instant recognizability within his singular profession, but something much more prosaic.

"It sure is hot today," she said musically, her words drifting down between her ample breasts. "I saw your cooler. Is there any chance I could have a sip? Just water would be fine."

Pushing his shades rakishly up onto his forehead, he smiled up at her. "Sorry. Can't help you there."

"Oh." Her expression fell and she started to turn away. "Sorry to bother you."

"No, no." He sat up so fast he nearly lost the shades. "I mean there's no water." He fumbled with the cooler's latch. "What would you like: RC, Sprite, or beer?"

She knelt down next to his beach towel, an altogether enchanting series of movements that he perceived as one. "An RC would be great."

He handed her the chilled can, wishing he had an insulating jacket, and ice, and a glass. Not to mention champagne. "My name's Max. Max Parker." He gestured toward the parking lot and the street beyond. "I live here. My apartment's right across the street."

"Hi—I'm Sherri." She followed the gesture. "You live right here? At the beach? Cool!"

If he had scripted the encounter himself it could not have been going any better. "Yeah, I've been here for a couple of years now. I'm a reporter."

"Really? Television?" Bright blue Midwestern eyes sparkled.

"No. Newspaper." He sipped his own soda.

"Oh." Her disappointment was as palpable as her pout was lubricious.

"Nationally distributed," he added hopefully.

The addendum still did not carry the cachet of television, but some of the initial sparkle returned to the visitant's eyes.

"You ever do any stories on the entertainment business, Max?"

"All the time," he replied offhandedly, as if Hollywood were his daily beat.

Her full interest returned. "That's great! You know, I'm an actress, like my sisters. We're from—well, you wouldn't recognize the name of the town, but it's west of Omaha. Would you like to meet them?"

Before he even had time to consider a reply, she was standing and waving, shouting up the beach. He looked in the direction she was facing, but the sun was in his eyes and he was loath to pull down the shades lest it minimize his view of even the tiniest part of her perfect figure.

Several shapes rose from the distant sand and came running, laughing and chattering as they approached, a tripartite cornucopia of irrepressible young feminine beauty. Like the redoubtable Sherri, two were blondes. The third was a redhead. The sisterly similarity was immediately noticeable. Remarkable, even.

Now where, he thought, had he recently encountered a similar situation?

While part of him was becoming distinctly warmer, and not from the broiling rays of the Southern California sun, the rest of him was growing cold. The internal conflict left him feeling distinctly uncomfortable.

The four giggling Omaha sisters looked enough alike, from their Kewpie-doll faces to their lush figures to their petite feet, to have sprung from the same floating scallop shell. One pair were clad in identical bikinis while the other two wore, respectively, a third identical swimsuit but of a different color, and the fourth a one-piece net outfit that was more not there than there. Two were slightly taller than their siblings, one had a mole on her left thigh, another green eyes instead of blue, and Sherri herself wore the only piece of jewelry among them: a black coral necklace. The slight differences were almost as disturbing as the astonishing similarities.

He found himself wondering wildly if they by any chance happened to be dating three contentious cat burglars, and were they interviewing him because they needed a fourth to complete the ménage?

He swallowed hard. The part of him that had been rapidly warming was quickly turning cold. "Let me guess: You've never set eyes on one another before today?"

The radiant sisters exchanged a look and laughed. Simultaneously, of course. "Don't be silly!" Sherri admonished him. "Girls, this is Max. He's a reporter."

Questions flew at him, none of which he heard. Searching faces and bodies for distinctions, he found only enough to emphasize their similarities. The four were not quadruplets, but they were far more alike than mere sisters. A growing unease was blossoming in his gut.

"Actually, we're staying in the hotel down the street," one of the girls told him. "It's pretty amazing. It's funny what you just said, because until we ran into each other in the coffee shop yesterday, we actually never had met before."

The ascending chill was spreading from his belly to the rest of his body. "How interesting," he commented flatly.

"I mean, it just blew us away," declared a third member of the quartet. "We're still trying to work it out. Our mother died two years ago, and all we can figure out is that we were separated at birth and raised by different families." She adjusted her position on the sand. "It's just like something you'd see on one of those tabloid news television shows."

"That's right," added the one red-haired member of the group. "Isn't it amazing that we could have all grown up in the same general area, near Omaha, and never run into one another until we met up right here in Los Angeles?"

"It's remarkable, all right," he agreed weakly.

"Of course," Sherri pointed out, "we're all trying to get into the movie and television business. Except Shari." Her mouth wrinkled up delightfully. "She wants to be an auto mechanic."

"That's right," chirped one of the blondes, who was equally as attractive as her three sisters.

"We all sat up most of the night talking," Sherri informed him. "It seems that even our families were a lot alike."

"Just fascinating." He fought not to back away as they pressed close around him. He noted that even their body odors were slightly different, not quite identical. He was afraid he was going to throw up, but not from the collective feminine aroma.

"I think you're kind of fascinating yourself, Max." The

redhead sidled close until her arm was pressing against his side. "I'm not doing anything tonight. You live here, so you know the city. How would you like to take me out and show me around?"

"Well, I don't . . ."

"And me," declared the blonde next to her. It developed that all four of them had a sudden urge to go out with him.

"All of you?" he stammered. "Simultaneously? Like in, together?"

The sisters exchanged looks. "Why not?" Sherri wondered. "If we all want to go out with you why shouldn't we all go out with you?"

"That's right," agreed blonde number three. She smiled invitingly. Corn-fed and fresh the four might be, but they were not shy. "Don't worry, Max. We'll go easy on you."

The redhead was shaking her head. "That's just what I was going to say. Honestly, it's amazing how alike we think."

"Yeah." Max rose quickly to his feet, nearly losing his footing in the soft sand. He fumbled with the contents of the cooler. "Here, each of you take a soda. I'm sure you're all equally thirsty."

"As a matter of fact . . ." admitted the redhead as she reached for the proffered can, "I am. You're so thoughtful, Max. It's like you just *knew*." Her eyes glittered in the bright sunshine. "It's almost like you're part of the family."

"Oh, don't say that." Sending sand flying, he hurriedly

snatched up his towel and snapped the cooler shut. "Look, I'm really sorry. I may even be really crazy—but I can't go out with you. Not individually or together." He took a step backward and nearly fell on his butt.

"But why not?" The redhead rose from her crouch like a speeded-up stop-motion film clip of a blossom opening, a svelte vision of down-home Great Plains loveliness. "We all like you. Don't you like us?" The four of them were staring at him with the same wistful, slightly hurt expressions. It was comely. It was intriguing.

It was downright creepy.

"Sure I like you. Who wouldn't." He spoke a little too quickly as he continued to back away. "It's just that I'm not too sure about some things going on in my life right now and it wouldn't be fair to lay it off on you ladies. Maybe another time, when I've got my head in order."

"Whatever you say, Max." An obviously disappointed and not a little confused Sherri concluded with a full-figured parting shrug, a gesture that did nothing to diminish his libido. Then her three sisters shrugged, in precisely the same manner, and that fully accomplished anything that the first shrug had not. Abandoning all pretense at politesse, he turned and ran.

"That's a very nice but very flustered young man," the redhead insisted.

"Exactly what I was thinking," added the sister on her left.

"Of course," agreed Sherri, and with that the four of them

once again fell to giggling, an a capella chorus of unrestrained feminine amusement.

Heedless of the heat, Max ran through the sand, across the parking lot, and nearly managed to get himself run down by a cable-company service truck while sprinting across Ocean Avenue. Taking the outside access stairs two at a time, he did not slow down until he was inside the familiar confines of the elevator. Fighting to catch his breath as it ascended, he bolted through the open door the instant the lift reached his floor. The hall was empty, but he ran anyway. He did not stop running until he was back inside his apartment with the door locked and securely bolted behind him.

Any other time, any other place, he would have gladly sacrificed the balance in his bank account for a date with any one of the Omaha sisters. The opportunity to go out with two of them would have made him wary. In his current state of mind, the presence of four nearly identical, interchangeable lovelies constituted incontrovertible overkill. They were not quite as indistinguishable as the three burglars had been. The differences were slight but noticeable. But the similarities were too similar, the duplication too uncanny. Considered in the light of the previous night's intruders, they constituted a coincidence the likes of which made him want to run screaming, and not with unrequited passion.

It was bizarre. It was frightening. It was weird. And the only situation in which he had recently found himself that equaled it in weirdness was the evening he had spent in the company of a certain Barrington Boles, gentleman surfer and would-be mad scientist. Good ol' Barry Boles and his parallel-world Lego set. Focusing on Boles and his abortive demonstration was a hope, not an explanation, but at the moment it was the only one Max had. Other than the possibility that he needed glasses, of a very special and unimaginable type.

He needed some answers, and he needed them fast.

Abandoning the apartment, he risked traffic citations several dozen times as he raced up the Pacific Coast Highway and through Malibu, putting the Aurora through some maneuvers the engineers at GM had never envisioned. There was a different guard at the compound gate. Patient and skeptical, he refused to buy any of Max's stories. Nor did the reporter's obvious agitation help any. But the guard did agree, despite his better instincts, to ring Boles's house. Evidently he was having a good day, or was in a particularly benign mood—or maybe it was the desperate, panicky look on Max's face, the expression of a man drowning out of water.

Be home, Max implored the unseen inventor. *Don't have run off to Madagascar or someplace. Be home.*

Still dubious, the guard put down his receiver and looked out at the distraught visitor. "He says to go on up."

Max barely restrained the Aurora long enough for the electric gate to swing aside and admit him to the private compound. He forced himself to take it slow climbing the winding road through the preserve of expensive homes lest some idle matron call Security down on a visiting reckless driver.

His anxious tone and words to the guard had produced the intended effect. Front door standing open behind him, Boles was waiting for him as the Aurora squealed to a halt in the circular driveway.

"Good to see you again, Max." The inventor wore a golden California senior's smile as he approached the car. His tan was the stuff of Chicago dreams. "What's so important that it brought you back so soon? The gate guard said you looked downright nervous."

"Nervous?" Max shut the door and hurried around the front of the car. "Yeah, you could say I'm a little nervous. I was robbed last night."

Boles's expression turned instantly sympathetic as they entered the house. "No kidding? That's a damned shame."

"Damned might be the right description." Max looked around and without being asked, fell onto a massive leather couch. Until that moment he had not really stopped running, physically or mentally. Now he was exhausted, but adrenaline flow kept him alert and talking as Boles took a seat opposite.

"So tell me what happened." The inventor offered M&Ms from a silver container. Max waved them off.

"I get home last night and find a guy trying to take my TV for a walk. As I'm confronting him another guy shows up. He looks exactly like the first. I mean, exactly. While they're arguing about who's who, a third kibitzer comes through the door and guess what—he looks just like the other two. Same build, same look, same voice, same clothes—they even argued alike. If you take their words and their actions at face value, they'd never met before that moment."

He eyed the candy uncomfortably. What he needed was a good, stiff Scotch, not chocolate. But as long as he had Boles's attention, he did not want to send him off to search the household bar. Health freak that the older man was, it was entirely possible that the only alcohol in the house resided in the medicine cabinet anyway. He put the craving out of his mind.

"Eventually they calm down. Then they tie me up and work things out among themselves, the downside being that they leave not just with my TV but also my stereo and my computer."

Boles was nodding sympathetically as he listened. Not once during Max's deposition had he laughed, or even smiled. "Fascinating. Maybe even remarkable. But what has it got to do with me?"

Max rolled his eyes. "Wait, there's more. Today I go down to the beach and after ten minutes of lying in the sun this absolutely stunning lady materializes and tells me she's thirsty. So I sit up right away and give her a cold soda. We start talking, everything's going exceptionally well, and then guess what? It seems she has three sisters. Three sisters who all look almost exactly like. Not as alike as the three burglars, but close. And you know what they tell me as I'm sitting there with my blood starting to congeal? They tell me that they'd never met before, didn't even know of one another's existence, until they met in a hotel restaurant the previous night." He gazed fixedly at the inventor. "I don't suppose any of this means anything to you?"

"Of course it does!" Boles was on his feet now, gesticulating excitedly as he paced rapidly back and forth. "They're paras! First the thieves, then the girls." He halted and stood staring at a high shelf of books, shaking his head slowly. "It works. The damn thing works."

"There's that word again." Max sat up straight, his eyes never leaving his host. "Paras. Want to tell me what it means?"

Boles looked over at him. "As I told you when you were here yesterday, my intention was to break through the barrier, or barriers, that separate parallel worlds, and find a way to enter one. The system did just that, but instead of allowing us to enter, it permitted the inhabitants of those parallel worlds to cross over into ours. And not just those of one parallel world, but in the case of your burglars, two, and in the case of the young women, three." His eyes were alight. "Who could have imagined such a result? Astonishing! Extraordinary!"

"Weird. Almost as weird as the stuff I write. I wonder while we're sitting here how many other people out there are running into newfound twins and triplets and quads and so forth."

"I can tell you. Zero. Nobody." Boles's excitement gave way to an intense, focused curiosity. "You and I were the only ones present when the field was activated. I was behind the console and you were, as I recall, quite close to the field arch. It is not only possible but likely that you are the only one who has been affected, Max."

The reporter's expression narrowed. "Affected? What do you mean, 'affected'?"

Boles weighed his answer carefully before replying. "Based on what you've just told me, my guess is that instead of being narrowly focused and harnessed within the confines of the arch, the field seems to have expanded far enough to encompass your position where you were standing at the moment of maximum sustained convivial interaction. Furthermore, the result seems to be that instead of you entering the field, the field seems to have entered you. Interesting. Parameters will have to be redefined. Somewhere in the equation a letter needs to be flopped."

"Flop my ass," Max muttered. "Talk to me in English. What's this about a field entering me? What are you trying to say?"

Boles was scrutinizing him in much the same way an entomologist in Peru might look upon an entirely new, highly attractive, but possibly toxic species of beetle.

"What I'm saying is that you may now be a kind of nexus, Max."

The reporter looked alarmed. "Hey, I was raised a Presbyterian and I don't even want to be that. I'm still not following you."

The inventor struggled to compose an explanation simple enough for any layman to comprehend. Even a tabloid reporter. "You are the gate now, Max. The effect has settled within you—or around you. Without detailed study I can't be certain of any specifics. You, or rather the effect now centered on you, drew not one but two parallelities, or paras, of that burglar into your orbit. Into your apartment.

"I want you to stop and think a minute. Did you go anywhere near the restaurant where those four 'sisters' claimed to have met?"

"No! From here I went straight home. I didn't stop, I drove straight . . ." He broke off, sudden realization chiseling at his memory. "The hotel they were staying at is right on Ocean. I went right past there."

Boles nodded sagaciously. "Obviously that was close enough for the field to affect them. No telling how many others your passing influenced. Fortunately, the strength of the field and its consequent effects appear to be of a highly intermittent nature."

"I don't get it. I didn't feel a thing. I *don't* feel a thing."

"Evidently you won't," Boles told him. "If you were going to feel anything, you would have by now. It's others, in other worlds, who are suffering the effects of what happened to you."

"But I don't feel affected." Max's initial fear was giving way to a growing anger. He was used to being in control of what was happening around him, not the unwilling carrier of some cryptic, fluctuating physical effect. If what Boles was saying was true, he was more out of control of his surroundings than any man had ever been.

"If I've been infected somehow by this whatever-it-is, I want it removed. This effect, or field, or whatever you want to call what I'm carrying, I want it wiped out, erased, neutralized, and cured. Right now."

"I'm afraid I can't do that, Max." Boles sounded genuinely apologetic.

"You can't? Why not?" His voice rose. "I'll sue!"

"That won't change things or put the universe back the way it was before I activated the field. You can't litigate physics, Max. I can't fix things because I don't know precisely how the effect was generated, much less how or why it locused in you. I was trying to open a gate, not make you into one. I can't fix what I don't understand." When the downcast reporter turned to stare worriedly out the broad picture window behind the couch, Boles was moved to comment further.

"Don't look like that." The inventor pleaded with his guest. "I know this has to be disconcerting for you. I'm not trying to dismiss your condition as hopeless."

"Oh, now that's encouraging," Max mumbled disconsolately.

"It's obvious that you've got a problem. But I'll work on it, I promise you that."

"Great!" Max dropped his head into his hands and used the heels to rub hard at his forehead. "So what am I supposed to do in the meantime? While you're trying to figure out how to reverse this, or terminate it, or whatever?"

"Do?" Boles eyed him curiously. "Why, the same things you always do. Live your life, write your stories. Are you in pain? Have you suffered injury because of the effect? Has your health deteriorated?"

"Only my sense of confidence in the stability of the world around me." The reporter looked up. "Otherwise, I feel okay."

The inventor looked satisfied. "Then what are you bitching about?"

Max considered before finally offering an indignant reply. "I lost my TV. If those—what did you call them? If those paras hadn't shown up and decided to cooperate instead of fighting for dominance, I wouldn't have lost my stereo and my computer."

"I'll buy you new ones. I am sort of responsible for what's happened to you."

"Sort of!" Max sputtered.

"Would you like a drink?"

"Sure, why not?" Max mumbled. "Anything's okay, so long as it's cold and full of alcohol."

Boles carefully filled two glasses with ice and amber-colored liquid from a corner bar, in the process answering Max's earlier question about whether or not the inventor was too health-conscious to consume liquor. He presented one glass to his guest and kept the other for himself. Max swallowed urgently.

"This is all so very interesting." Boles was thinking aloud again.

"So were the first A-bomb tests, but I don't know anybody who wanted to study them from ground zero." The harsh yet sweet liquid burned the reporter's throat.

"I'm pondering possible ramifications. If two of your nocturnal visitors were paras, then that means they have gone missing on two parallel worlds. The same holds true for the four 'sisters,' only their absences are much more likely to be noted. Because they're here and this world is apparently so analogous to their own, they will all be familiar with it. Oh, there'll be plenty of confusion when they try to apply for the same job simultaneously, or pay bills with one bank account, but I suspect they'll manage to sort it out. By way of explanation, each of them will ascribe their personal situation to confused memories or some such. That's what people do.

"But they will have left behind holes in the para worlds they were drawn from. Disappointed boyfriends, angry employers, puzzled parents, and more. It would be fascinating to be able to visit those parallel worlds and observe exactly what the effects of such disappearances are."

"I've got it," Max informed him sarcastically. "Why don't you fire up that monstrosity in the basement again and see if it will infect *you* with the unsolicited ability to attract people from parallel worlds?"

Unperturbed, Boles smiled. "For a tabloid reporter you have a delightfully droll sense of humor, Max."

"Which I am rapidly losing. Isn't there anything you can do?"

His host shook his head regretfully. "Not without a great deal of additional study, I'm afraid. I can offer one positive thought."

"What's that?" The distraught reporter was ready to clutch at the tiniest hint of optimism.

"The effect may be temporary. Given the limited amount of energy available for the experimental run, it most probably is. Even as we sit here discussing the matter, it may already have run its course. The notion of a cure being required may already be irrelevant."

"Yeah. Right. How will I know if it has? Run its course, that is?"

"I should think the answer to that would be self-evident. Go about your business and see if you run into any more multiples, any more paras. If not, then I think we can safely assume that the effect has worn off. The possibility that any measurable results from the propagation of the conjectural field might be extremely transitory in nature was one that always concerned me. It appears that if confirmed, my greatest worry may turn out to be all for the best."

"But what if it's not transitory, or at least what if it takes a couple of days to wear off, or fade away, or dissipate, or whatever it is that it's going to do? What if the effect is sustained for a while and I do run into more of these paras? How many should I expect to have to deal with?"

The shrug Boles gave him somehow managed to contain within it all the imposing majesty of experimental physics past and present—or at least something more than insouciant indifference.

"Who can say? Theoreticians have speculated for hundreds of years on the possible existence of worlds that parallel our own. It's only recently that the math and computing power has become available with which to shape actual hypotheses. I won't try to explain the algorithms I used to help design and build my system." His tone grew cold and deep. Suddenly he sounded less like a gracefully aging surfer and more like a highly motivated if slightly addled prophet.

"There could be hundreds of parallel worlds, Max. Millions. Numbers beyond imagining, many exactly like ours or so nearly alike as to be indistinguishable, others different in minor or extreme ways we can't begin to imagine. For example, you mentioned that the four sisters differed from each other in very minor but distinctive ways."

He nodded. "That's right. Three were blondes, but one had red hair. Another had a mole, here"—he tapped his right thigh—"but the others didn't." He smiled thinly. "I really wasn't paying much attention to petty differences. There was too much else to look at."

Boles was nodding thoughtfully. "Parallel for sure, but not

always identical. A single strand of DNA in one person might be enough to comprise the sole difference between this world and another. At a different level more pronounced differences would appear. A mole, for example. So much possibility for variation!" He downed a long swallow from his glass, but it was an empty gesture, one designed solely to recognize the presence of the tumbler and its contents. His heart and his mind were elsewhere.

"Resume your life, Max. Right now that's the best advice I can offer you. As long as you are the one drawing paras into our world, into this world, the effect on your existence, and mine, should be minimal. As the locus, you are likely to be the only one who notices them. I know this is upsetting to you, but neither is it like you've been cast down into the lower regions of Purgatory. How bad can it be if the worst that happens is that you lose some home electronics that I will gladly reimburse you for, and that four beautiful women want to ask you out on a congruent date?"

Max summoned up his last vision of the four Omaha sisters, sitting on the sand, bright sunshine glinting off their para hair, reflecting from their identical para eyes, casting teasing shadows across their startling para bodies. Maybe being a locus for parallel worlds wasn't such a bad thing, after all. Especially if Boles was right and the effect would wear off of its own accord.

If that was the case, he reflected, he needed to return to

that hotel and look up his most recent para acquaintances before they snapped back into their pertinent parallel worlds. In the absence of any harmful side effects, it was an experience he ought not to miss. Especially if they all thought like sister Sherri. Some simultaneous notions might not be such a bad thing.

Get on with your life, Boles was telling him. Could be that the old boy's attitude was as right on as his science was way off. In any event, it would not do any good to sue him—not even in California. What kind of accusation could be brought? "Plaintiff was made an attractant to parallel worlds without his consent and with malicious intent?" Any lawsuit that made even oblique reference to Boles's bizarre scientific theories would be laughed out of court. Even in California.

"I do have one idea for canceling or negating the effects of the field if it doesn't dissipate on its own," the inventor was telling him. "It's awfully premature and I hate to mention anything so wild."

"What do you call my condition now?" Max challenged him, waving his glass. By this time it was empty save for melting ice cubes.

"From a scientific point of view, enviable." Boles's reply contained not a trace of irony. "I wish I had been the one affected, not you."

"Finally. Something we agree on." Max's concurrence was

heartfelt. "Let's give your idea a try, whatever it is. The results can't be any wilder than my current reality."

"It isn't going to be that easy. Certain preparations have to be made. The system must be modified and checks run." The inventor considered. "Come back next Tuesday."

Sure thing, Doc, Max mused sourly. *After all, I'm way overdue for my yearly reality shot.*

IV

Other than being passed by two apparently identical black Mercedes E-600 sedans headed north on Lincoln Avenue, a wary Max was not assaulted by any blatant parallelities on his way to work Monday morning. At the office friends and acquaintances remarked on his unusual pallor and a lack of the familiar energy that customarily seemed to radiate from him. Max barely acknowledged their stares and whispered comments. Anything that caught his eye and smacked of unnatural redundancy, from people to pencils, caught and held his attention.

He turned in the medium story for publication, the clever embellishments he had added in the course of reliving his visit to the bereaved Collins household cheering him as he reread them. The brilliance of his own writing never failed to inspire him. He hesitated over the Boles story, finally dismissing his concerns with a mental shrug. A story was a story, whether it involved him personally or not. He had written selectively about the colorful and lively demonstration of Boles's equipment, downplaying the laughable aspects of the inventor's theories. There was a chance that the sharp-eyed Kryzewski would sniff out the omissions, but Max could not laugh at that which he no longer found funny.

By lunchtime, his presence among familiar surroundings and friends had combined to reinvigorate much of his usual easygoing, wisecracking persona. He was almost relaxed, when he saw the twins.

They were seated several tables across the room, in one of the darker sections of the Thai restaurant where he and his friends had gone to eat. The two young men were nearly but not quite identical, and the sight of them was like a big bucket of ice water in his face. Excusing himself from his puzzled companions, he stumbled over to the table that drew him like a fly to a *Rafflesia*.

"Pardon me," he mumbled, interrupting their conversation. They looked to be about twenty, twenty-one. Probably UCLA students on their day off, or on break from class. Sandy-brown hair, slim builds, faces verging on the innocent, they looked up at him curiously. Simultaneously. "I know this sounds crazy, but how long have you guys known each other?"

The two youths exchanged a glance; then the one on the left looked up over his dripping cheeseburger. "Are you kidding? How long does it look like we've known each other?"

"All our lives, obviously." The other brother snickered at the blatantly dumb question.

"So what you're telling me is that you grew up together? You haven't been separated and didn't just happen to bump into one another yesterday?"

"What's with the interrogation?" Turning bellicose, the first youth set his sandwich aside.

"Yeah, what's this all about, mister?" inquired his brother. "You some kind of reporter doing a story on twins? Rich and I have been in a couple of twins' stories before, back home." He smiled. His personality, if not his face, differed significantly from that of his twin. "We're from near Cincinnati."

"Yeah, that's right." Max was weak with relief. "I'm some kind of reporter. Always looking for a story."

Now that their visitor had explained himself, the other brother responded enthusiastically. "What do you want to know? About how much we think alike? Actually, except for looks we're not that much alike. Steve and I have always had pretty different tastes. Some people find that surprising, but you know, just 'cause you're twins and look alike doesn't mean you're, like, the same inside."

"That's right," agreed Rich cheerfully. "For example, I can't stand Smashing Pumpkins, and Steve loves 'em. On the other hand, Steve's a Hootie fan, but as far as I'm concerned, they can . . ."

"I get the idea. I'm afraid that won't work for me. I'm sort of on the lookout for duplicates who are alike in everything.

Sorry to bother you." Much eased in mind, Max turned to rejoin his friends.

"Hey, wait a minute," Steve called to the reporter's retreating back, "what about the story?"

Max did not respond. Not every set of twins or triplets or quads in the world was the result of a wealthy scientific dilettante's maladjusted experiment gone awry. Hopefully Boles was right in his suppositions and the effect had already worn off. That did not mean, Max reminded himself, that the beauteous Omaha sisters were fled from their beach hotel. Tonight he would do his best to find out. Feeling very much more like himself, he was finally able to relax and enjoy the rest of his lunch. His friends noticed his newly upbeat mood immediately.

He considered telling them about what he had been through the past couple of days, but decided against it. No one would believe the truth anyway—he hardly believed it himself. Parallel worlds populated by plethoras of parallelities, he told himself. Say that fast three times. Live that fast three times.

"What are you grinning at?" Amee asked him. She was a petite, recent immigrant from France with the tenacity of a pit bull and a waspish pen—an ideal addition to the *Investigator* team.

"Just feeling good," he told her expansively. "Not to dwell on it, but I've had a rough couple of days."

"Two bylined stories in less than a week." On the other

side of the table, Harrison grumbled and played with his frijoles. "I should have such a rough couple of days."

Max bestowed a friendly smile on his friend and fellow scribe. "Just take my word for it: If you knew what I've been through you wouldn't want to trade."

The rest of the day went exceptionally well—which was to say, normally. No pairs of paras confronted him in the hallways or offices, his two stories were gruffly praised by Kryzewski, and a contact in El Monte whom he had not heard from in months and whom he had pretty much given up on phoned in with a tip on a voodoo faith healer who was working the lower-middle-class neighborhoods in the area south of the San Bernardino Freeway.

By the time he got home he was feeling positively jaunty. He'd had a rough experience but now it was behind him, the actuality of it reduced by a normal day to a scarcely credible memory. He'd have to take a moment to call Boles and tell him the good news. The proposed Tuesday return visit would thankfully not be necessary.

To cap it off, the door to his apartment was properly locked and sealed. No acquisitive evening visitors this time. He slipped the key into the deadbolt.

"Mr. Parker, Mr. Parker!"

He started, but the voice came from down the hall and not from within his apartment. Furthermore, it was one he recognized. Looking to his left, he saw Ginger Bonley from number eleven waving anxiously in his direction. A sweet old widow in her late sixties, toughened from several years of living on her own at the beach, she often made presents to the building's other tenants of favorite cuttings from her forest of houseplants. Max's kitchen boasted two beautiful coleuses and a climbing Schefllera courtesy of Mrs. Bonley's horticultural expertise.

She started toward him, gesturing with one hand and occasionally glancing back over her shoulder as if Beelzebub himself were after her. He put the door key back in his pocket.

"Ginger, what's wrong?" He thought suddenly of the thieving triplets. They were just as likely still to be in the vicinity as were the Omaha sisters.

She was having trouble catching her breath. One hand continued to flutter at him while she held the other pressed against her narrow chest. "My apartment, Mr. Parker. In—my apartment!"

"What's in your apartment?" He looked down the hallway past her but saw nothing. "If you've got a problem why don't you call the manager?"

"He—he's not here." She clutched at his wrist. "You come, Mr. Parker! Please, you come."

"Okay, sure." He let himself be led along.

The door to number eleven stood open wide. While she cowered apprehensively behind him, he peered in. From what he could remember of the last time he'd paid her a visit, the apartment appeared undisturbed. Throw blankets covered old, unstylishly comfortable furniture. No one had messed with her TV. Houseplants hung from ceiling hooks and thrust upward from elegant enameled pots, giving the room the air and appearance of an English Victorian seaside salon.

"It's a little stuffy in here, that's all," he told her reassuringly as he entered. "Stuffy and humid. You should really keep a window open more often, Ginger."

Her fingers clutched at him. "No, no, it's not that! There's nothing wrong with the air. You don't understand . . ."

Avoiding the sharp edges of the black lacquered coffee table, he strode through the room and unlatched the big sliding glass door. Since eleven was in the back of the building her apartment had no ocean view, but the water could be seen clearly from out on the small concrete patio. He shoved the door all the way open and turned to smile across the room at her.

"You just need some fresh air in here, Ginger. It helps keep the head clear. Now, come on out and have a seat. I'll make you some coffee if you like."

"You're so kind, Mr. Parker." She warily entered her own living room and closed the door behind her. Her attention, however, was not on him but on the door that led to the back bedroom. "I guess—I guess they're gone."

"Guess who's gone?" He frowned as lingering images of identical burglars once more entered his mind.

"They must have gotten out somehow while I was talking to you in the hall." Ignoring the look he gave her, she took a tentative step toward the bedroom.

And was immediately swarmed by a screeching, squealing, hysterical cascade of yellow. With a soft scream she threw up both hands to protect her face and head, turning away and trying to duck.

The feathered avalanche winged past Max, beating at his face and upper body as it exploded through the open patio door. Instinctively he threw up his arms, diverting the stream of feathers and beaks around his head. The entire assault lasted only seconds. Then, except for a lingering smell of stale birdseed, it was over.

Breathing hard, he turned to look out the open door as the intensely yellow cloud dissipated, its individual components scattering in all directions. In less than a minute it had vanished, save for a few stragglers who had chosen to perch on palm fronds or telephone wires to take more deliberate stock of their situation and surroundings. If not for their continued presence he might have accounted the entire experience a mad dream.

Mrs. Bonley was standing next to him, eyeing the high wire where half a dozen of the escapees now reposed. "I guess that's the end of little Bidgee." She looked up at her stunned neighbor. "I don't understand it, Mr. Parker. There must have been more than a hundred of them. Where could they all have come from? I only had one canary."

"I—I don't know, Ginger. Maybe a pet store delivery truck had an accident nearby and all their cages broke open."

But there had been no accident involving a pet store delivery truck, he knew, or a pet store, or some unsuspected private aviary. He did not need Barrington Boles's brain to figure out what had happened. The para effect was still in full flow, only this time it had reached out to not one parallel world, or two or three, but to more than a hundred.

It made perfect sense. Parallel worlds would naturally be inhabited by more than para humans. There would also be para cats, and para dogs, and probably para whales and cockroaches. Only that could explain the sudden manifestation in Ginger Bonley's nearby apartment of a hundred para canaries. Flocked in her bedroom, they had made a break for freedom as soon as they had detected an opening to the outside.

Elsewhere, in many identical or near-identical elsewheres, a hundred para Ginger Bonleys must simultaneously be bemoaning the inexplicable loss of their plumed pets. Somewhere, a hundred innocent para cats might be concurrently catching hell. The birds had all looked exactly alike, but then, every canary he had ever seen had looked just like every other canary he had ever seen. Scattered and dispersed throughout West L.A., he doubted any coincidences would be remarked upon. To the best of his knowledge, genetic researchers were not in the habit of catching stray canaries to see if they could use them to make a perfect DNA match.

What next? he thought uneasily. A thousand para Pekingese

pitter-pattering the streets of Beverly Hills, two thousand para coyotes massing for a joint assault on the mountain residences of Mulholland Drive? He was a locus, a nexus, helpless to manipulate or mitigate the effect that had settled in, on, or around him.

"Mr. Parker, are you all right?" A concerned Mrs. Bonley was looking up at him, brushing fitfully at the canary poop speckling her hair.

Grim-faced, he stepped around her and into the living room. "I'm fine, I'm all right. Will you be okay?"

"I suppose." Not surprisingly, she looked and sounded slightly shell-shocked. "If they all came from a broken pet shop truck, how did they get into my apartment? All the windows were closed."

"Maybe you forgot and left one open." He was already out in the hall. "It doesn't matter. They're gone."

"Yes, they're gone." She snuffled softly. "Along with my little Bidgee."

He was moved to compassion, a condition that afflicted him but infrequently. "I'm sorry about your birds—your bird, Ginger. But it's not like you lost a dog you've had for twenty years. You can always get another canary. And you still have all your plants for company."

"Yes, I suppose so." She was absently rubbing her chin with the forefinger of her left hand. "After what just happened, I just don't know if that's such a good idea." She looked at him wide-eyed. Ginger could be a little strange. Also, she was from Arkansas. "Do you think they were evil?"

"What?" he mumbled absently, his attention still held by the few remaining birds perched on the telephone line. "No, I don't think they were evil, Ginger. Some things in this world are just hard to explain, that's all."

And you wouldn't understand the explanation if I took a day to lay it all out for you, he thought. *Even if it does make more sense than claiming that they were Satan's canaries.*

What next? he wondered as he stumbled back to his apartment. Around him, the most ordinary everyday objects began to take on ominous overtones. Was he to be overwhelmed in his sleep by a thousand para pillows? Dare he check his pantry for something to eat without expecting to encounter a million para roaches?

Back inside his living room all was calm, serene, and blessedly normal. If he could not relax, at least the chilling panic was beginning to leave him.

He attempted work, but without success. Every time he tried to outline a story, or fix on something appealing from his file of tips and proposals, he found himself blocked by visions of his para selves on a million parallel worlds sitting in the same room bending over the same laptop computer, struggling fruitlessly to conjure the same empty words. From his encounter with the Omaha sisters he knew that slight differences were likely to prevail among his innumerable para selves.

The morose mood into which he had fallen notwithstanding, he found himself smiling at the thought that perhaps one or two of the uncountable horde of Max Parkers might be having better luck than he was.

He prided himself on enjoying his free time to the fullest, but even after he quit trying to get any work done, the rest of the day turned out to be a waste. He managed to cook and consume a fitful supper, wondering what his para selves might be eating and how many might be suffering from indigestion due to variations in his frequently uninspired para cooking.

After the sun had set and darkness had enveloped the shore, he donned shorts and a sweatshirt and made his way down to the beach. A cool breeze was blowing in off the Pacific and he encountered only one homeless person (was it that long ago that people used to call them winos? he mused) as he trudged across the deep sand toward the water.

Ignoring the KEEP OFF sign fastened to one leg of the lifeguard tower, he ascended the weathered wooden ramp and sat down, folding his legs beneath him as he rested his back against the door of the locked cubicle. Perched twenty feet above the sand, he gazed at the string of lights that ran south toward the bump of the Palos Verde peninsula and north toward the affluent curving coast of Malibu. Barrington Boles's house was located farther north, around the point. He found that he was glad he could not see it.

The intermittent but rejuvenating breeze had already

swept any lingering smog inland, dumping the pollutants of greater Los Angeles on the unlucky inhabitants of the San Gabriel and San Bernardino valleys. Overhead lay a black sky in which the most prominent stars competed for attention with the pulsating night lights of the great city.

Tilting his head back against the wind-worn, sand-blasted, faded green plywood, he stared upward. Billions of galaxies, the astronomers claimed, within which could be found trillions of planets. Did each and every one of them boast their own infinitude of parallel worlds? Did the concept of universal parallelity espoused by Barry Boles allow for an infinity of worlds multiplied by infinity?

In school he'd had difficulty with any group of numbers that extended beyond three places. Algebra had absolutely defeated him, and trigonometry he had always imagined to be more difficult to learn than Sanskrit. Therefore, the actual numbers he was contemplating presently had less than no meaning and he could barely imagine them in the abstract. It was enough to know that the universe was Big, and if Barrington Boles was right, it could now be multiplied by the figure Bigger Still.

And at the moment it seemed to him as if it was all, all of it, centered on him.

It was too much to think about. His brain was not equipped for the contemplation of such concepts. Such notions acquired life and substance only in the minds of mathematicians and theoretical physicists. To Max, a quantum state was one where gambling was licensed, and Schrödinger's cat lived somewhere on Laurel Avenue.

He lowered his gaze and watched the white rims of waves roll in and splinter into hissing, dissipating foam. There was nothing he could do but wait it out, wait for the field to vanish of its own accord. At least until Tuesday, he reminded himself. Boles had told him that if the effect persisted, to come back Tuesday. He had an idea, the inventor had claimed.

It better be more than an idea, Max thought tensely as he looked down at the fingers of his right hand. They did not glow, did not flicker with reality-distorting energy. Whatever else the Boles field was, it was not visible.

Three para burglars he could cope with. Four beautiful para sisters he could handle. A hundred emigrating para canaries made for a shocking but not dangerous sight. Thus far his encounters with intruders from parallel worlds had been relatively benign, but what if the next one was not? What if, in pursuing a story in the Hollywood hills, he found himself confronted by a hundred para rattlesnakes? What could a doctor do if someone with a cold sneezed in his face and instead of finding himself conventionally infected, his body suddenly bulged with a billion para germs? Tuesday began to look more and more like a day of salvation.

Meanwhile he would just have to be patient and cope. Act normally, Boles had advised him. Easy to say, when you were not the one looking sideways at every person, every living thing, every object, expecting it at any moment suddenly to multiply and reproduce.

His tormented wave-caressed solitude was interrupted by the hacking sound of a lonely vagabond retching a little ways up the beach.

Much to his surprise, upon finally returning to his apartment and falling into bed, Max enjoyed a restful and sound sleep. All the angst and excitement of the previous day had exhausted his body as well as his mind.

Rising early, he took a long shower. Following this with fresh coffee and a schmeared bagel left him feeling better than expected. Work would keep his mind occupied and off his unfortunate condition, and the hectic atmosphere at the office would help to pass the time. Tuesday no longer seemed so far away, or unreachable.

He even enjoyed battling the traffic on the way to work. The bad driving habits and worse manners displayed by his fellow commuters were another refreshing sign of normalcy in a world that had recently suffered from an excess of abnormality. Even though he was a little late arriving, no one had parked in his space. By the time he headed up in the elevator he was convinced he could get through the worst of whatever the Boles Field could throw at him.

In the hall he ran into Serra from subscriptions. The other man eyed him oddly, to the point that Max was moved to comment. "Something wrong, Carlos?" He checked his fly, which was circumspect.

"Uh, I guess not." Serra glanced back the way he had come. "Man, I knew you were a go-getter, but I didn't know that you *ran* from meeting to meeting."

Max blinked. "Say again?"

"Never mind." Serra pushed past him. "Got to go, man. The BHL are waiting on me." He winked. "Feeding time at the local post office."

Max felt that the tabloid-hungry blue-haired ladies who actually subscribed to the *Investigator*, as opposed to buying it at the checkout stand of their local supermarket, could wait until he had received a more detailed explanation of Serra's comment, but the other man was already at the elevator. Some kind of fluke, he told himself, or else the assistant subscription manager was having a little fun at his baffled coworker's expense.

As it developed, he apparently wasn't the only one.

"Whoa!" Turning a corner, he nearly ran over Heather Cerkas. Barely five feet tall, blond, pretty, and petite as a Parisian chanteuse, she was a bundle of inexhaustible energy who always seemed to be a dozen places at once around the office. The unforced analogy was one that made him suddenly uneasy.

"Sorry." As he tried to go around her she reached out and grabbed his arm.

"Wait a minute. How did you . . . ?" She broke off, looked behind her, then slowly released her grip.

"How did I what?" He grinned gamely. "Whatever it is I'm

not guilty, unless it's something good, in which case I readily confess."

"I'm not sure confession is called for." She was eyeing him most peculiarly. Not unlike Serra, in fact.

"Look, what's going on here?" Mounting exasperation threatened to ruin his good mood. "What's the gag?"

"That's what I'd like to know," she replied elliptically. "When you figure it out, be sure and let me in on it." She pushed past him.

"Hey, wait a minute!" But Cerkas showed no more inclination to linger than had Serra.

Maybe I should go out, go back to the car, and start over again, he told himself. What was with everybody this morning? But it wasn't everybody, he told himself. He'd passed plenty of people he knew and had swapped hellos or good-mornings with them without any incomprehensible ancillary commentary whatsoever. So two of his dozens of colleagues and acquaintances had decided that today was going to be "Let's weird out Max" day. Two out of dozens. Well, screw 'em. He had better things to do than wonder at their sick motivation.

His assigned modular cubicle had high walls of smooth gray fiberboard. These were decorated with favorite clippings of his own stories as well as those of colleagues and competitors he admired. Scattered among them like incisive confetti were Max-anointed political cartoons, gags, photos, and personal memorabilia. Notes for stories, memos from management and coworkers, current relevant newspaper and magazine clippings, all bunched up around the computer on his faux wood desk like so much proprietary dandruff. There were also two multibuttoned phones, a compact fax-copier, a miniature Christmas tree decorated entirely with tiny pigs, and the current centerfold from a particularly notorious magazine on which female coworkers had scribbled insulting comments.

In short, everything was normal and as it should be save for one notable exception: his computer was on. And not only was it open, but it was open to one of his private files. Openmouthed, he stared at it. First off, people who worked at the *Investigator* did not mess with one another's machines. It was an unforgivable breach of office protocol, not to mention accepted professional courtesy. Second, his personal encoding system was supposed to be unbreachable by anyone of lesser skill than a CIA encryption specialist.

Furious, he looked around to see who might be watching for his reaction, but no joker was staring over a partition at him or standing in one of the passageways giggling. Still fuming silently, he closed down the file, debated whether to take a seat and try to start work, and ended up stomping off tightlipped and frustrated in the direction of the men's bathroom.

Outrage dominating his thoughts, he angrily banged open the door and stomped over to the first sink. A couple of sharp twists brought both faucets on full flow. Allowing the hot and cold to mix, he splashed some on his face and fumbled for the roll of paper towels. As he turned away from the basin to dry his face, he heard a reverberant flushing sound and saw himself come out of a cubicle. At approximately the same time the himself who was buckling his belt saw himself holding a handful of absorptive recycled brown paper to his own face and halted. Identical jaws dropped simultaneously.

"Holy shit!" Max mumbled.

Equally flabbergasted, himself stared back. "Who the hell are you?"

For an instant Max was really not sure. As the once strong sensation of self began to flee madly, he hastened to rein it in. "Max—Maxwell Parker."

The other's expression twisted sardonically. *Do I look like that when I'm about to get sarcastic?* Max found himself wondering. *I guess I do, because I am.*

"What a hysterically funny coincidence," the other declaimed, not smiling at all.

Max's reply was as controlled as it was emotionless. "No it isn't."

V

"What are you," the emerging Max inquired, "some kind of clone?" His gaze traveled the length of the figure standing at the sink. "What are you doing in my clothes? And when did you start parting your hair on the right?"

"I'm not a clone, these are my clothes, and I've always parted my hair on the right." The alternate hair parting was the only visible difference in his other self. It was just like looking into a mirror, only in this case the mirror talked back. With an edge in its voice.

Max turned. At any moment their transient privacy might be lost, leading to questions he did not want to have to try and answer. "Listen, I'll explain it all as best I can, but not here. We need to find someplace quiet away from people who know us."

His counterpart hesitated only briefly before replying with a suggestion. "How about El Cortez?"

Max nodded agreeably. It was the same place he would have picked. Naturally. The Mexican restaurant was a personal favorite. The booths were dark, the service discreet, and at this hour no one from the office would be there. "I was just about to suggest that myself."

"Of course you were," murmured his twin. "This is insane."

"No, it's science. It's been my experience that science is never insane, just maddeningly complex." He walked to the door, paused a moment before stepping through. "Unlike people. Since I don't like to think I'm going insane, and also to keep things on as even a keel as possible, how about if I call you Mitch?"

"Wait a minute." The other man objected as quickly as Max would have himself. "How come I have to be Mitch? Why can't you be Mitch? Or Murphy, or Marty, or whatever the hell you like?"

Max stared stolidly at himself staring back at him. "Do you have a clue as to what's going on?"

"Well, no," his other self admitted.

"That's why." Max put a hand on the door. "Wait five minutes. By that time I'll be clear of the building." He smiled thinly. "No point in inviting questions neither of us can answer. I'll meet you at the restaurant."

"Back corner booth?" said Mitch.

"Where else?" Max headed toward the elevators.

No one intercepted him as he left. For a moment he considered waiting for his double. If he took the Aurora, Mitch would have to walk. But it wasn't far and besides, the Aurora was *his* car. Of course, Mitch would doubtless think of it the same way.

This early in the morning the restaurant was virtually deserted except for the habitual barflies. Mitch arrived fifteen minutes later, miffed and winded in equal measure.

"I thought somebody stole my car," he explained as he slipped into the other side of the booth. "Then I realized that you probably took it."

"I considered leaving it for you. But you know how it is: first Max come, first Max served."

"You're handling this a lot better than I am." Munching on corn chips and salsa, Mitch looked distinctly unhappy.

"That's because I know what's going on."

"Yeah." His other leaned forward. "Mind filling me in?"

"You're not going to like it."

Mitch made a face. "I don't like it already."

Over drinks, chips, guacamole, and salsa, Max explained as best he could. He did not have to repeat anything, since Mitch understood intuitively. Talking to yourself, Max reflected, had certain advantages.

When he had finished the story, Mitch leaned back in his chair. His expression was akin to that of the man who had just seen the proverbial purple horse prance past. It looked like a horse, neighed like a horse, and smelled like a horse—but the suspicion remained that there was something seriously unequine about it.

"So what you're trying to tell me is that I'm one of these things you call a para?"

"Not me," Max reminded him. "That's Barry Boles's term."

Mitch straightened and took a deep breath. "If what you're telling me is true, I expect we'd both like to strangle the bastard."

"Of course we would. But that's not going to solve your problem or make mine go away. Fortunately, we're not encumbered by any close personal relationships at the moment, so nobody will miss you for a while."

"If I only show up for work in this world and not in mine, I'll get fired," Mitch reminded himself.

Max tried to reassure his other self. "Don't panic. You know how often we go off on assignment. Kryzewski will think MacKenzie assigned you, and MacKenzie will think it was Kryzewski. That state of affairs won't last indefinitely, but everything should be resolved and back to normal within a couple of days. Tuesday, to be exact."

Mitch swirled his drink unhappily. "*If* this Boles can fix things." Max had no ready reply to that. "This sucks. I want back to my own world."

"Nobody wants that more than I do," Max told him feelingly. "Of course, nobody would. I mean, if you can't get sympathy from yourself, where can you? But for now it looks like you're stuck."

"So what do we do?"

"We?" Max frowned. "Why 'we'?"

Mitch looked up sharply. "Don't tell me you're thinking of turning your own self out on the street?"

"To tell you the truth, I hadn't really thought that far ahead. But I guess you're right." Max brightened. "How about we explain you as my visiting twin brother from back East, whom I haven't seen in years?"

"I guess that's okay." His duplicate sounded less than enthusiastic. "I still don't see why I can't be Max and you be Mitch."

Max held his ground. "I've already explained; you're my para."

"Is that a fact? What makes you think that you're not *my* para?"

Max struggled to contain his exasperation—not to mention his increasing confusion. "Look, if we start fighting about individual nomenclature we're both going to wind up in the loony bin. Just indulge me, will you?" He smiled encouragingly. "After all, you'll be indulging yourself."

"I don't feel very indulged," his other muttered. "But what you say about drawing unwanted attention makes sense."

A relieved Max smiled. "How could it be otherwise? You said it—more or less."

"Okay, fine. So now I'm 'Mitch.' But only for the duration." The exasperated para downed the rest of his drink. "This is a great place, except they never put enough salt on their margarita glasses."

"You don't have to tell me," Max replied promptly.

"I know," said the para.

Max did his best to put a positive spin on their unprecedented situation. "This *could* be interesting, if we don't let it get us down."

"Easy for you to say," grumbled Mitch. "You're not the one missing a world."

They left separately, Max letting Mitch pick up the tab after first checking to insure that their credit card numbers were identical. They matched perfectly, except that Mitch's photo ID showed his hair parted on the wrong side. Needless to say, the bored cashier did not pick up on the subtle and almost invisible difference.

Having paid, Mitch wanted to drive. Out of curiosity, Max let him, and sat back in silent astonishment as his para negotiated exactly the same route back to the beach that Max himself would have chosen.

If not for the eerie overtones that made it feel as if he was talking to himself (but wasn't he?) he might have enjoyed the situation. It was like having the world's best valet. Mitch drove, Mitch opened the garage, Mitch parked the car. Too bad, he found himself thinking wryly, that neither one of them could cook.

As much as he had come to accept the situation, it was

still something of a shock when Mitch pulled a set of keys from his pocket and opened the door to the apartment.

"Home," his para murmured as they stepped inside. "My home, your home, our home." He looked over at himself and smiled. "I'm glad all the bills are paid on our other place. My place. Everything will be all right for a while until this Boles person can restore me to my reality. Meanwhile," he said as he headed for the kitchen, "all that sitting around in El Cortez has made me hungry."

"Not me." Max trailed him. "We may be alike, but it looks like we're not locked in a do-everything-together two-step."

"Damn good thing, too." Mitch was examining the contents of the refrigerator, verifying that its contents were identical to his own. "Otherwise we might go crazy." He was nodding approvingly as he spoke. "Salami, mayo, relish, our favorite brand of tuna—you've got all the right stuff."

Max nodded solemnly. "What else would you expect from yourself? I don't have to ask if there's anything in there you'd like to eat. If you're going to make a sandwich, and I suspect that you are, there's half a loaf of cracked wheat bread in the pantry. Just go easy on the groceries. It looks like I'm buying for the two of us now."

While Mitch threw together tuna and bread (about the extent of their combined knowledge of gourmet home cookery, Max reflected), his counterpart opened a beer and took a seat in the den. They subsequently discovered that they liked the same television programs except that Mitch preferred the local news on channel four instead of two, and he rooted for a different local basketball team. These less-than-earthshaking revelations provided just enough leeway in conversation to separate them as individuals, despite the overwhelming similarities, and allowed each man room enough in which to establish an identity apart from his para.

Ready to retire at the same time, they went through the motions of preparing for bed in exactly the same fashion save that Mitch brushed with an up-and-down motion while Max preferred to stroke from side to side. The king-sized bed was more than adequate for the both of them, and neither man had any compunction about sleeping with himself. Graciously, Max allowed Mitch to have the right side of the bed, which both men favored.

"This doesn't mean I'm buying lunch again tomorrow," Mitch pointed out as he climbed between the sheets. "Remember, my bank account's also in another world."

Max checked the alarm before turning out the light. "Talk about your convenient excuses . . ."

Dressing the following morning was no problem. Everything that fit Max fit Mitch, and they took turns at the bathroom sink and mirror. Breakfast was a matter of simply making two of everything.

"Remember now." Max led the way down to the garage. "You're my twin brother Mitch from back East, visiting the

West Coast for the first time since I started working for the paper."

The para indicated that he understood. "I'll be careful not to say too much or I'm liable to reveal too much knowledge of L.A. for a supposed stranger."

Max nodded approvingly. "That's just what I would do."

"Of course it is. And we're going to have to stop remarking on that as well."

They entered the deserted garage. "You've got it easy," Max told him. "I'm the one who still has to work."

"What makes you think that's going to be easy?" the para complained. "What am I supposed to do while you're working? I can't just sit around and do nothing all day." At a sudden thought, Mitch brightened. "I know. I'll help you. We can collaborate. We're already collaborating on the Boles story."

Max did not need long to consider the offer. "Sure, why not? I'll attend the story conference this morning and you can do research." He followed the suggestion with a lopsided smile. "I know you know the passwords for the computer."

Mitch looked pleased. "We'll amaze even those who thought you were a fast worker. Some of them are liable to think there are two of you." Both men chuckled, as was appropriate. They found the same things equally amusing.

In response to Kryzewski's queries Max was forced to stall on turning in the final draft of the Boles story by explaining that he was still working out certain angles and verifying specific details. That did not mean he was completely tied up with that one particular story, however. In response, and reflecting the fact that it was a slow news day, he was directed to work up something on Judy, the renowned painting elephant. The assignment suited Max perfectly, since it meant that he and Mitch could spend the rest of the day out of the office and away from startled stares and prying questions.

"What can we do with an elephant that paints?" Mitch leaned back in the passenger seat as Max accelerated up the on-ramp, heading east toward Griffith Park and the Los Angeles Zoo.

"Beats me. There have been stories on this elephant before, in the daily media. It's pretty bland stuff." Max looked at his para. "That's why Kryzewski assigned me to it. I'm supposed to be good at finding new angles to old news. So don't just sit there. Think of something inventive."

"What do you think I'm doing?" Mitch replied irritably. "Two heads are only better than one if the first leaves the second alone once in a while."

"Let's concentrate on different approaches. I'll work the elephant angle, and you try to come up with something based on the paintings she does. Something like 'Noted Freudian Seeks Vindication Through Elephant Art,' or 'Ponderous Pachydermal Paintings Pure Pontification, Praises Poet.'"

"Fair enough," agreed Mitch.

"Of course it is." Once up to speed on the freeway, his double focused on his driving. "We're a fair kind of guy."

Max had no trouble gaining admission to the zoo with his press pass, but the attendant wanted Mitch to pay, insisting that the pass was only good for one. They solved the problem by having Max enter alone. After checking around for Security personnel, he then moved quickly to a chain-link fence and handed his pass over to Mitch. Presenting the pass at the other main gate, he was readily admitted, unseen by the first attendant.

Judy's keeper was delighted that they had come to do a story on her charge. With every news release, the price of the elephant's colorful abstracts rose. That meant additional income for the zoo, and not incidentally, more notoriety for the four-legged artist's handlers. Her delight was mitigated when Max informed her that they represented the *Investigator*.

"The *Times* has already done a couple of stories on us," she informed them. When neither of them responded to this she added reluctantly, "I suppose any publicity is good for the zoo. You're not going to do anything unpleasant like say she paints pornography or something, are you?"

Mitch responded with a reassuring smile. "As I understand it, her 'paintings' are all abstruse swatches of color. Pretty hard to read something controversial into that."

"People love to read about the anthropomorphic aspects of animals." Max chuckled encouragingly. "The pig that lives in the house, the dog that likes to ride motorcycles, the bird that rings the doorbell—that sort of thing. That's where Judy fits in. She's entertaining, not controversial."

"Well, your paper is certainly 'entertaining.' " The young female keeper directed them to a small electric cart. "Not that I ever read it," she added hastily. "I just see it at the checkout stand in the supermarket."

"Of course you do." Mitch struggled to keep any hint of condescension out of his voice. He winked at Max. Nobody ever actually bought the *Investigator* and its cousins. All those millions of copies that sold weekly were always purchased by Someone Else.

It was a short ride in the service cart to the spacious elephant enclosure, where Judy proved to be more congenial and cooperative than the majority of Max's human story subjects. At her keeper's command to "Paint, Judy!" the pachyderm delicately selected a brush from a bucket and turned her attention to a nearby rack that held cans of paint. Choosing her own colors and working with unmistakable deliberation, she proceeded to execute broad streaks and splotches on an easeled canvas. From across the way, ordinary, less privileged zoo-goers looked on raptly.

"Her paintings sell for thousands of dollars." The keeper repeatedly patted the elephant on her side and trunk.

"Who gets the money?" Mitch had his own recorder out and Max was watching him admiringly. *We're all professional, I am*, he thought.

"It all goes to the zoo. Mostly for educational programs

and elephant upkeep." The keeper's affection for her multi-ton charge was evident.

Max glanced knowingly at his other self. "Come on, now. Are you telling us that Judy doesn't have her own bank account? After all, it's her money."

"Yeah." Mitch was warming to the possibilities. "She probably has thousands stashed away in a numbered Swiss account."

"No, no, in the Seychelles," Max corrected him. "That's the closest tax haven to East Africa."

Mitch nodded. "Wouldn't surprise me if she has somebody working the peanut futures at the Chicago Commodities Exchange for her."

Heretofore open and friendly, the keeper was now eyeing them anxiously. "This is going to be a serious story, isn't it? I mean, I know the kind of paper you guys are working for, but you're not going to make fun of Judy, are you? She's a genius, not a freak."

"I wouldn't dare make fun of her, or her manifest artistic abilities," Max insisted somberly. "After all, if I wrote a less than respectful story and somebody read it to her, she'd never forget it." Next to him, Mitch chuckled appreciatively. "Seriously, I've seen plenty of so-called innovative gallery art that isn't half as interesting."

"And she works for peanuts," Mitch reminded him, proving himself incapable of resisting the obvious. "I'd buy one of her pieces myself. If I had the money. If I had a blank wall."

"You sure can't afford it," Max told him. "And I ought to know."

They were interrupted by a commotion on the far side of the enclosure, beyond the protective moat and wall. Mitch strained to see.

"Wonder what's going on over there?" Behind him, the keeper left Judy to her painting and joined them for a better look, standing on tiptoes and shading her eyes with one hand as she tried to see.

"Something's not right. There's some kind of trouble. I . . ." She broke off as the intercom clipped to her belt buzzed. Max and Mitch waited silently while she listened.

"Yes . . . yes sir, right away, sir." Snapping the unit shut, she looked up at her two guests. "There's a zoo emergency. All visitors must be evacuated now. I'm afraid I'm going to have to cut this short." Without waiting for a reply she turned and ran off back the way they'd come. Baffled, and unwilling to be left alone with even an artistic elephant, they followed her at a more measured pace.

"What's wrong, what's the matter?" Max called after her, but she was already too far in the lead to hear. Not wanting to be left behind, they lengthened their strides to catch up.

In the service alley behind the elephant enclosure they found her waiting impatiently behind the wheel of the electric cart. Wordlessly, she watched them climb aboard, barely waiting for Mitch's feet to clear the pavement before she engaged the engine. With a jerk, the compact vehicle started off down the narrow paved track they had taken previously.

"If I'm not diverted, I should be able to drive you all the way to the entrance. The office there has been secured. But stay alert." She did not look at them as she spoke. Instead, her eyes kept darting from side to side, intently examining the lush, dense landscaping that gave the zoo grounds the look and feel of a real forest even in the midst of a vast city.

" 'Secured'? 'Stay alert'?" Uneasy, Max stared out the right side of the cart. "Alert for what?"

"The chimps." Her expression was grim as the cart, driven much faster than it usually was on such rounds, bounced over the undulating asphalt. "The chimps have gotten loose."

"How do we tell them apart from the general public?" Mitch asked, unable to resist. He beat Max to the punchline by half a second.

Their guide was not amused. "You think this is funny? Chimpanzees are powerful, dangerous animals, with incredibly strong arms and long canines. The ones we have here aren't trained, like movie chimps. They're still more than half wild. If one gnaws half your face off, you won't think it so funny." With Mitch looking suitably abashed, she returned to her driving, negotiating the narrow twists and curves in the path with practiced ease.

They were starting to encounter panicked visitors. Not many, because early on a weekday morning the zoo was typically uncrowded, but enough to indicate that an alarm had been raised.

"Where are these renegade chimps now?" Max found himself watching the trees. Arriving to do a filler about a painting elephant, they found themselves quite by accident on the cusp of a breaking story of considerably more interest. He could see the headlines now, right up on the front of the next issue of the *Investigator*.

"KILLER CHIMPS TERRORIZE L.A. ZOO! RUN AMOK ON FREEWAY! DODGER STADIUM THREATENED BY CHEETAH AND BREAK-OUT RELATIVES!"

Bannered over a photo of someone like their middling attractive young hostess, with her clothing ripped in suitably strategic places, the story would without a doubt sell double or triple the usual number of copies. And he would have the chance to do a legitimate news story, for a change. Now, if only he and Mitch could get a glimpse of a couple of the proverbial raging chimpanzees, they would have all the verification they needed.

They did not have to wait long, and when the encounter finally took place, it involved rather more than one or two of the resourceful primates.

Rocking around a sharp bend, they came face-to-face with not one, not two, not a dozen, but perhaps fifty fully-grown adult chimps. Presently, this mob of 99.9-percent-same-DNA close cousins was tearing apart a mobile snack stand from whose vicinity the prescient operator had long since fled. Ice-cream bars were ripped open and slurped, popcorn was flung madly about, and vicious battles over colorful bags of peanuts raged in at least two separate locations.

The cart slowed as its driver changed direction to avoid the fracas. "I don't understand. This isn't possible."

"Don't take it so hard," Mitch told her. "Every once in a while a cage is breached somewhere in the world and its inhabitants get loose. It's just your turn today."

"It's not that." Wearing a dazed expression, she studied the anthropoid free-for-all as they drove carefully past. With plenty of food at hand, the rampaging chimps ignored them. "There are too many of them." She shifted her attention to Max. "There are only twelve individuals in the whole zoo chimp family. That includes males, females, and infants." She gestured with one hand. "Not only are there too many of them, but they're all adult females. I've spent a lot of time working with our primates and I know all our chimps by name. These I can't even tell apart."

Tell them apart. Max looked at Mitch. Neither man spoke; neither had to. Each knew what the other was thinking.

Fifty chimps where there ought to have been no more than twelve, and all looking alike. The rush of a hundred identical canaries had been unsettling, but in its perverse and unnatural fashion, almost beautiful. Certainly their presence was harmless. Fifty or more para chimps on the loose were something else entirely. As their hostess had explained, the husky primates constituted a very real danger, not only to one another as the peanut war demonstrated, but to fleeing visitors and overwhelmed zoo staff alike. He stared back over his shoulder as the howls and screeches receded behind them, glad that the menacing escapees had found something to hold their attention.

Mitch leaned forward and whispered. He needn't have bothered. Their guide was too preoccupied to pay any attention to their conversation anyway.

"Don't take this to heart, Max. You have no control over this field, or effect, or whatever it is. Things could be worse. You might have sucked in fifty para bull elephants, or fifty rhinos."

"I know, I know. But it's getting harder to try and ignore. If we hit the beach later and decide to go for a swim will the field around me pull in fifty para whales? Or a hundred?"

"You're asking me?" Mitch sat back, occasionally looking back the way they had come to make certain the boisterous chimps were not in pursuit. "If we did and that happened, it wouldn't surprise me if they were all white, with wrinkled brows lined with broken lines and bent harpoons."

"This isn't a literary conceit, Mitch," Max replied darkly. "This is happening."

"Pardon me if from time to time I try to pretend that it's not." He shifted in his seat and scratched reflexively at his chin, precisely as Max would have done.

We may do things alike but at least we don't do everything simultaneously, he mused. That would have been too much to take. He fought down the urge to scratch.

They passed another group of some twenty chimps being driven back in the general direction of the overwhelmed primate enclosure by a phalanx of keepers and other zoo personnel who had been recruited for the purpose. Intelligent and agile, the chimps were proving difficult to round up. Several scampered gleefully up nearby eucalyptus trees. From their inviolable perches they rained insults, urine, and branches down on their outnumbered assailants. In the distance, the high-pitched complaint of approaching sirens could be heard.

"Reinforcements," Mitch observed.

"I don't suppose the director had any choice," their hostess commented. "The chimps can't be allowed to get out of the zoo. They could run around in the rest of Griffith Park for weeks, months even, attacking hikers and picnickers." She was chewing her lower lip. "Our people have tranquilizer guns. I don't know where all these chimps came from, but I'd hate to see any of them end up dead."

"Police and sheriff departments have tranquilizer rifles, too," Mitch pointed out. "For darting wandering coyotes, and bears, and mountain lions, and citizens tripping on PCP." Some of the sirens were very loud now. "Hopefully they're coming with that in mind."

Not only that, Max knew, but on a number of parallel worlds in a plethora of parallel zoos, a host of distraught parallel keepers must be lamenting the sudden disappearance of their own chimpanzees, no doubt worrying anxiously over their present location and condition.

"Where do you think they all came from?" Mitch was watching their guide carefully. Max threw him a sharp look, but the question was a perfectly natural one for a reporter to ask.

They slowed as the service cart approached the main gate area. There was no panic, but frantic visitors were struggling to file through the exits while anxious cops came pouring through the entrance gates. Hauling nets and specialized rifles, they were accompanied by local veterinarians and other volunteers. Television news crews from most of the metropolitan stations were not far behind. Somehow the story no longer seemed quite so important to Max.

"I don't know and can't imagine. Maybe they escaped from some movie star's illegal private primatarium, or an unlicensed medical research lab." The guide climbed out of the cart. "I'm going to have to leave you here. They'll be needing me for the roundup."

"Git along little monkeys," Mitch quipped. "They had to come from somewhere."

She looked back over her shoulder as she ran toward the main administration office. "Maybe it's part of a more elaborate agenda. You might try contacting the representatives of the more radical local animal-rights groups. This could be their way of making a statement." She disappeared into the office before Max could ask her any more questions.

Mitch was eyeing him expectantly. "What now—brother?"

Max studied the confusion. Most of the zoo visitors had been hustled outside. A small army of cops and medical personnel continued to stream onto the grounds. Their thoughts focused on rampaging chimps, nobody paid the two "twins" the least attention.

"I guess we might as well get out of here. It'll make a great story." He started toward a deserted exit gate.

"Sure will." Mitch sounded equally unenthusiastic. "You write it, I guess, and I'll do the polish."

"Oh sure, put all the work off on me!"

"Why not? You're the one who's going to get the credit. Remember, in my world I'm absent without leave."

"Okay. You can have the story." Max pushed through the revolving gate.

"Fat lot of good it'll do me. No chimps are going berserk in my L.A."

"That's right," Max realized. "I didn't think of that."

Wending their way through the advance guard of emergency vehicles that had assembled outside the main entrance, they circled to the left to avoid the surging crush of nervous, uneasy visitors who had been hustled out of the zoo. Piling into their cars, families and couples honked and beeped at one another in their haste to get clear of the parking lot. To Max's relief, his new car was right where he had left it, untouched and safe from the near-panic. The Aurora responded instantly when he thumbed the unlock button on the remote door key entry system.

In fact, all eight of them did.

VI

They were lined up as neatly as in a showroom lot, side by side and facing the same direction. All eight gleamed with the same champagne-gold paint, and displayed the same sharp ding on the passenger's-side doorframe, an identical pattern of collected dirt, and the same beige upholstery. Three had license plates that differed by one digit. One had a map bag on the backseat. While curious to see what kind of maps it contained, Max was more anxious to flee the increasingly frenetic atmosphere of the zoo parking lot.

Mitch had gone on ahead and was trying doors. Released by Max's remote, every one of them was open. "I guess we can take any one of them." He smiled wanly. "They're all ours."

"Somewhere, six of us are missing their cars." Max fingered the door handle of the nearest Aurora. "I'd sure like to leave in my own."

"Why yours?" Mitch rejoined him. "Why not mine?" Leaning over and peering through a window, he tried to find some small detail that would separate his particular vehicle from the rest. Max joined him in the search.

They were able to eliminate the three cars with the variant license plates plus the one with the map pocket on the backseat. That left four, so identical that they might have been prepped for sequential scenes of automotive destruction by a Hollywood special-effects team.

Mitch slid behind the wheel of the nearest. "I can't tell any of the others apart. Might as well take this one."

"I guess that's okay by me." Max stood by the door. "Except that I'm driving."

Mitch smiled up at him. "Of course you are. Aren't I already in the driver's seat?"

His counterpart was not amused. "Don't start. Isn't everything messed up enough for you as it is?"

Himself stared back up at him. "Are you saying I don't know the way back to the office?"

"We're not going back to the office." Max's expression was grim. "We're going out to Boles's. He said he might have a solution to my—to our problem. You ought to meet him anyway." A thin smile split his face. "The reality of your presence will lend emphasis to the situation."

Unable to come up with a counterargument, a reluctant Mitch slid across the seat and allowed Max to take up position behind the wheel. "I'm used to dealing with perpetual motion fanatics and flat-earthers, but not some freak whose invention actually works."

"He's no freak. Actually, he's a pretty nice guy, for a rich SOB." Max turned the key in the ignition and the Aurora roared to life. "I could like him, if he hadn't screwed up my life so badly."

"Our life," Mitch corrected him as Max pulled out and headed north.

Utilizing a back service road enabled them to avoid the horn-blaring traffic that was crowding the main entrance to the zoo's parking lot. There was no one around to challenge the Aurora's right to use the restricted roadway. Every zoo employee had been called to do battle with the inexplicable outbreak of chimps.

On the way out of Griffith Park, as they were heading for the nearest on-ramp to the Ventura Freeway, the Aurora passed a trio of the energetic primates scampering hell-bent for the hills of the mountainous park. Some unsuspecting hikers were in for an afternoon surprise, Max reflected.

They stayed on the Ventura all the way to Malibu Canyon Road, having no need to cut back through the west side of the city. This being Los Angeles, traffic never entirely disappeared even at midday, but once they were past Topanga it finally began to thin.

They wound through the mountains before heading down the other side toward the gleaming blue Pacific. Since Max was concentrating on the twisting, ancient road, it was Mitch who let out a start and sat up sharply in his seat.

"Did you see that?" He was staring out the passenger's-side window.

"See what?" Max slowed, but kept his attention on the pavement.

"Bighorn sheep. A whole damn herd of 'em!"

Max had to grin. "There are no bighorns in Southern California. You know that. Where do you think you are? Colorado?"

"Yeah, I know it." Mitch settled back in the seat. "But I saw them."

"You saw ordinary, everyday, domestic sheep. Maybe this bunch was healthier than usual. There are probably several hobby herds around here. Rich folks in these hills keep everything from lions to llamas." He broke off as he concentrated on making a tight curve without stressing the tires.

Mitch glanced over at him. "There's nothing wrong with our eyes, as you damn well know, and I'm as familiar with the hobby wildlife of Southern California as you are. I'm telling you, they were bighorns."

"All right, they were bighorns. Let me know when you spot the first grizzly."

"Don't worry," Mitch told him without a flicker of sarcasm. "I will." He turned his gaze back to the window.

They reached the coast highway without encountering

any oversized bears or any more heavy-horned sheep, by which time even Mitch was beginning to wonder if he'd imagined the noble flock.

They both saw the condor, however.

It approached from behind, soaring over the front of the car, tracking the highway in search of fresh roadkill. His eyes wide, Max leaned forward against the wheel. Alongside him, Mitch did likewise.

There was no question in either man's mind as to the bird's identity. Its wingspan was immense, far greater than that of the state's largest buzzard. When it settled down to roost atop a telephone pole they could clearly see the svelte, hooked beak and domed, featherless skull.

"Watch it!" Mitch yelled.

Max jerked hard on the wheel, bringing them back into the northbound lane from which the Aurora had strayed. The blaring echo of a car traveling in the opposite direction briefly assailed their ears before fading rapidly behind them. Max found he was starting to sweat. So, not surprisingly, was Mitch.

"What's going on?" his passenger muttered darkly. "What the hell's happening?"

Max stared forward, his fingers tight on the wheel. "Bighorns and condors. We might see that grizzly yet." He looked over at himself. "I have a feeling that we're not where I belong anymore, Mitch. Or you either, judging by your reactions." He thought long and hard before continuing.

"I wonder if instead of creatures and things slipping from parallel worlds into mine, we've gone and slipped into a para world that's just slightly different from the one you or I are used to. We're not talking duplicates of existing people or critters anymore, but entirely new stuff. There are no bighorn sheep or condors in the Santa Monica Mountains." He scrutinized the road, the houses they were passing, the power and telephone lines.

"Everything else is the same, everything's normal, except that in this slightly different para more of the indigenous wildlife seems to have survived."

"Wonderful. An entirely new predicament to worry about." Mitch considered thoughtfully. "If that's really the case, then it's a better world than the one you or I live in."

"Maybe." Max was hesitant to agree. "If those are the only differences. Actually, there's only one I'm concerned about."

"What's that?"

Max met his double's gaze. "What if in this parallel world there's no Barrington Boles? We could be stuck here permanently."

Mitch sat back in his seat, staring out the window at the pavement ahead. It was the same Pacific Coast Highway that he knew so well, flanked by the same trees, the same fast-food restaurants, the same Malibu-trendy boutiques and shops. The same cars plied the side streets, driven by ordinary citizens intent on the familiar tasks of everyday life. Only in the Aurora was reality distorted, only in the minds of its passengers had it been displaced.

"Well," he observed finally, "if that's the case then at least we know we'll each have one friend. But I'm not sharing Lisa."

Max frowned. "Lisa? Lisa Sanchez from down in advertising? You're dating her?"

"Sure. Aren't you?"

"I've been trying to get her to go out with me for months. She always says she's too busy."

"Not for me she isn't." Mitch grinned.

"You smug son of a bitch. Tell me: How is she? Do we have a good time?"

"A great time." Mitch proceeded to explain exactly how. After all, it wasn't as if he was revealing intimate secrets to a stranger. Or worse, spilling the details to a representative of his own newspaper.

They were almost relaxed when Max noticed that something important had gone missing. Point Dume, to be precise. The small, rocky peninsula, a dominant local landmark, was nowhere to be seen. The Seabreak Motel sat where it belonged, as did the Malibu pier and its attendant restaurant and parking lot, but instead of rolling up against a thrusting cliff, the beach continued northward in a gentle, unbroken line.

Mitch missed the distinctive geological formation as well. It was another indication of how radically different a para they had slipped into. But the highway continued to unwind ahead of them, familiar and unbroken. A sign showed that Trancas and its attendant beach and community were not far ahead, exactly where they belonged. A peninsula had gone missing. Nothing to get excited about.

"Wish we could lose a few other parts of L.A." Unable to do anything about the situation in which he found himself, Mitch was doing his best to get into the spirit of things. "There's a building full of lawyers in Beverly Hills I could do without."

"Why stop there?" Max was feeling a little light-headed. "Why restrict ourselves to the L.A. basin? Why not wish away Libya, or Iran? If there can be a para where there's no Point Dume, why not one with no Hussein or Gaddafi?"

"Or no U.S. of A.," Mitch added. That thought sobered them up fast.

The elite beach community of Trancas looked undisturbed, exactly as Max remembered it from his last visit. He was ready to believe they had slipped back into his own world until he saw the guard booth at the entrance to the gated community wherein dwelled the meddlesome Barrington Boles. The cubicle was painted a soft oceanic blue instead of the bright sunny yellow he remembered. But the guard was the same, as was the road that led to Boles's hilltop aerie.

"He won't be surprised to see me," Max explained as the Aurora ascended after they had been passed on through the barrier, "but *you* ought to give him a start."

"I hope the bastard faints and hits his head," Mitch growled.

"He'd better not," an alarmed Max reproached his double. "We need that head. It's our only chance of putting things right and returning to normal, to our own worlds."

He pulled into the circular drive, noting with relief as he did so that the house and grounds were unchanged. Even the flowers and the rest of the landscaping were exactly as he remembered them. Overhead, the sun bathed the surrounding hills in warm, hazy Southern California light. In the distance the Pacific shone deep blue. Under such conditions it was hard to stay angry at anything. A condor went soaring by overhead on vast black wings, reminding them why they were there.

It was with great relief that Max heard Boles's voice respond over the intercom speaker set into the wall next to the door. When the inventor appeared in the portal a few moments later, the anxious reporter managed to summon a smile.

"Hello, Max. Nice to see you again."

"Not as nice as it is to see you."

The inventor frowned. "I don't understand." At that moment he caught sight of Mitch, who was standing slightly off to one side. The older man's jaw dropped slightly but perceptibly. "I didn't know you had a twin."

"I don't." Max gestured in Mitch's direction. "But I have a para. As you should know."

"As I should . . . ?" Boles halted, then stepped back. "I think you'd better come in. Both of you."

The den was just as Max remembered it. He sat down in a

chair this time, leaving the couch to Mitch and the opposite chair to their host. Boles's gaze kept shifting from one to the other.

"This is incredible. Simply incredible."

"Yeah, that's kind of how we see it." Mitch helped himself to a handful of cashews from a dish on the big coffee table.

"You're sure you're not twins?" the inventor inquired guardedly. "You're not pulling some kind of elaborate gag on me so you can make a fool of me in your paper?"

"Wasn't I straight with you when I was here before?" Max looked longingly at the cashews.

"Yes. Yes you were." Boles still did not sound quite convinced. "But after the failure of the system I couldn't keep from envisioning the ridicule a publication like yours could heap on me."

"Excuse me?" Max looked up sharply. "Failure? What failure?"

"The inability of my device to produce the effect I claimed for it, of course."

It was comfortably warm in the room, just as it had been outside, but that did not prevent a chill cold as a death-creep from running down Max's spine. "I don't know what you're talking about. Now who's trying to pull a gag? Your machine worked exactly like you claimed it would. I'm stuck with this field or whatever it is unpredictably and erratically affecting the world around me. Ever since I left here I've been running into parallel people, parallel things, and parallel occurrences."

He gestured at his double, who was munching away happily on the contents of the nut dish.

"We're calling him Mitch, but he's me in every respect. He's not my twin, he's a para. Until we can figure out a way for him to return to his own parallel world he's staying with me. It's not exactly an imposition. After all, we're more than best friends." He leaned forward slightly and stared hard at the would-be scientist. "So don't sit there and try to tell me that your infernal device didn't work. Mitch is living evidence to the contrary, and I can offer you plenty more."

Sincerity dominated the inventor's reply, was writ large on his face. "This is just plain unbelievable. I'm telling you, Max, that you walked out of here a few days ago mildly disappointed in my failure but otherwise unaffected. As much as I'd like to claim credit for it, my setup didn't work."

Max sat back and waved at Mitch. "Then how do you explain him, and everything else that's happened to me? I've had to deal with para women, para burglars, para cars, and even para chimpanzees. Not to mention at least one alternate para world in which condors and bighorn sheep still thrive in Southern California. Everything keeps changing around me, and without warning. There are no condors surviving in Mitch's para Southern California either, so that means that not only did he slip from his world into mine but that together we slipped into a third."

"You slipped into a third, all right," Boles agreed readily.

"And in this one, my machine did not work. Don't you see?" he finished earnestly.

Max finally did, and the shadow that he felt falling over him darkened. He and Mitch were in still another parallel world, all right. Only in this one, Boles's device had not worked, did not work. Which meant that he was not talking to the same Boles who had told him "he had an idea" on how to fix things and to come back Tuesday. That Boles was waiting on him in his own, original world, waiting futilely for a reporter who had gone slip-sliding away to show up at his house. He could not try out his corrective idea because the subject on whom it was to be tried had gone away—to a parallel world in which the inventor Boles had yet to succeed.

Obviously, Max now realized, he had to return to his own world line and to that particular Boles, or at least to a para in which Boles's device worked. But how? He did not know how he had slipped from his original world into this one, much less how to get back. Were parallel worlds like an enormous deck of cards that existed in a continuous state of shufflement? How could he gain the attention of the dealer, or was the effect purely random? It was already clear that he had no control over his movements between worlds. He could only hope that he would wake up one day and find himself in one where Boles knew what he was doing.

What if the para effect wore off while he was still in this world, still accompanied by the unlucky Mitch? Would they both be stuck forever in whatever para Fate happened to drop them in, like a spinning coin finally bereft of its momentum? If that happened then both of them would simply have to cope. But he did not want to cope. He wanted home, wanted his own world back, a world wherein he was the only Max and condors did not roam the skies above the absent Point Dume.

One thing was plain enough. Much as he might want to, this para of Barrington Boles could not help him.

"Do you know how my para self worked out the final settings?" Boles was asking him. "What about the final parameters of the distortion arc?"

Max sighed tiredly. "I don't have a clue what you're talking about. I didn't think the damn thing would work, so I didn't pay attention to any of the operational details. I thought all the lights and electrical discharges were real pretty, and that was about the extent of my formal observations."

"Too bad." Boles turned reflective. "Though it is encouraging to know that in another world I succeeded. If you could tell me how, maybe I could duplicate the results here, and then figure out a way to get you back to the world line where you belong."

"It probably wouldn't matter." Max stood. "The frequency of shifts, the intensity of the effect, seems to be increasing. By the time you got it worked out I'm likely to be in another para altogether. With luck, one where you knew what you were doing."

Shaking his head slowly, Boles rose from his chair. "I have a feeling none of my selves knew what they were doing. If they did, you wouldn't be here. For what it's worth, I'm sorry."

"Sorry, hell!" Max took a step toward the inventor. "I ought to strangle you."

Mitch hurried to intervene. "Don't even think about it. Kill him and you might affect every other Boles up and down the line. Then we'll have no chance of putting things right."

"Yeah, you're probably right."

"I always am." Mitch smiled reassuringly. "Aren't we?"

It was a bad idea anyway, Max decided. Though older, the inventor was bigger and in much better shape.

"You can stay here if you like while I work on the machine." Boles was trying his best to be encouraging.

"No thanks." Max turned in the direction of the front door. "This place gives me the creeps. You give me the creeps." He gestured expansively. "Lucky me. Now the whole world gives me the creeps, and I don't even know which one I'm in. Stay here? I'd rather camp out in the shadow of Chernobyl." He turned to leave. Mitch hurried to follow him.

"Don't mind him," he told their host in passing. "He's just upset. As am I."

Boles followed them toward the door. "Pardon my questions, but surely you understand my fascination with the success of my other self. Tell me, do you feel the same emotions simultaneously?"

"Pretty much. We are the same, after all, except that he's locked into this field, or disturbance, or distortion, and I'm just kind of a fellow traveler. He's the tornado sweeping between parallel worlds, and I'm one of the pieces of debris that's been sucked up and dragged along in his wake. Sooner or later the tornado will run out of energy and fall apart. When it does, I hope it drops me where I belong."

"So do I," murmured Boles emphatically. "In a way, you two are fortunate. I don't imagine I'll ever get to meet any of my para selves."

"If you do, I hope it goes better for you than it has for us." Mitch gestured at the angry figure nearing the front door. "We're not really crazy about ourselves. It's more a matter of mutual toleration."

Little was said between the two M. Parkers during the drive down the hill. Max barely grunted at the guard as they paused and waited for the gate to swing up. Nor was there any impetus to conversation as he pulled out on the coast highway and headed south, back toward L.A. Evening was advancing upon the coast and the sinking sun turned the smog-saturated sky a pale shade of incandescent orange.

"There has to be something we can do," Mitch avowed, as much to break the tension that had gripped the interior of the Aurora as in hopes of receiving a reply.

"Like what?" Max stared morosely straight ahead, hands clamped to the wheel. It was late, after rush hour. Most commuters were already home enjoying the long daylight-savings-time sunshine. This far north of the city, there was still little traffic. They would not hit much until they reached Malibu.

"You could wish upon a star," Mitch suggested.

"Very funny," Max responded flatly. "I'm glad you find our situation so amusing."

"God, but you're a pain when things aren't going your way."

"You should know."

After that nothing was said. Mitch pressed back in his seat and stared at the road ahead, wondering if in his own world he had already been fired.

His attention was drawn to a bright light in the southwestern sky. It was reflective and moving toward them. As soon as he was certain it was not a hallucination, he mentioned it to his companion.

Max leaned forward against the wheel and squinted. "Must be a plane coming in."

"There's no airport in Malibu," Mitch pointed out. "At least, not in my Malibu." The object was growing larger even as they spoke.

"Yeah. Not in my Malibu, or in yours, maybe, but how do we know there isn't one in this Malibu?"

"Good point." Still, the more Mitch stared at the approaching light, the less it reminded him of a descending aircraft.

Its true nature manifested itself as Max slowed to take a sharp curve where the highway ran right along the sea. The object fell precipitously, resolving itself into a three-story tall ovoid lined at top and bottom with a succession of elegant flutings and flanges. As it settled to earth on a jackstraw of seemingly haphazard metal projections, what appeared to be a cold fog wafted lazily from its equator. No windows or ports of any kind marred the otherwise smooth, bronze-hued surface.

"It's a weather balloon," Mitch suggested breathlessly.

"Don't try to be funny. We've got a story here. Maybe even a legitimate one." His throat constricting, Max hit the brakes and pulled the Aurora off on the small, narrow shoulder that separated the pavement from the otherworldly, metallic apparition. Gravel crunched beneath the radials.

Together, both men leaned forward and stared up at the silent monolith. "Nothing's happening," Mitch murmured. Mist continued to emanate from the seemingly solid surface, dispersing in the form of gentle curling gray wisps into the warm evening air. Behind them, a car shot past, traveling too fast in the opposite direction. This being Southern California, it did not even slow. Not having seen the ovoid descend, the car's driver probably thought it was part of some new advertising scheme—or a movie prop.

Actually, Max was more than half convinced that that was exactly what it was. His conviction lasted until the aliens emerged.

There were only two of them. A round platform descended from the lowest point of the ovoid, depositing them on the rocky ground. Neither he nor Mitch could see where the platform was attached to the rest of the monolith.

Upon reaching the surface, the two aliens appeared to converse briefly. Both stood slightly over six feet tall and were clad in elegant, flowing robes of dark magenta. Their elongated, humanoid faces were the color of aged yellow pine, deeply wrinkled by vertical furrows. A single dark slit in the middle of each face might be an extensive nostril, or some other organ. The flanking coal-black eyes were protuberant, pupilless, and the size of hens' eggs. A single oral aperture was small, round, and toothless. One stood slightly taller than the other and displayed a dark streak of navy blue down the left side of its face.

The flowing robes concealed whatever passed for alien feet, but the unencumbered hands were clearly visible. The same shade of burnished yellow-brown as the somber faces, these were correspondingly long and flexible. The four fingers or tendrils that sprouted from each knobby wrist joint were spindly and fragile-looking.

"They're coming toward us!" Mitch announced tersely.

"I can see that." Max grabbed the handle on his side and pushed the door open. "We don't want to hide from them."

"We don't?" Mitch hesitated before joining himself outside the car. Side by side, they observed the aliens as they approached, shuffling forward, their long graceful robes barely shifting with their subtle movements.

"How do you interview an alien?" Max already had his recorder out and running.

"Why ask me?" Mitch was fascinated by the somber extra-terrestrial faces. More than anything, they suggested to him the central figure in Edvard Munch's famous painting *The Scream*, only on downers.

"I thought maybe aliens had visited your para."

Mitch shook his head. "That's another area where our paras are the same. Nobody in my world believes in mysterious alien visitations—although I've probably gotten ten or eleven stories out of ET sightings and the babblings of those nuts who claimed to have been abducted."

"That's how many I've done," admitted Max. The aliens were very close now. Their black eyes glistened moistly. He could see no evidence of eyelids or of sexual dimorphism. "Maybe this isn't a para experience. Maybe we just happen to be in the right spot at the right time. After everything we've gone through, it's only fair that we get a real story out of it." He checked his recorder to make sure it was operating properly.

"I wonder how they communicate?" A thoroughly absorbed Mitch was staring at the small, round mouths.

"Through intelligent conversation. How else do sapient species communicate?"

The response came from the nearer of the two creatures, the small oral opening at the bottom of the face expanding and contracting like a resonating diaphragm as it spoke. The voice was soft, muted, and overlaid with a quite perceptible amalgam of exasperation and irritation.

Confronted with such unexpected extraterrestrial fluency, the average wayfarer might well have found himself flustered to the point of speechlessness, but Max was conditioned to respond no matter how bizarre the situation.

"You speak our language!" He thrust the recorder out slightly in front of him.

The voice of the other alien was somewhat harsher than that of its companion. "Of course we speak your language! We have been speaking it for some time, as you well know." Turning to its companion, it proceeded to launch into an extended diatribe, the contents of which remained a mystery to the two enthralled human onlookers.

This lack of understanding soon lost its charm. "Excuse me," said Max, interrupting in what he hoped was an appropriately deferential manner, "but what's going on here?"

Ceasing their private discussion, the aliens looked back at them. "That is what we were contemplating asking you. First you act as if you have never seen a Mithrathian before, then you propound the most absurdly infantile query regarding means of communication."

Max and Mitch exchanged a glance. "Actually," Mitch informed them, "we never have seen a Mithrathian before."

For reasons unknown this set the two aliens to furiously debating all over again, though this time it proved unnecessary to interrupt them. They soon ceased of their own accord.

"This is very distressing." The taller of the pair now sounded more concerned than critical. "We were wondering if your odd, inexplicable, and unprecedented reaction might in some as yet unfathomable way be connected with the disappearance of the spaceport."

Max blinked. "Spaceport?"

"Yes." Raising a slim, deeply furrowed arm, the shorter of the two aliens pointed inland and slightly to the south. "Shathri Moi, which you humans refer to in your local dialect as Angeles Metroplex Spaceport."

It was Mitch's turn to respond. "I'm sorry to have to disappoint you guys, but there's no spaceport in the Santa Monica Mountains, and no place called Shathri Moi, either—unless there's a new subdivision going in I haven't heard about."

"How can this be? Or not be?" the taller alien wondered aloud.

"To be or not to be," Max muttered softly. "That is the spaceport." He was feeling more than a little giddy. It was unsettling enough to encounter real aliens. Encountering English-speaking, badly confused aliens who had apparently lost their way was much worse.

"How long is this spaceport supposed to have been here?" Mitch inquired gently.

"For many of your years. It is near the place where our people first made contact with yours. The port can accommodate half a dozen Mithrathian ships at one time. There should be at least one other already docked, but during our approach we were unable to make contact with its crew, just as we were unable to make contact with the port itself. We finally decided to set down here to evaluate our options."

"Yes," concurred the other. "At least the sea is where it belongs, and acting as it should."

Revelation appeared simultaneously to Max and Mitch. "I think I can explain," Max began. "I can try to, anyway. You probably won't believe me, but then I've been having a hard enough time believing it myself."

VII

The aliens listened quietly, taking the news with admirable calm. They were clearly dubious, as anyone would be, but the more Max explained the more they came to accept the insanity of what he was saying. It helped that Mitch was present to corroborate his para's statements.

"So you have acquired about you a field that affects the links between multiple parallel worlds, causing objects and individuals from those worlds to slip into yours or you to slip into theirs." The taller alien contemplated the two humans unblinkingly.

"That's how things are," Max admitted. "Believe me, I wish it were otherwise. It's getting to the point where I don't know what belongs where, what's right, or whether I'm in my world or another."

"An extraordinary claim for so primitive a technology."

The shorter alien remained doubtful. "I would find it difficult to believe were it not for your honest naiveté and the utter absence of Shathri Moi." Black eyes lifted toward the chaparral-cloaked hills. "Spaceports do not vanish."

"It's clear enough to me what's happened." Mitch now had his own recorder out and humming. "You guys have slipped into this world just like we have." He nodded in the direction of his distraught companion. "We don't have any way of measuring the extent of the field Max is embedded in, how far its effects extend, or even what shape it takes around him. Could be a sphere that expands and contracts, or something that shoots off flares the way the sun shows prominences. It's like a tornado: it can tear apart a house but leave the settings on the dining-room table undisturbed."

"Assuming all is as you claim," murmured the taller alien, "what are we to do?"

"There's nothing you can do," Max told them sadly. "Unless I can find the original of the man who created this effect and get him to cancel it out or turn it off or whatever the hell it is he has to do to return things to normal, all we can do is hope that it wears off of its own accord."

"Not a sanguine scenario," declared the shorter alien. "Aberrations in the structure of the physical universe tend not to be vanquished by wishful thinking. You cannot fill in a black hole with spadefuls of dirt."

"Too bad." Max gazed out to sea, where the sun had already set. The dark oval shadow of the alien craft loomed over them. "You seem like nice folks. I'm sorry you got sucked into this. It's nice to think that in another para aliens have actually landed, that they're friendly, and that everyone is getting along."

"You would like Mithrath." The taller alien sounded wistful. "It is a beautiful world, different from your own but with sufficient points of similarity for humans to find visiting there most pleasant. Likewise, we find your own Earth quite exotic— though this business of parallelities is pushing matters."

Something began to glow softly within the fabric of the robe that covered the second alien's midsection. Both of the slender visitors turned and inclined their elongated skulls backward.

"What is it?" Mitch tried to follow their skyward gaze. "What's happening?"

The taller alien replied without altering his posture. "It appears that we may not be so isolated as we feared. Even as we speak, a second ship of Mithrath approaches."

"That's about right," Max whispered under his breath. "We go from having no contact with an alien civilization to a crowd."

A second ovoid was dropping precipitously toward the coast, its base and crest glowing softly. It settled gently to earth quite close to the first vessel, there barely being enough solid ground between the water and the highway to accommodate two interstellar craft and one late-model Aurora. As the two Mithrathians and the humans looked on expectantly, a platform descended from the base of the new arrival and a pair of creatures stepped off.

After surveying their surroundings for a brief moment they started directly toward the waiting quartet. The new visitants wore long robes and had the same furrowed skin and dark eyes.

"Fellow Mithrathians," declared the shorter of the two aliens. "It will be good to have company, and perhaps they will have suggestions as to how we might deal with the astonishing and unprecedented circumstances in which we presently find ourselves."

While the two humans looked on in fascination, the four aliens entered into an elaborate exchange of greetings. Not long after this commenced, however, one of the first pair made a noise that sounded like a young elephant assaulting a bassoon. Its obviously upset companion hurried to comfort his shorter companion. Simultaneously, the two new arrivals began arguing vociferously among themselves.

Mitch leaned over to whisper to Max. "What happened? All of a sudden this doesn't look like it's going so well."

"I agree." Max had already taken a wary step backward. "We'll just have to wait until they're ready to give us an explana . . ." He broke off, his eyes widening.

Mitch frowned at him. "Not you, too. What the hell's going on?"

Max raised an arm that felt heavy as pig iron and pointed. "Look at the taller of the new arrivals."

Still frowning, Mitch complied. "Looks just like a Mithrathian, surprise, surprise. What about it?"

"See the dark blue line running down the left side of its face? It's an exact match to the facial streak on the taller of the two aliens who landed here first."

Mitch squinted into the gathering darkness. "Yeah, I see it. So what? So they both have blue streaks on their faces. Am I supposed to be impressed by your knowledge of alien beauty marks?"

"Same height, same build, same streak." Max's tone was flat. "Same kind of ship coming down in the same place." He turned to face his double. "Suggest anything to you?"

The full range of expressions that crossed Mitch's face in a very short period of time was wonderful to see, as if he were running through all the options of his own personal morphing program.

He swallowed hard. "Are we talking para aliens here?"

"Why not? I'm a para, you're a para, they're a para too. I've driven through para landscapes, dealt with para people, talked with a para Barrington Boles. Why shouldn't aliens have paras as well?" He gestured at the now seriously upset quartet of Mithrathians.

"First two of them arrive on this world, where they don't belong any more than we do. Then two more of them appear who just happen to be perfect doubles of their predecessors." He spread his hands. "In a cosmos of infinite para possibilities, it makes perfect para sense."

Mitch put his hands to his head. "And this is beginning to drive me para crazy. Look, I'm not a philosopher or physicist or mathematician. I'm just a reporter for a midrange tabloid newspaper, and I'm losing track of what's supposed to be where."

"How do you think I feel?" Max replied emotionally. "No, you don't have to think about it; you know. I'm as mixed up as you are. I'm beginning to wonder if I'd recognize my own reality if we were dumped back in it right now. And would it really be my reality, or yours?"

Mitch managed to get ahold of himself. "That one we know how to answer. We just find the world with the Barrington Boles whose machine worked."

Max smiled thinly. "I wish it were that easy. There might be dozens, hundreds of parallel worlds where Boles's machine worked. It doesn't necessarily follow that any particular one of them is my world. We could find a Boles whose machine worked and ask him to put things right, but what if it's not the exact right para and a third one of us is running around somewhere else, or at work, or out researching a story? Unable to tell us apart, Boles might turn his machine onto the wrong me. Then there'd be two of us wandering around all screwed up, or two of us permanently in the right para and none of us in another."

"Stop it, stop it!" Trying to clear his head, Mitch focused his attention on the baffled, bickering aliens.

"Yeah, I know." Max joined him in waiting for the distraught

Mithrathians to calm down. "Ponder the possibilities too much and they'll drive you nuts."

"Now there's an explanation I can live with," declared Mitch fervently. "We're already crazy, see? So none of this matters. Not all this nonsense about Barrington Boles and his parallel worlds, not you and me, not these lost aliens: none of it. When you're insane, everything makes sense, no matter how wacko it seems."

Max eyed him unswervingly. "You believe that?"

"No," Mitch admitted resignedly. "No. I don't feel demented. But in a crazy sort of way it would be comforting if that happened to be the truth."

"You want comfort, try goose down. Unfortunately, we're both too rational to seek refuge in madness. When your career involves dealing daily with the deranged, it's hard to lose sight of your own sanity."

Nodding, Mitch indicated the four aliens. "I wasn't kidding when I made the tornado analogy. Whatever else you can say about this effect that you've captured, or that's captured you, one thing we know for sure: It's a mighty impressive, strong thing. If anything, I'd say the presence of para aliens suggests that it's getting stronger, not weaker."

"Let's try real hard not to dwell on the ramifications of that," Max replied. "I had enough trouble dealing with the reality of four identical girls."

"You never did go into much detail about that," Mitch

reminded him. "Why don't you fill me in now? It would beat listening to aliens argue."

"Jaded with extraterrestrial contact already?"

Mitch jerked a thumb in the aliens' direction. "They're interested in their own problem, not ours. I'd rather hear about four identical beauties."

Max had to smile. "A man after my own heart."

"A man with your own heart." Mitch settled himself down to listen.

At about the same time that Max had exhausted his extensive lexicon of adjectives on the memory of the four pluperfect paras, the aliens finally came to terms with their situation.

"It is clear," professed tall alien number one, "that we can do nothing to alter our condition. Everything depends on you slipping back into the world from whence you came, or at the very least into one in which this human Boles has developed a device that works, and persuading or helping him to return the alignment of realities to normal."

"Yeah, that's about how we see it," agreed Mitch.

"I'm sorry you were drawn in." Max shrugged helplessly. "I have no control over the field's effects."

"Heartfelt apologies are of little use in influencing the flux of cosmic forces," murmured short alien number two. "However, as one sapient to another, let me say that I appreciate your concern."

"What are you going to do?" Mitch eyed the four curiously.

"Since you have no formal presence established on this world, your appearance would, um, startle the natives."

"We concur in this. Therefore we will retire to a concealed orbit from where we can monitor developments on the surface. Should we slip back into the respective parallels from whence we came, we will immediately either set a course for home or land at the missing port. In either event, we will probably not see you again. Though in a proper parallel world, where our presence is not only accepted but expected, we could doubtless track down your para."

"Let's not make things any more complicated than they are," Max suggested quickly. "It's reassuring to think of one or two of my paras enjoying a normal life, uncomplicated by paradigm shifts between worlds."

The alien executed an elaborate incomprehensible gesture. "We will respect your wishes. No one is going to believe us anyway."

With that, the two pairs of aliens returned to their respective ships. Max and Mitch watched in silence as first one ovoid and then the other took to the skies, disappearing in the general direction of the North Star. Or maybe it was Venus. While they often filed stories on the amusing vicissitudes of astrologers and their ilk, neither Parker had ever been very good at real astronomy.

Behind them, occasional cars flashed back and forth along the coast highway, following close upon the bright beams of their headlights. In front, the Pacific rushed heedlessly shoreward, foaming excitedly among the boulders beneath the level rocky outcropping where the spacecraft had landed. Was it the real Pacific, his Pacific, Max wondered? Or some para Pacific in which dwelled oysters with their shells turned inside out and squid that blew songs through their siphons?

What if it was a Pacific from which pollution had been banished? In that event he felt he might be tempted to remain. Except that he knew he could not stay, even if he found himself in a para he preferred to his own. As he had told the Mithrathians, he had no control over the situation in which he found himself. Only Barrington Boles had control over that—and then only maybe.

"What now?" Mitch wondered aloud as he turned away from the place in the sky where the alien spacecraft had disappeared.

"You hungry?"

"Of course I'm hungry. As are you. Aren't you?"

"Yeah. I guess along with everything else we share the same appetites." Opening the door to the Aurora, Max slid into the driver's seat. "The fish-and-chips place just north of the canyon road looked halfway decent. I could do with a little fried grease about now." He flashed a half smile. "Call it a tasty, if not a tasteful, reminder of reality."

From the passenger seat Mitch looked across at his companion. "Seems fitting. I wonder what para cod tastes like?"

"Better than para noid, I hope." Max gunned the engine. "Because that's the way I'm starting to feel. Every minute, I fear slipping without warning into a different parallel world, or having part of it fall into the one I happen to be inhabiting at the moment." Backing up a couple of car lengths, he waited for a passing truck to clear the curve before pulling back out onto the highway.

"It's funny." Mitch relaxed in his seat, content to let Max do the driving. "Many's the time I worried about being an unstable personality, when all along I was the stable one and it was the universe that was unstable."

"Why don't I find that a comforting notion?" Max responded sardonically.

The warm light from inside the little eat-in, take-out restaurant spilled welcomingly through the picture windows and out into the parking lot. Only a couple of other cars marred the Kabuki pattern of white stripes on black asphalt. Max regarded himself, seated comfortably in the other seat.

"Want to eat inside or in the car?"

Mitch grinned and shrugged slightly. "You know the answer to that. You should know the answer to everything, at least where you and I are concerned."

"Then I don't have to ask you what you want. Dinner plate with fries, ketchup unless Thousand Island dressing is available, malt vinegar for the fish, and plenty of napkins because we're both indifferent diners."

"Actually, I kind of wanted a steak." Gratified by the look of uncertainty that slipped over Max's face, Mitch hastened to reassure him. "Just kidding. Cod and fries sounds great. You're paying, of course."

Max grinned back as he slid out of the car. "Of course we are. Be right back."

The pleasant matron behind the counter took his order quietly and efficiently, waiting on him with the same courtesy she would have accorded any of the movie stars who lived in the immediate vicinity. While he was waiting for the deep fryer to perform its task of inserting cholesterol and fat into otherwise healthy fish, Max examined his surroundings. Two couples munched their way through their own beer-battered suppers, as oblivious of his presence as of the fact that he wore chaos like a diadem. It wasn't visible, which was fortunate for his health. He was quite aware that he could be lynched as readily in this para as in his own.

Perhaps lulled by the warm evening and the onset of night, the world chose to remain stable in his eyes. No grotesque aliens sauntered in the door to place an order, no octopi jetted brazenly through the pungent air of the dining room, no condors roosted outside awaiting the next victim of arteriosclerosis-induced stroke. Everything looked, sounded, and smelled normal. The thick, odoriferous aroma of fish frying was as myrrh in his nostrils.

It was not long at all before the matron returned with his double order. He paid with a credit card. Cradling the garishly decorated, steaming cardboard boxes of fish and fries, he used his right foot to push open the door that led to the parking lot. He was more than a little gratified to see that the Aurora was right where he had left it.

A figure was seated behind the wheel. Well, if Mitch was bored and wanted to drive the rest of the way home, that was fine with Max. He was flat worn out.

Sliding into the vacated passenger's seat, he juggled one dinner box in his companion's direction. "Here you go: malt vinegar and Thousand Island for the fries, just like we like 'em."

"Just like who likes them?" a voice that was manifestly not Mitch's demanded to know. "And how did you know that I like malt vinegar with my fish and Thousand Island with my fries?"

Max gaped at the individual seated behind the wheel. The individual stared back. It was not Mitch, but it was still him, still Max. Or rather, another Max para. There was no mistaking the similarities: in the eyes, the forehead, the hair, the mouth. But there were distinctive differences—some subtle, some less so. For one thing, he had never seen himself in full makeup before. Either he had slipped into a new para, or part of that para had slipped into him.

This time, he was a she.

I hope you slipped home safely, he thought to the vanished Mitch. *Back to where you belong. I hope at least one of us is happy again.*

"Who are you?" the young woman demanded to know. "And what the hell do you think you're doing in my car? I was just going in to get something to eat."

For the second time a resigned Max shoved the spare box of fish and chips in the driver's direction. "This was for somebody else, but since you've taken his place I guess they're for you. You know you'd rather eat in the car anyway."

"As a matter of fact, I would, but I don't see what that's got to do with your intrusion. Now how about you move your ass out of here before I start screaming at the top of my lungs?" Her tone softened as she stared more closely at him, as if struggling to recognize a long-lost relation. "Do I know you?"

"Better than you think, lady. Better than you think."

Her name was, unsurprisingly, Maxine, and she did not faint as he commenced his explanation—in between mouthfuls of hot cod and crispy fries. What mollified her initially was his seemingly uncanny ability to anticipate every one of her objections and questions. Besides, she was hungry too, and a free meal was a free meal. He considered asking her about the aliens but thought better of it. If, as in his own, no aliens had made contact with mankind in her reality, then any allusions to them would hardly inspire confidence in the rest of his story.

"And that's what's happened. Or rather, what's happening," he told her, concluding his tale of worlds slip-sliding and melding unpredictably.

"I never heard anything so ridiculous!" She waved a hand at him, semaphoring with a french fry. "Superficial similarities are one thing, but you can't be me!"

"Believe me," he sighed, "I know how confusing this must look, not to mention how utterly impossible it must sound. Me, I'm getting used to explaining the situation to other mes." He scratched delicately behind his left ear.

She stared. "Does that spot always bother you?" He nodded. "Me, too." Reaching out with her free hand, she let the fingers trail along the lines of his face. His reaction to her touch was—confusing.

Like her voice, her features were far softer than his, more delicate. Not that his face would ever have been mistaken for, say, that of Jack Palance. *She's not you*, he reminded himself. *You share the same genes but the blueprint is different. Concentrate on the matter at hand. Focus.*

It was difficult to do so. Dealing with Mitch had been straightforward enough. But this version of himself was really stacked.

He looked away. Though still highly dubious, she was beginning to relax a little, his presence no longer making her nervous. When he turned back to her he recognized the look in her eyes. He'd seen it in the bathroom mirror often enough, though not framed by mascara and eye shadow.

"I still think you're crazy," she told him, "but I also think I could get to like you."

"Of course you like me," he replied uneasily. "I'm you. You have to like yourself."

"Not necessarily," she corrected him. "I know plenty of people who don't like themselves. Who'd punch themselves out if given the chance."

Difficult though it was, he met her gaze. "And do you want to punch me out?"

"No. In spite of your story, I think you're okay." She leaned toward him slightly. "Go ahead: Convince me. Tell me more about us."

By the time he finished reciting intimate details from their mutual childhood that no one else, not even their parents, could possibly have known, she was persuaded in spite of herself.

"Parallel worlds. Multiple realities." She shook her head and her shoulder-length hair rustled. He'd always wondered what he'd look like with long hair. "It's an awful lot to ask someone to accept over a take-out meal of fish and chips."

"I've had to accept it. Mitch accepted it." Reaching out the open window, he tossed his empty dinner container into a nearby trash barrel. "You might as well get used to the idea too."

"How long does the effect last?"

"With me, I can't say. As for the paras around me, they've been changing constantly. Sometimes the slips are small, like with the burglars or the bighorn sheep. Sometimes they're major, like with the aliens." He eyed her appraisingly. "The para we decided to call Mitch and I found ourselves thrown together for a couple of days. Now he's gone, and you're here. I have to say that I wouldn't mind being stuck with you for a while. You're a lot prettier than Mitch."

She did not blush or look away. Why should she? He never had. "You realize what you're saying."

"What? That I'm giving myself a compliment? Wouldn't be the first time."

Climbing out of the car, she disposed of her own after-dinner trash, giving him the opportunity to admire the full gracefulness of her form. It was like looking at himself in a fun-house mirror.

"I thought the reality of the aliens was weird," he told her when she returned. "This is weirder." He checked the dashboard clock. "Don't you think it's about time we got home?"

She made a face. "What makes you think I'm taking you home with me?"

He gave her the address of their building, unhesitatingly describing everything from the location of bad oil stains in the parking garage to the cracked plaster in the hallway to the interior of their apartment itself. His impossibly intimate knowledge of their living arrangements overcame her hesitation, if not her lingering discomfiture at the situation.

"I guess you're right. It is your apartment as much as it is mine." She started the engine. Or at least, she appeared to. The car hardly made a sound as she backed it out of the parking lot and pulled back out onto the highway. That's when he noticed the peculiar arrangement of the instruments in the dash.

"This looks like my car," he told her, "but the gauges are all different, and half of them are missing." Though they were speeding along at a sedate fifty-five, the Aurora hardly made a sound. "What does it run on?"

"Run on?" She barely glanced in his direction, keeping her eyes on the dark road ahead. "It's fully charged, if that's what you mean."

"Charged? It's an electric?" The comparative silence of the speeding vehicle was uncanny.

She gave him a funny look. "All personal vehicles have been electrically powered for the last twenty-two years. Don't tell me that in your reality you're still using those horrible internal-combustion engines that make everyone deaf and pollute the atmosphere?"

"I'm afraid so." He went quiet, wondering what other technological advances might define this para from his own. He found that while he did not miss the smell of gasoline, the absence of the satisfying, deep-throated rumble beneath the hood distressed a certain primitive part of him.

Night-cloaked Malibu and Santa Monica looked as familiar as always. To further vitiate his identity he took to describing every street scene and corner before they reached their building, up to and including the code that was programmed into the remote garage-door opener. It was not necessary. In spite of herself, she was convinced. As they parked and exited the car he found himself wondering if she had a certain mole in a certain place that in her case did not exist.

While they rode up in the elevator, after both tried to push the same floor button at the same time, he slipped his arm around her waist. She jerked away, her expression a reflection of repulsion and curiosity.

"That's sick!"

He did not look away. "What's sick, Maxine?"

"Hitting on yourself." She shook her head. "This is just too bizarre."

"You think *you're* having a problem with this? I'm the first para you've ever encountered. I've already had to deal with a male para of myself—an exact physical duplicate, plus aliens, *para* aliens, strange wildlife, a para Barrington Boles who doesn't even understand what's happened to me, para burglars, potential para dates . . ."

"What did the dates look like?" A look of sudden horror came over her face. "No, I didn't say that. I'm straight."

"Of course we are. Only, under present circumstances, what constitutes straight and what constitutes bent?"

The elevator opened and they headed up the hall. While she was by now completely persuaded, it did not hurt that his key opened the door to the apartment. It looked exactly like his, except that certain masculine appurtenances had been replaced by feminine ones.

"Coffee?" He smiled reassuringly at her. "Don't worry. I know where everything is."

"Coffee—yeah, sure." She slumped down on the couch, and he could not help but notice that they had great legs. Her, not the couch. "I suppose you might as well spend the night." She gestured resignedly. "If everything you've been telling me is the truth, then this is your place as much as it is mine."

"That's right." The coffeemaker, he noted with relief, was right where he had left it. Unlike the Aurora, it exhibited no unfamiliar technological traits.

When the brew (his favorite Goroka-Kenya blend) was ready, he presented her with a prepared cup. Sipping delicately, she favored him with a slightly twisted smile. "One cream, two sugars. It's perfect."

"Of course it is." He sipped from his own mug. "Did you think I wouldn't know how we like it?"

She sighed heavily. "You're on your way home from a relaxing drive up the coast and your whole world turns upside down in the parking lot of a fish-and-chips place." She edged closer to him. He did not draw away.

"At least you're still in your world," he told her. "To me, this is just a para of mine, and I don't know how to get home. Maybe you're confused, but I'm the one that's lost. Lost in place." He grinned crookedly. "Where's Doctor Smith when you need him?"

She allowed him to put his arm around her. He knew

exactly how to do it, where to let the fingers fall. When she snuggled closer she knew precisely how to do that, as well.

This is Maxine, he told himself. Another human being. Another individual, another person. It was not him, but someone else entirely. Well, maybe not entirely.

It was the first time in his life that he had ever made love without hesitation and without having to wonder if he was doing everything right.

VIII

While she made the coffee in the morning he did the toast and eggs: medium brown for the toast, over easy for the two eggs, half a glass of pineapple-grapefruit juice on the side. They ate in silence until their mutual unease dissolved into smiles and laughter: nervous giggles for her, deeper chuckles for him.

"How was it for you?" It was a morning-after question he had never had the guts to ask any of the other women he had made love to, but deep down he felt—no, he knew—that Maxine would not be offended.

She grinned at him over the top of her coffee mug. "You have to ask? I always wondered what it would be like to make love to someone who knew exactly what to do without having to be prompted. Now you've spoiled me." Reaching across the small table, she put her hand on his.

"After what we've been through we deserve to be spoiled a little." He energetically mopped up runny yellow yolk with bread. "This could get to be habit-forming."

In both look and tone, her response was one of mild reproach. "Today is a work day. Or is it different in your para?"

"I'm afraid not. The things I'd like to see changed, that I'd be comfortable with having turned upside down, stay the same." He smacked his lips, wiping at his mouth with a napkin. The napkins he bought at Ralph's were plain, generic white. Maxine's were stamped with little bouquets of flowers. "I suppose we'd better report in. I don't want any of my selves fired even if they're only para selves."

She pushed back from the table. "I'd appreciate it if you didn't talk like that. Remember, to me you're my para, not the other way around."

He nodded. "Sorry. It's hard to think about manners when you're trying to concentrate on not going crazy. If it's all right with you, I'll drive. I'd like to check out the handling on the electric."

"Internal combustion." She shuddered visibly. "I'll bet the skies of your Los Angeles are barely clear for half the year."

He saw no point in correcting her. Anyone who could clear the skies of his Los Angeles for half the year could get elected mayor for life. Or maybe emperor.

A very few of the buildings they drove past looked different, but not sufficiently to slow him down. Some familiar advertisements were missing, but as far as he was concerned that was all to the good. Every vehicle on the street, from private cars to buses to delivery vans and even large trucks, traveled in eerie near-silence, whining in concer only when they accelerated.

It was an extraordinary experience to be able to drive up Lincoln with the window open while listening to the conversation of passing pedestrians or the songs of birds flying by overhead. There were far more birds than he was used to, as well, and a plethora of species instead of the usual dominant and domineering ravens and pigeons. Another legacy of the cleaner air in Maxine's world, he noted.

Clearly, more than Maxine and her car were significantly different in this para. It meant he could expect to encounter further differences. On a whim, they compared the contents of his pocket and her purse. Except for certain feminine accessories that she carried and he did not, the contents were identical. Even to the signature, her credit cards were identical to his, her assorted forms of identification matched; she even carried the same kind and amount of money.

"Who's the president?" Turning east on Wilshire, he found nearly every light and corner and storefront as familiar as day. Only the day itself, devoid of the usual smog and companion pollutants, was radically different from what he was used to.

"John Thomas Michaels, of course." She leaned back in her seat and he admired the silhouette a slight but significant realigning of genes had produced.

"Local boy from Orange County, right?"

She nodded. "And before that, Bill Clinton."

He was feeling more and more comfortable. "Check. And before him, George Bush, and before him, Ronald Reagan."

She looked over abruptly. "Ronald Reagan? The actor?" Amusement at his witticism was writ plain on her face. "I know we share the same sense of humor, but it's not usually so droll."

"No, really, I'm serious. Ronald Reagan was the fortieth president of the United States. Two terms, in fact." He turned to face her. "Are you telling me it's different for you?"

"You're not joking, are you." She became thoughtful. "It was during Stevenson's terms in office that Purnululu power spread worldwide. That's when the internal-combustion engine disappeared and gave way to electrics."

"Purnululu power?" He admired the deep blue sky. Living as he had all his life in Los Angeles, it was a color he saw only in pictures, or when he traveled beyond the atmospheric limits of the city.

"I'll be damned; you've never heard of it, have you? You haven't a clue what I'm talking about."

He spread his hands and looked helpless. "Sounds like an ad for a new music group."

"It's rather more important than that. The principles were formalized by a consortium of Australian researchers working out of Perth and Brisbane. They led to, not exactly cold fusion, but a new, clean, and incredibly cheap way of generating electricity."

"Bet that calmed things down in the Middle East."

She frowned. "The Middle East has been calm for years. When Purnululu power was made widely available, the price of crude oil dropped to something like six dollars a barrel. Deprived of any financial leverage, even the more extreme Arab governments were anxious to make a lasting peace."

"So there was no Gulf War during the Bush administration? Saddam Hussein's Iraq didn't try to take over Kuwait?"

She smiled, shaking her head in disbelief. "Why would Iraq want to take over Kuwait? There's nothing in Kuwait but sand and oil, and the world has plenty of both." She turned away from him, staring out the front window. "I think I'm glad to live in this para and not yours. The world's been a much better place since the Aussies took over."

Now it was his turn to gape. "The Australians and not the Americans are the world's dominant power?"

"Of course. What would you expect from a country that controls the world's supply of cheap electricity? Their GNP overtook that of the U.S. at least ten years ago and the gap has been widening ever since. The nice thing is, nobody minds, since the Aussies don't bring the historical baggage of an imperial or colonial power to the world stage. They're good stewards of international standards of behavior and the competition has forced American beer to become fifty times better than what it used to be." She turned thoughtful.

"There was some minor outcry in certain parts of the

States last year over the hundred-dollar bill they issued with the Norman Lindsay painting reproduced on it, but that's quieted down." She considered a moment longer. "I still don't think I'll ever get used to McMutton burgers, though."

It was a lot of severe historical revisionism to try and digest all at once, and he was grateful when the familiar structure that housed the offices of the *Investigator* finally came into view. He was about to pull into the underground parking area when Maxine hastened to interrupt.

"Wait a minute, where do you think you're going?"

"Down, of course. To park."

"You can't park here. At least, I can't. Go to the lot around the block. Take the next corner."

Confused and not a little upset, he followed her instructions, cruising regretfully past the familiar entrance. "I don't get it. I've been parking downstairs ever since I started working for the paper."

She stared at him. "Paper? You work for a paper?"

"And you don't, I take it." He searched for an entrance to the parking lot behind the main building.

"I started writing for a paper, sure. Then I found out that people would pay me ten times as much money just to look at me. Well, to look at me while I was performing."

His voice darkened. "Just what exactly is it that you 'perform'?"

"Hey, calm down. I'm an actress. A legitimate actress,

though I will do the occasional nude scene. But only if it's essential to the story line." She shook a finger at him. "You don't have to explain your reaction. Remember, I know how your mind works as well as you do. I'm just not that used to dealing with it from a male perspective."

Great, he thought. *I meet my perfect female self, a literal counterpart, and she's doffing her britches for the camera.* He knew he should have been flattered, but for some reason he wasn't.

The warehouse-like structure on the opposite side of the parking lot from the *Investigator* building had frequently been used as a studio by small production companies, but Max had never been inside. He'd often seen equipment and catering trucks lined up in the lot or on the nearby streets. As these were a common sight in Los Angeles, he'd never stopped to watch or kibitz with the crew. He had always been too anxious to get to or from work.

They parked in an unreserved space and she led him inside, gaining admittance for him by propounding the simple ruse that he was her brother. Looking at the two of them, no one would have disputed it. The atmosphere inside the warehouse was hectic, with two productions shooting scenes simultaneously in different parts of the building. Maxine's appearance was the occasion for numerous greetings and waves, whereas Max drew more than a few startled double takes from extras and technicians.

"I have to go to work," she told him. "First wardrobe, then makeup. But I'll be back. Meanwhile you can wait for me here." She opened the door to a small but comfortable dressing room equipped with a lounge, TV, refrigerator, and other comforts.

He was more than a little impressed. "You've got your own dressing room?" He admired the modest furnishings. "We must be doing well in this business."

Standing in the doorway, she laughed softly. "We are. In fact, if the critics are to be believed, our career's about to take off. If you find yourself stuck in this para maybe I can get you some work. Identical twins are always in demand for commercials and such, and God knows there are no twins more identical than you and I."

Except for me and Mitch, he reminded himself, and me and a billion other paras. He wondered if they were all this successful, across the multiple para lines. It was intriguing to contemplate the possibilities. What might he be in the next one over? A respected, highly lauded surgeon, perhaps, or a famous painter.

Stop it, he ordered himself. It was a waste of time to fantasize unreasonable expectations. Acting he could see himself doing, especially in Maxine's comely form, but he knew his limitations. More than likely, those extended across parallel worlds as exhaustively as did his undeniable abilities.

"Be back in a little while," she assured him. "I'll check in on you before they call me. As long as you keep quiet you can probably observe the filming."

"I just might do that," he replied. "What kind of a picture is it, anyway?"

"*Babe Meets the Road Warrior.*" She looked apologetic. "Sony Pictures wrested the rights to both franchises away from George Miller. I can't say that I'm crazy about the script, but it's a substantial part and I only have two scenes with the pig." She smiled reassuringly. "It'll be good for my career. Anything with an Aussie connection sells tickets." She closed the door quietly behind her.

Left alone in the dressing room, he took further stock of his surroundings. The Australian edition of *Premiere* lay on the small end table along with *The Economist* and the trades. Deciding that he might as well make himself comfortable, he flopped down on the couch, picked up the TV remote, and switched on the set. Flipping through the agglutinated angst of morning soap operas and talk shows, in which he detected several strong Aussie accents among the principal players, he settled on a slice of inconsequential chat froth taped in Sydney. The media personality being interviewed was American, the interviewer Australian, the set florid with Asian colors and accoutrements.

As these novelties began to pale, he found himself drifting off. The couch was wide and comfortable, the room well insulated from the industrial-strength showbiz bustle outside, and he was exhausted mentally if not physically. When Maxine was ready to do her scenes he would take her up on her offer to watch the shoot, he told himself sleepily. She said she would wake him. Meanwhile, it would not hurt to give his over-burdened mind a rest.

As he knew from experience, talk shows made excellent soporifics. Stretching out on the couch, he kicked off his shoes and let the banal drone of fruitless argument between uninteresting people with nothing to say lull him swiftly to sleep.

For the first time in days, his slumber was not troubled by disquieting dreams. When he awoke, he felt greatly refreshed and ready to deal with whatever the cosmos pitched his way. His shoes were where he had left them, at the foot of the couch.

Except—the couch was different, as were his surroundings. Different, and yet startlingly familiar. He instantly recognized the refrigerator in the corner, the table and scattered chairs, the posters and cartoons tacked to the walls, the pantry area with its built-in coffeemaker, even the stains on the floor. As for the couch, he had spent many a fruitful moment reclined on it before.

Or had he? Aware now that reality was not always what it seemed, he sat up slowly and donned his footwear. The employees' lounge was heartrendingly familiar. Of Maxine there was no sign.

Moving to the door, he opened it not onto the bustling backwash of a small studio but a hallway frequented by familiar faces. There was no sign of filming in progress. The studio, like Maxine, was gone. Though he needed a good deal more proof before he would allow himself to accept the comforting reality of his surroundings, it was possible, just possible, that the Boles Effect had dropped him not into another para, but back into his own world line.

Stepping out into the hall, he oriented himself and headed off to his left. Through the occasional windows that opened onto the outside he recognized the same hazy urban panoramas he had casually committed to memory during his two years at the paper.

Well-known faces looked up and smiled or volunteered nonchalant greetings, as if nothing was amiss and all was right with the world. This world. For them, nothing was faulty, nothing had gone awry. Their reality was and always had remained undisturbed. Sterling Feeney, from down in Composition, stopped to chat.

"Hey Max, saw that piece you did on the fortune-teller and the dead kid. Good stuff! You have a real feeling for atmosphere in your stories and . . ." He broke off, his expression becoming one of concern. "You feeling all right? You look a little out of it."

A little out of it, Max thought. *Yes, you could say that I've been a little out of it.*

"I'm fine, Stir-fry. You know us writers. When we're caught staring off into the distance it doesn't mean that we're rude or not listening; we're just hard at work."

"Yeah, that's the excuse you always use."

"What about you?" he asked the compositor. "How are you doing these days?"

"Me? I'm swell."

"Nothing out of the ordinary happen in your life lately? Nothing extraordinary crop up in your neighborhood or fling itself in your face?"

Slightly baffled, Feeney regarded the reporter uncertainly. "Are you getting at something specific, or are you just having me on?"

"Forget it." Raising his gaze, Max looked past the shorter man. "Seen Maxine around?"

"Maxine?" Feeney considered. "Don't know any Maxine. She work here?"

"I thought she did. With another writer named Mitch."

Feeney shook his head slowly. "Haven't seen any stories with a byline from a guy named Mitch. Has Kryzewski hired some new people?"

"Probably not." He pushed past the bemused compositor. "See you round, Sterling."

Back, he thought as he heaved a long mental sigh. I'm back. It was just as Boles had hopefully hypothesized; the effects of the field were transitory and had worn off of their own accord, leaving him back in the world where he belonged. There was no need now to revisit the eccentric inventor, except perhaps to show him that he could relax and that there was no longer any cause for alarm. Like a bad headache quickly cured, the effects of his experience could no longer be felt.

Passing others in the hall, he was now able to greet them cheerfully. His cubicle beckoned, familiar and changeless. Before he could slip inside and take his seat, he ran into Hammel coming the other way.

"Max, good to see you. You been out the last couple of days."

"Working." Max smiled back at the staff artist. "You know how it is. Sometimes you get hooked on a story and can't let go. I've been busy with follow-ups."

"Must be some story." For an artist, Hammel was positively loquacious. "There's a chance I can score four tickets for the Lakers Friday night. Want in?"

Basketball, Max thought. *Total mental immersion in mindless professional sports. One of the most benign social pursuits. Funny the things you miss when you're being skipped from world to world, like a flat stone across the surface of an endless pond.*

"That's a rhetorical question, isn't it? I'll even spring for the parking."

"Hey," Hammel blurted in surprise, "what makes you so generous all of a sudden? You sell a column to a syndicate?"

Max pursed his lips. "Let's just say that I'm feeling expansive."

"Glad to hear it. I was told that you'd spent the last couple of days home sick." Lowering his voice, he moved closer. " 'Fess up now: You really been working, or you just decide to take a couple of days off?"

"I've been working." Max frowned slightly. "Who told you I'd been home sick?"

Hammel stepped back and shrugged. "Just heard it around. Glad to see it isn't true." He stepped around the reporter. "My place, Friday, right after work. We'll grab something to eat on the way or if the traffic's bad, we'll eat junk food at the Forum."

"Who else is going?" Max asked absently. Something the artist had said continued to bother him and as a consequence he was finding it hard to concentrate on the conversation. Why would Hammel or anyone else think he'd been home sick?

The staff Rembrandt looked back over his shoulder. "Not sure yet. Probably Stan, maybe Gina from my department if I can talk her into it." Volunteering no further information, he disappeared around a corner.

Max was still mildly troubled by the unsubstantiated rumor that he was suffering from some unknown illness when he entered his cubicle. It was unchanged, exactly as he remembered it, even to the number and position of cut-out editorial cartoons pinned or taped to the movable walls. Slumping down in his chair, he switched on the computer. All of his files were undisturbed, exactly as he'd left them. In fact, everything was as he'd left it.

I haven't been home sick, he told himself. *Not I, me. But someone else might have been. A para Max could have been home sick.*

If that was the case it should be simple enough to check up on. All he had to do was pick up the phone and call himself.

The receiver lay in its bracket, faux ivory and quiescent. Everything was going so well, everything seemed so familiar and comfortable and normal, that he hesitated long and hard. Perhaps someone around the office had simply chosen to interpret his absence as due to illness, thus initiating an unsubstantiated rumor. Or possibly it was just the result of some simple misunderstanding.

The phone continued to repose in its holder, calling to no one but him. He started to reach for it, held off, reached again, drew back his fingers. Around him, all was as it should be, he told himself. There *was* no ill para waiting for him at home, lying in his bed, watching his TV, making Carrey faces before taking his medicine. He was here, at work, where he belonged—and nowhere else.

He had new stories to develop, old ones to edit. Later, he would go to lunch with his friends. Tonight, he would drive home (in a car that made some fitting noise, he promised himself) and catch up on his reading, maybe see what was on cable. Friday he would attend the Lakers game and scream himself hoarse while other, much taller men engaged in a game whose skills were denied to him. Such was life. *Así es la vida.* Resolutely opening the file on Boles, he set to work composing a suitably tawdry, enticing story out of the notes and memories of his visit.

The few interruptions he suffered were normal and, as such, were welcomed. At a quarter to twelve he went to lunch with several friends, none of whom evinced anything out of the ordinary. No triplets or quintuplets or any other kind of unnaturally interchangeable plets sat down across from him. The good food and energetic conversation relaxed him further.

Back at the *Investigator* building everyone went their separate ways, returning to their own cubicles or departments. On the way back to his desk Max waved to casual acquaintances and spoke to close ones, glancing in turn at Werther and Hammel, surreptitiously eyeing Elena Alonzo's most excellent legs, sharing a joke in passing with Steve Dalhouse from photography, staring at the heavy, broad figure of the dark green shape with the tentacular, cephalopodian head and the ichorous skin as it shambled past and got onto the elevator. It was going down, he noticed as he halted in midstride and gawked, his lower jaw hanging as loose as if every connecting cartilage and tendon in his face had suddenly snapped.

What in the name of all bastard Creation was that? He found himself wondering.

Hallucination, he told himself firmly. A consequence of everything he'd been through the past couple of days. An aftereffect of the effect. He stumbled toward the elevator and waited for it to return. In moments it arrived, disgorging three fellow workers. Two of them gave him funny looks as they hurried past.

The elevator looked normal enough. So had those who had exited. Blinking, he turned to continue on his way. The file he had opened on his computer needed to be closed. He took one step and slipped slightly. Catching himself, he looked down at the floor.

A thin path of glistening mucus led along the passageway and up to the elevator, which by now was on its way to another floor.

Tolerably dazed, he returned to his cubicle. Around him, the room hummed with the sound of keyboards working, paper being shuffled, people moving about. Here and there conversation or subdued laughter rose above the general, familiar buzz of work.

What he had observed entering the lift had been slightly larger than man-sized and grotesque in the extreme. Its skin had been leprous and warty, the face—there had been little in the way of a face. Just a mass of languidly writhing tendrils flanked by a pair of bulging, glassy eyes. The apparition had not been even remotely human.

Hammel materialized suddenly behind him and the twitchy reporter jumped a clean inch off the floor. "Whoa, take it easy, pal. Just wanted to let you know everything's set for Friday."

"What?" Max mumbled.

The artist stepped into the cubicle. "Friday? The Lakers game?" His smile flattened. "You feeling all right, Max? You're sweating."

Using the back of his arm, the reporter wiped at his moisture-beaded forehead. "I don't know. I guess so." Swiveling in his chair, he looked up at his friend. "I just had a waking hallucination. A real Tim Leary prizewinner."

Hammel laughed. "Man, did you slip something into your lunch I didn't see? You been raiding the recreational pharmaceuticals again?"

"No, dammit! I haven't taken anything." Max could feel his heart pounding behind his shirt. He was unable to keep himself from glancing repeatedly in the direction of the elevator.

"Okay, okay! Calm down." Hammel grew more serious, less jocular. "Is something wrong?"

"I don't know." Max nodded to his left. "I think I just saw something like a bipedal squid get into the elevator."

The artist turned in the direction Max had indicated. "Bipedal squi—oh, that must've been Ce-Sathaq."

Max's eyebrows rose. "You want to run that by me again?"

"Ce-Sathaq," repeated Hammel. "Surely you've met him by now? He came over last week to replace Toroth-Mek." Leaning forward, the artist searched his friend's face. "You sure you're all right? You don't look well at all. Like you might be feverish."

"No fever," Max assured him. "Who—or what—is a Toroth-Mek? Or for that matter, a Ce-Sathaq?"

"Man, you are out of it. You hit your head or something?"

"I—now that you mention it, I have been missing some things lately. I don't think it's anything serious."

Hammel looked less certain. "Mild amnesia? You fall and hit your head in the shower or something? Ce-Sathaq's our new Cthulhi. You know how the Great Old Ones feel about the media. 'That which is not dead can eternal lie, and with strange eons, even death may die.' " He shook his head. "I've heard plenty of excuses for a lack of original programming and the substitution of constant reruns, but that one takes the cake. But what can you do?" Leaning closer, the artist dropped his voice to a whisper.

"I mean, that's the way things are now, ever since the Awakening, and there isn't a damn thing anyone can do about it. Not in this lifetime, anyway. Maybe not ever. It's kind of sad for the human race, but there's no going back. And it isn't so bad, is it? You get up in the morning, perform your daily obeisance, recite the sacred litany, and go on with your life. Sure there are the sacrifices, but the Old Ones aren't greedy. They just want the respect that's due them. Sort of like intergalactic homeboys.

"There's always a good side to everything. No more wars, after all. Not with the Great Old Ones in control of the planet. Just so long as it isn't your kid who's chosen for the weekly sacrifice, right? And neither of us is married so that's not our problem. Not for now, anyway."

Hammel's words fell on Max's mind like tax day on an unrepentant gambler. No matter how hard he tried he could not make sense of what his friend was telling him.

"I guess I have had a mild spell of some kind. Refresh my memory, Dave. Bring it all back for me."

"Yeah, well, if you had to disremember something I guess the Awakening wouldn't be a bad thing to forget. Can't live that way, though. Nobody can, much as they might like to. I mean, reality's reality, right?"

If only you knew, Max thought painfully. *If only you knew.*

IX

"You don't remember anything about the Awakening?"

"Not a thing," Max assured him heartily.

"It was all the fault of that picture they were making. That damn picture. The one about the Necronomicon. Some fool producer got ahold of a copy of the real thing, not one of the cheap fictional fakes, and thought it would make the basis for a good horror film. You know the way the business is. They'll jump on any gimmick. So a script was drawn up, and principal photography started, and when they read the critical words for the hundredth time, all very innocent and all, the Earth trembled and the skies opened up and the Great Old Ones awoke and began their triumphant return.

"And now the human race is stuck with the cephalopodian bastards. The whole lot of 'em." He jerked his head in the direction of the elevator. "Ce-Sathaq is a Cthulhi, a servant of great Cthulhu. Being a sea-being, Cthulhu's dominion extends over all the coasts and coastal cities of the world." He was studying his colleague's face closely. "You sure you don't remember any of this?"

"No, nothing." An openly dazed Max shook his head.

"Well, you'd better seek professional help if I can't bring it back for you, or you'll forget to do your daily ablutions and recitals. That could mean real trouble. The Cthulhi aren't telepathic, but they have their ways of finding out who is being properly obeisant and who's slacking. You know what happens to the slackers." The artist shuddered visibly.

Max did not know and, based on his friend's reaction, chose not to inquire after details.

"So that's how it's been ever since the Awakening. Cthulhu demands homage from those living near the sea. Hastur the Unspeakable and his minions run the mountainous parts of the country, Shub-Niggurath is up in the north woods where the climate and ambience suits him, and so on down the line. Or maybe I should say lineage. As usual, they don't always get along and then it's the humans who are caught in the middle who suffer." He looked thoughtful.

"It's really not so bad. Except for the day when we lost Minneapolis there hasn't been much of what you'd call mass affliction. The Great Old Ones want respect and the occasional juicy young sacrifice, and that's all." He shrugged.

"In a lot of ways, Congress was worse. And those of us here in the L.A. basin have benefited ever since Cthulhu decided to make R'lyeh a part of L.A. I mean, what's one more suburb in Southern California, even if the architecture is cylopean and non-Euclidean? Where else in the country would that kind of eclectic construction fit right in? In New York they used to sell thousands of little bronze and plastic replicas of the Statue of Liberty, before Cthulhu tore it down. Now they sell replicas of the great obscene obelisk in R'lyeh instead. I mean, what's the big deal?"

"This Cthulhu thing—what's it look like?" Max inquired.

Hammel made anxious shushing motions with both hands. "Hey, are you nuts? Don't call him a 'thing' or you'll find yourself in worse shape than a sacrifice. I've heard stories—but never mind, you don't want to know. He looks like his Cthulhi, of course, only much worse, and he's as big as the Forum. You *really* don't remember any of this?"

"No." *Because it's not my para*, he thought. *Thank God it's not my para.*

Have to get out, he told himself. *Have to get away.* Suddenly, being stuck in a parallel world occupied by his female self, or in his own world with a para Max or condors or even aliens for company, no longer seemed such an imposition. Any of those situations were infinitely better than this one, where the world had been taken over by gigantic hideous horrors from beyond.

The trouble was, he couldn't just jump between paras, or buy a ticket out, or click his heels together and say "There's no place like home" three times to resolve the situation.

What would happen to him if he died here? To his real self? Probably, his paras would live on, including no doubt the one who occupied his life position here who was lying home sick in bed. But he, him, the one Max that was Max to the Max, he would perish, permanently and forever.

He could not allow that to happen. He had stories to write, fabulous useless products from the Sharper Image and Hammacher Schlemmer to buy, beautiful ladies to charm, literary and journalistic awards to win. He wanted to travel the length and breadth of his own world, not that of others.

The noise of some increasing commotion reached them from the far side of the room. Rising, both men peered down the passage that led between cubicles. A hideous black winged monstrosity with no face was devouring the thrashing carcass of someone up from the mail room. Having cleanly removed the top of the young man's skull, the creature was now gnawing out his brains. As the unfortunate's struggles grew weaker, interest in the room waned and people started shuffling back to their work.

Seeing the horror on Max's face, Hammel took pains to explain. "That kid's been known to scrawl anti–Great Old Ones graffiti in the men's rooms. He was warned. Those damned byakee birds—you can't hide from 'em. I always wondered how they could eat without a mouth." He summoned up a smile. "You still on for the Lakers game Friday? I mean, if you're not feeling up to it I can always find somebody else to go."

"No, I'd like to go. I'm okay, really." Rising from his chair, Max walked past his friend. "I just need to step out for a little while, get some fresh air."

Alarmed, Hammel looked around nervously. "Where are you going? If you're not sick you can't just take off. It's not like the old days. The pre-Awakening days. You know the work rules."

Aiming instinctively for the elevator, Max abruptly changed direction and headed toward the fire stairs. "I just need some outside oxygen," he called back to the artist. "I'll be back in a little while."

"You'd better be." Hammel was looking around uneasily, searching the passageways between cubicles. "I can't cover for you on this one, Max. I have to get back to my own department. I've spent too much time talking to you already. Someone's liable to notice and make a report. I'm sorry, but you know how it is. Or you should." He started off in the opposite direction, smiling weakly. "Friday, don't forget. You're paying for parking."

Max did not reply as he yanked open the protective fire door that led to the stairwell. Stark, cool, and spray-painted a dull white, the emergency stairs corkscrewed their way groundward below him. After leaning over to make certain the shaft was empty, he started down. Despite his efforts to move quietly, his steps rang loud on the metal stairs. Detecting in the distance what he perceived to be an occasional tormented moan, he hurried his descent.

Outside, the world appeared normal. There was the familiar line of specialty shops on the opposite side of the street, the big Ralph's grocery store on the next block up, cars and pedestrians advancing and retreating to the clockwork rhythm of the streetlights. The placid Southern California sun shone brightly overhead, unnaturally unimpeded by the familiar layer of smog. Nothing he saw or heard indicated in any way that humanity was no longer in control of its own destiny or that live sacrifices were required weekly to appease the gluttonous appetites of grisly invaders from Outside.

Nothing except the billboard over the Osco drugstore that advertised discount vacations to glorious R'lyeh, with its antediluvian otherworldly architecture and magnificent unpolluted beaches. To Max, the supposedly enticing holiday images raised up in the sunshine looked anything but inviting, though his fellow pedestrians appeared undisturbed by their appearance. Coming as he did from a different para, perhaps he had truer perceptions. He decided that the local populace was either locked in a collective, willing suspension of disbelief, or else a somniferous pall of unreality had seeped into everyone's brains. The result of mass hypnosis to keep the *untermenschen* in line, he decided, or some other deceptive effect he could not imagine.

It had to be so. Otherwise how could a lighthearted, easygoing guy like Hammel talk so glibly about systematically scheduled human sacrifice? If Max's concerns were valid, then voicing them might inadvertently single him out as an independent thinker, a defining social characteristic that had no future in this world.

Sure enough, as he took long, measured strides up the street in the direction of Westwood, sirens and lights flared behind him. Ignoring them, he walked on, resolutely not looking back. If it was him they were after he ought to be able to disappear before they discovered his absence. He hoped they, whoever "they" were, wouldn't go from the office to his apartment to arrest, or eviscerate, or whatever it was they did to those who resisted the hypnotic sway of Great Cthulhu, his possibly ill para.

The bloodcurdling inhuman wail of the sirens grew louder. In spite of himself, he looked back. Expecting to see one or more police cruisers drawn up in front of the·*Investigator* building, he was shocked to find himself staring instead at a large, lugubrious lump of gelatinous protoplasm from which protruded, at seemingly random locations, a plethora of bulging eyeballs and toothy, snapping mouths. A throng of armed, uniformed Cthulhi were sliding off it and shambling into the newspaper building. Along the crest of the heaving, pulsating mass, a line of red lights spun silently.

Resuming his retreat as he continued to gape at the extraordinary sight, he stumbled into the back of a well-dressed older man hugging a briefcase. "Sorry."

"It's all right." The tall, patrician figure lengthened his stride to match that of the younger man. "Keep walking. Don't look back. You don't want to draw their attention."

Noting absently that the man smelled of fine cologne, Max fell into step alongside him.

"What is that thing with the lights on it?" It was hard for Max not to glance over his shoulder. Behind them, the sirens wailed less insistently now.

His temporary companion looked down at him. "You must be from the heartland or something. That's a Los Angeles Police Department Shuggoth. Not as fast as some of the old-fashioned cruisers, but it can push anything out of its way. Of course, if you run from a Shuggoth you had better make certain you get away."

"Why is that?"

"Because when they catch you, you don't get arrested. You get enveloped and consumed." He looked thoughtful. "It does tend to cut down on the transient jail population." Disregarding his own advice, he looked back the way they had come. "Oh my. It seems that there are minions coming this way." His eyes widened as he saw his fellow traveler in a new and less convivial light. "They must be after you!" Holding his briefcase in front of him like a shield, he stumbled away from the inoffensive Max.

"Hey, take it easy, I haven't done anything." Looking back now, Max saw that a number of the Cthulhi had come out of the *Investigator* building and were heading up the street in his direction.

"Stay away from me! I have a virgin daughter!" Clutching

his briefcase, the panicked executive hurried off down a side street.

Max did his best to stay inconspicuous, but it soon became clear that the Cthulhi, though still not entirely sure of their quarry, were beginning to narrow their search. Several of the cephalopodian creatures were within half a block of him. They paused only briefly to check the faces of terrified pedestrians before moving on. Max knew he had to hide, to get out of their sight, but if he was giving off some kind of unknown mental incongruity that they could detect, where could he find safety?

A subway entrance beckoned. In this para, the L.A. line had been extended, logically enough, to the western part of the city. He ducked down it quickly, wondering if his money would be accepted in this para, fearing that his coins would not operate the automatic turnstiles.

Perusing papers and magazines, their brains turned to temporary tapioca by uncountable variations on the ubiquitous plugged-in Walkman, or dealing with children, passengers-to-be stood waiting for the next train. A cautious glance back up toward the street showed several of the ghastly Cthulhi hovering near the entrance and debating, their facial tentacles writhing like packs of mating snakes. Then two of them started down the access stairs.

Max looked around wildly. There was still no sign of the next train. As inconspicuously as possible, he made his way to the far west end of the tunnel and ducked down the narrow serviceway that ran along the tiled wall parallel to the tracks. Looking back, he could see the circle of light that marked the location of the station receding behind him. Wishing for a flashlight but not daring to stop, he hurried on into the darkness. Track switching lights provided some perspective without adequately illuminating his surroundings.

Fortunately, it was impossible to lose the narrow walkway. Extending his arms out sideways allowed him to touch the tunnel wall with his left hand easily and the walkway guardrail with his right. As long as he didn't hit a protrusion or hole in the concrete path he would be all right.

An unlit tunnel swerved off to his left. Emergency siding, he thought, or a branch of an as yet uncompleted line. Afraid to cross the open tracks ahead, he turned and followed the new corridor. There were no colorful switches here to guide him, but occasional shafts of light soon appeared in the distance. The illumination was pouring through some kind of skylight or service access to the surface, he decided, grateful for even the tiny amounts of light.

Behind him, he heard a distant roaring. It might have been a train, or it might have been something equally massive but far more organic in nature. Whatever it was, it was coming up the main tunnel in his direction. He had no intention of retracing his steps in hopes of identifying it. He hurried on.

A fair amount of time had passed and there was still no sign of the Cthulhi or, for that matter, subway service technicians, construction workers, or anyone else. For the moment, at least, the tunnel was his.

Hurrying along the unyielding path proved hard on his feet. Eventually, he was forced to slow to a pained walk. With luck he'd lost his pursuers, at least for a while. Ahead, a greater volume of light beckoned. Too bright to signify the presence of a station, it probably indicated the location of a new access under construction, perhaps even preliminary excavation. Questions might be forthcoming when he, a solitary pedestrian, came tromping out of the darkness, but he felt confident of his ability to slip away before the authorities could be notified. With so much else being familiar and recognizable in this para, there was no reason to assume that his press credentials would not be accepted as legitimate. They had gotten him out of difficult situations before.

The nearer he drew to the light, the more it became apparent that this was a station or service entrance still under construction. Chunks of steel and blocks of concrete lay strewn about, along with broken rock and piles of crumbled scree. Wiring for overhead lights dangled loosely from the ceiling and the tiled steps shone uncompleted. It was dead silent not only within the station but up on the street as well.

Either a large area up on the surface had been roped off to keep the curious away from the construction site, he decided, or else he had left the busy Wilshire corridor behind. Perhaps this station was being built in a quiet residential section. That could account for the exceptional silence. With a backward glance to reassure himself that no threat was immediately forthcoming from that quarter, he started cautiously up the broken steps.

The world into which he emerged was not the one he had just left.

It took him only a moment to realize that the condition of the subway station at his feet was due not to an incomplete state of construction but to one of untimely destruction. It was not a station half built but one completely destroyed. As was the street, and the structures that had once lined it, and as far as he could see, the heretofore familiar city around him.

Most of the buildings he knew so well from innumerable drives up and down the roadway had been razed to the ground. Only the fragments of foundations and in places, nothing more than black scars, remained to show where they had once stood. The Ralph's was gone, as was the *Investigator* tower, and every other store and apartment building and office block that used to line the boulevard.

Turning a slow circle, he saw only a few tattered remnants of well-known office spires sundering the horizon like so many shattered teeth. To the north the Santa Monica Mountains rose from a listless gray haze. The familiar hillsides presented a blasted and bleached appearance, as if the green and brown chaparral that normally covered their slopes had been scoured from their flanks by some gigantic razor, leaving only the folds and creases of obscenely naked gullies behind.

To the east nothing stood: not the carefully aligned steeples of the Wilshire corridor nor the distant, taller skyscrapers of downtown. Even the San Diego and Santa Monica freeways were gone. As he stood staring, a chill wind sprang up, making him bunch his shirt tightly against his neck. Scraps of paper, some with burnt edges, and gray ash went flying erratically past him.

At least the mountains gave him a means of orienting himself. At his feet, the ruined subway station beckoned. No way was he returning to that dark hole. Not knowing what else to do, he set off westward down the street. No Cthulhi waited to embrace him with their revolting tentacle-ridden faces. Not in this para. Somewhere he thought he heard a dog bark, but it might have been only the wind driving scraps of wood against heaps of metal slag. The wind howled forlornly around him as he staggered off in the general direction of the Pacific.

It had been a long, long time since he had walked so far in L.A., but he had no choice. No buses rumbled past, no immigrant-piloted taxis hailed him. In all that destruction and devastation, nothing moved that was not carried by the wind. Perversely, the blasted solitude gave strength to his tired legs, and he lengthened his stride.

Eventually, undisturbed by man or machine, he reached the coast. He knew it was the coast because he recognized the bluffs on which he stood. Far below lay a thin, shattered strip of asphalt that had once been the Pacific Coast Highway. Beyond was the beach, and beyond that was the ocean.

Should have been the ocean.

The Pacific had vanished. As far as he could see, from Malibu in the north to Palos Verde in the south and all the way to the western horizon, was nothing but sand and dried mud baked hard and unyielding by the sun. For all he knew, the desert that had once been an ocean bottom extended all the way to Japan.

What unimaginable catastrophe had devastated this para? he wondered. What had reduced a great city to little more than ashes, and had dried up even the ocean itself? Dumbfounded, aware that he was confronting a disaster beyond his limited imagination to envision, he stared at the silent, barren horizon. Neither it nor the wind offered up any explanation.

There was nothing to be gained by standing on the edge of the bluffs until he collapsed. Experiencing a sudden urge to view the remnants of his home and wondering at the same time if he would recognize them, he turned south, intending to walk the rest of the way down the coast to the site of his apartment building. From Wilshire, it was only a little more than a dozen blocks.

As he turned to go, there came a voice. It was no auricular hallucination: he heard the words clearly and distinctly. Breaking into a run, he followed the sound, and a few moments later found himself confronting a scrawny, starving individual seated with his back against the dead stump of one of the numerous palm trees whose green fronds had once waved exuberantly from the crest of the bluffs.

The man wore only the shreds and tatters of what had

once been denim pants. He had no shirt, his hair was unkempt and uncut, and the filthy, shaggy growth of his beard reached down to the middle of his chest. Sores and blisters covered his body, the suppurating redness showing noisomely through the mascara of accumulated, caked-on soil. He had been talking to himself, loudly enough for Max to overhear.

"Christ, man, what happened to you?" Max gestured at the devastation around them. "What happened here?"

"Stranger, are ye? Then there's still a place where the Sicknesses haven't struck everyone down." The man trembled as he spoke, and his voice shook in time with the vibrations of his desiccated body. "No matter where you be from, how can it be that you are ignorant of what occurred?"

"Everyone forgets things." Max spoke as gently as he could. The poor fellow was obviously in the last stages of physical and mental exhaustion.

"It was the Effect that did this, o' course. The thousand-times-be-damned Effect." His lips were quivering so badly he could hardly form the words.

Max leaned closer so that the man would not have to expend as much energy talking. "The Effect? What Effect?"

"Why, the Boles Effect, naturally. This is what happens when a man who doesn't know what he's doin' goes monkeying around with the unifying forces o' the Universe. Curse his careless soul to Perdition forever!"

The Boles Effect. Max swallowed, squinting as the cold wind kicked up ash and debris. "Barrington Boles?"

Rheumy, bloodshot eyes stared up at him. Max was not sure they were focusing. But the survivor's uncertain gaze did not waver.

"Was there any other? Course, the meddlin' bastard's probably dead now. Not that it does the few of us that are left a world o' good." A constrained cackle emerged from the depths of the diseased throat. " 'World o' good,' get it?"

Keeping his back facing the wind, Max straightened slightly, admiring the skeletal survivor huddled at his feet. "I would've expected someone in your condition and situation to have lost their sense of humor a long time ago."

The woolly head twitched. It might have been a nod. " 'Bout all that's kept me goin' this long. Though I don't know why I bother." Shaking badly, a diseased arm rose and pointed at the vanished Pacific. "Guess I keep hoping the sea will come back. I miss it more than I do the people. Back before the Effect ruined everything, back when things were normal, I used to come out at night and sit on the old wooden lifeguard stations and just watch it, listening to the waves breaking on the shore."

Max followed the unsteady finger. "I know what you mean. I used to do the same thing. I ..." He broke off abruptly. It felt as if an unseen and especially sadistic assailant had just smacked him in the stomach with a rubber mallet. Ignoring the stinging grit flying through the air, he stared wide-eyed at the seated, trembling figure.

"What—what did you do—before the Effect?"

"Do? Do." The man considered, as if remembering the smallest detail of what had gone before was a Promethean struggle. "Why, if I be recalling correctly, I used to write. Little articles of no consequence, short stories of no merit. They didn't matter much then, and they don't matter at all now." A hand characterized by broken nails and running sores reached shakily up toward him. "Max be my name. Maxwell Parker."

"No." Slowly Max backed away from the sickly, repellent figure. He could see it now—beneath the haggard tangle of hair, behind the wild beard. Could see it in the glassy, half-wild eyes.

He had met another of his paras.

With a cry he turned and ran, ignoring the coughing, hacking entreaties of the devastated stick-figure behind him, not looking back, not turning to see or to listen. He was running north now, his chest pounding, the wind-flung ash and debris stinging his eyes and exposed skin. Running north, toward distant Malibu and, beyond, Trancas. That was where he would find Barrington Boles, who, if a breath still lived within him, Max steadfastly intended to kill.

To what end? He slowed, finally coming to a complete halt. Suppose he did find Boles alive? How could he know if he was killing the right Boles, the right para? What was the point of it, when a million billion Boleses still lived on a billion million parallel worlds? With at least a few million of them working on the machine, how many would eventually get it right? How many would finally stumble on the secret of the field effect, resulting in the utter and total destruction of innocent paras like this one?

What was the point of it all? What was the point of anything anymore? Was he even the right Maxwell Parker, or was he nothing more than one of dozens of frantic paras all scurrying futilely about in a hopeless attempt to find their way home, when "home" could no longer even be properly defined? For all the sense anything made anymore, he might as well go back and wait to die alongside his poor, bemused, helpless local para. Distraught and disillusioned and pretty near his wits' end, he turned back into the wind.

Propelled by the angry, moaning mistral, something larger and heavier than ash or grit came flying through the dreary, sorrowing atmosphere. Intent to the exclusion of all else upon his redeeming vision of private justice, Max never saw it coming. It struck him on the side of the head and he went down, instantly rendered unconscious, face-first into the dead earth.

X

"Is he alive?"

"Hold off on that emergency request, chaps. I think he may be coming around."

"The poor dear! What could have happened to him?"

"See all the dirt on his clothes. He looks like he has been wandering around aimlessly in Death Valley."

Within himself, Max heard the words. They issued from different throats, male and female. None of them shook, none of them were afflicted with a diseased quaver. None of them were filled with the anguish of a ruined world. He fought to open his eyes.

The sun was shining, the sky was blue, and the air smelled of fresh, sweet growing things. While he was unconscious, he had shifted paras once again.

Hands pressed against his back and pulled gently on his

shoulders, helping him to sit up. Strong, healthy hands and arms. Blinking frequently and reaching up to rub grit from his eyes, he was finally able to open them.

Paradise spread out before him.

Well, maybe not Paradise, but a purer, cleaner, more agreeable vision of Los Angeles than he had ever imagined. He knew it was still Los Angeles, because there was much that he was still able to recognize.

His location, for example. He was sitting up where he had fallen, on the bluffs that overlooked the coast highway and the ocean beyond. The ocean, the glorious Pacific, had returned in all its unsurpassed deep blue splendor. As for the coast highway, it was still there. Only in this para it was paved not with asphalt but with grass. Fully enclosed silver-sided vehicles cruised along its wide, unstriped path, traveling silently a foot or so above the undisturbed emerald turf.

The palm trees that normally lined the edge of the bluffside park were back also; healthy and alive, their fronds swaying in a gentle, warm breeze. As in his para, pedestrians promenaded along the bluffs, taking in the view and the sea air. Their clothing differed from that favored in his own world but not radically so. It was not some wide-eyed 1930s vision of what contemporary casual attire should be. The fabrics and designs looked as natural and comfortable as the people who wore them.

He found himself the recipient of the solicitous stares and

attentions of the four passersby in their mid-twenties who had discovered him lying behind a tree. There were two men and two women; one black, one Asian, the other two white. All fairly glowed with health and beauty. He allowed them to help him to his feet.

He stood where he had fallen. The green carpet of the park extended all the way to the first buildings that fronted on the promenade. In place of the blacktop that in his world defined the strip of street known as Ocean Avenue, there was another extended lawn. More of the silent silvery hovercraft cruised noiselessly north and south above the undisturbed greensward. Some had their transparent canopies down, and teenagers shouted to one another from the interiors of passing vehicles.

The buildings that began where the grass ended were enclosed by a crystal wall that varied in height. Gone was the eclectic but somewhat tawdry pastel jumble of fast-food restaurants, souvenir emporiums, T-shirt shops, and beach hotels that he knew so well. Everything was spotless, clean, wholesome, and beautifully maintained.

If this is the beachfront, he found himself wondering, *what must the rest of the city be like?* It was the diametric opposite of the unfortunate para he had just left.

Seeing that their foundling was alert and sensible, the shorter of the two young men performed introductions. "Glad to see you up and about, old man. You look in a bad way, don't you know. I'm Corey. This is Cheung, Lacy, and Bert." With each name, extended hands were offered. He shook each one in turn as he identified himself.

Lacy was giggling at him. "You look like you're fitted out for a costume party. How do you stand the heat in those pants? And those ridiculous shoes!"

Automatically defensive, Max glanced down at his two-hundred-dollar Reeboks. "What's so ridiculous about them?"

"They're so big and bulky," the diminutive Cheung pointed out. "And those little white ropes that hold them together. Eminently retrograde."

"The color scheme's not bad. See the cute little nonfunctional inserts?" Bert was making an effort to be understanding.

Max noticed that they were all wearing shorts, thin tops fashioned of different, slightly reflective materials, and sandals that seemed to adhere to their feet without the aid of straps, laces, or any other kind of visible binding mechanism. *Maybe they glued them on,* he thought. Lacy and Corey wore sunglasses that not only changed color according to the intensity of the light, but displayed intimations of moving landscapes across the interior of the lenses, like compact rear-projection televisions.

A much larger hover vehicle appeared, traveling from north to south. As it turned up Pico, it bent in the middle to make the corner, flexible as a snake. The people within were not affected. Overhead, the sky shone a deep, untrammeled blue. There was not a hint, not a suggestion, of smog, much less the gray-white ash of total devastation.

Off to the north, something like an amethyst needle thrust impossibly far into the azure sky. Small white clouds trailed inland from its tip.

"What's that?" he found himself wondering aloud.

The two young women looked at one another and giggled. They seemed a bit old to be engaging in so much giggling, he thought. It was the one called Cheung who supplied an answer.

"You really are from out of town, aren't you? That's the observatory, silly."

"Is that a fact? And what does it observe?" he inquired tartly.

"Weather patterns, seismic disturbances, the feeding habits of the local cetacean and pinniped populations, bird migrations—that sort of thing." Bert's smile was infuriatingly condescending. "It's been there for a quite a few years now, old man."

So this time I'm a hick in my own hometown, Max reflected. *So enlighten me.* "I'd think it would be an awkward place to be in a bad quake."

"Not at all, old boy," Corey assured him while the women continued their damned giggling. "The foundation is buried quite deeply in bedrock, and counterweighted besides. It sways, quite a bit sometimes, but it's quite impossible to topple. There's quite a good restaurant on top, below the scientific station. You can see all the way to San Diego."

"Quite," added Bert unnecessarily.

"So on a clear day you can see Mission Bay." Max gawked at the three-thousand-foot-tall tower.

Bert made a face. "Oh, I say, old chap, is there any other kind?"

"You never have any smoggy days?"

" 'Smoggy'?" Cheung frowned and, for once, did not giggle. "Oh, you mean that air pollution certain places used to have back around the early part of the century. I wouldn't have guessed you were a history buff, Max."

"I'm not, not really. In—some places—I understand that the smog didn't get really bad until after World War Two."

His new benefactors looked at one another. "World War Two? But there was only one world war," Lacy insisted.

Max hesitated, not wishing to make any more of a fool of himself than he already had. "We didn't fight the Germans and the Japanese back in the forties?"

Corey was eyeing him cautiously now, perhaps wondering if their filthy friend might have escaped from a place not spoken of in polite company.

"I say, old man, where *have* you fallen from? Why on Earth would America ever fight the Germans again, much less the Japanese? After Teddy Roosevelt won his third term and pushed through the plan to rebuild Germany following the world war, and the Emperor began to personally supervise the growth of the Keiretsu in Japan, this old world finally started acting sensibly. Except for that momentary hiccough in Russia. But everyone knows this. Have you been living as some kind of hermit since you were born, or something?"

"Or something," Max admitted. The women had backed

several steps away from him, much as they would have from a large, drooling animal encountered unexpectedly in the woods. "Listen, I'm not crazy, though if I told you the truth about myself you might think otherwise."

"Well then," declared Bert, clapping Max on the back, "don't tell us. Not that we all can't use a bit of craziness in our lives now and then." He winked. "Bit of a social necessity, what?"

"So the rest of the city looks like this?" Max gestured at the gleaming crystal wall, the manicured grass thoroughfares, and the immaculate pedestrian promenade on which they stood.

"Pretty much," Bert told him. "There are the industrial areas, of course, but they're all out in Barstow and Palmdale."

Max eyed him intently. "And there are no racial problems in South Central?"

"Racial problems?" Bert looked bemused. "What might those be, old chap?"

I want to stay here, Max decided. Maybe he didn't belong; not now, not yet. But he could learn, adapt, survive. Let them giggle at him all they wanted. Writing was still an art that transferred effectively from place to place. His other-para perspective might even work to his advantage in this world. What was dull, daily truth to him might be received as quite the novelty here. If it would help him to blend in, he would even surrender his Reeboks for a pair of shiny, stick-on sandals.

In this para courtesy was still common currency, compassion for even a confused, misclad stranger willingly offered, and the environment—the environment was what it ought to be but what the people of his para could only dream about. Yes, he could live in this world. Settle down and find something to do. His belly growled complainingly. If it was as elegant as the rest of his surroundings, he couldn't wait to taste the food here.

"Listen, thanks for your help." He started away from them, heading south in the direction of his apartment building. He wondered what it would look like, and if his key would work.

"Are you sure you're going to be all right?" Lacy was smiling now, all honest sympathy. "If you're not feeling well we can call for medical."

"Yes," agreed the petitely attractive Cheung. "Or if you prefer, you can come home with one of us." She smiled encouragingly. Neither Corey nor Bert offered any objection.

Imagine an attractive young woman in his world asking a stranger who looked like his current disheveled self to come home with her, and her friends not objecting. It spoke volumes about the level of crime in this world. If there *were* any such social aberrations remaining, he mused. Perhaps serious crime here was as hoary a relic as air pollution. Tempted as he was, he badly wanted to immerse himself in the familiar trappings of his own home, his own life.

"Maybe another time!" He waved, and was gratified to see that they waved back. Not everything in this para was strange and unfamiliar, then. For one thing, certain gestures had been retained. Only the cleanliness was completely alien to him.

He drew a few curious glances from other pedestrians as he made his way across Pico and down the green fairway of Ocean Avenue. In place of the haphazard, occasionally ramshackle buildings he knew so well, there rose a neat line of new structures that were sleek and spotless and more modern than he could ever have envisioned. Yet for all that, they presented a warm and inviting aspect, and were not in any way cold or distant. Most were painted in soft Mediterranean pastels, and none was over four stories tall.

The replacement of pavement with turf encouraged the proliferation of birds and other small creatures. Astonishing to one who had spent all his life in the Los Angeles of his world, he thought he saw a fox peeping out from between two wonderfully Art Deco apartment buildings. It was stalking a rabbit. On Ocean Avenue. In the middle of Santa Monica.

Off to his right, the old familiar public beach was wider than he remembered it and looked as if it was vacuumed daily. The sea broke clean and invigorating against the shore. Gone were the vague chemical smells that often permeated the air along the coast. He wondered if the water was as unadulterated as the beach and the air. Based on what he had observed already, there was no reason to suspect otherwise.

Unable to believe his good fortune, he squinted out to sea where what looked from a distance suspiciously like an old-time clipper ship was making way for Marina del Rey. The sun momentarily blinded him and he had to blink away tears.

When he opened his eyes, the retro clipper was gone. The beach remained, and the sea, but he was striding along concrete instead of thick grass. A car came up behind him on the street, honked accusingly, and shot past. It reeked of noise, gasoline, and exfoliating rubber. His nostrils twitched. Out on the beach he could see isolated piles of garbage, and the gleam of scattered sunlight on lumpy plastic bags.

With the deepest, most regretful sigh of his life (except perhaps for that day his senior year in high school when he had shyly declined the voluptuous Arlene Marishabroda's offer to spend the night with him), he glanced reluctantly overhead. A faint brown haze, like a background wash applied by some skillful watercolorist, dimmed the blue of the sky. The atmospheric muck was heavier and darker inland. Much darker.

On the other side of the cracked, soiled pavement rose rank upon rank of apartment houses, old homes, and condominiums of varying quality. No matter which way he turned, he recognized every detail, even to some of the cars parked on the street. The shouts of gamboling children rose from the beach, carried inland on the salt-stained breeze. Somewhere, a man was screaming at his wife. A dog barked, its presence on the beach a violation of city statute.

He was home. Or, at least, he chose to believe he was

home. Time would tell. But for now, he *needed* to believe that, needed it desperately.

Yes, he was hopefully back in his own para, with every particular and finite sight fulsomely, tiresomely familiar. The field propounded by the Boles Effect had finally faded away.

He knew that after what he had been through he ought to be glad. Glad, hell—he ought to fall down and kiss the gum-dotted, cola-splotched sidewalk. But he could not. Could not, because the last para he had visited prior to his return was what the city of Los Angeles should be. Worse, he knew it was what it could be, because in another para, it was.

Be happy within thine own world, his inner voice admonished him, *lest you find yourself embedded forever in one that sucketh.*

At least he knew his key would work. He resumed walking the last couple of blocks to his building.

A woman on the exhausted side of fifty passed him, walking her poodle. It had been to the hairdresser; she had not. Behind a palm tree, a wino slept silently on a cushion of flowering purple iceplant. Three young boys came blasting by on their skateboards, heedless of pedestrian safety. He was home, all right.

Ahead, flanking one of the main walkways that led from the beach up to the street, a pushcart vendor was hawking espresso, café latte, bagels, Danish, and hot dogs. Reaching into his pocket, an eager Max fished for his wallet. Changing worlds was somewhat more exhausting than taking off and putting on a new pair of pants. His stomach growled again, just as it had for the elegant inhabitants of a better para. It was some time since he had last eaten, and he was borderline starving.

Other than not having a wide-brimmed hat, a broad mustachio, and perhaps an attentive trained monkey, the vendor looked like he had just finished working a Manhattan sidewalk. For the merest second Max stood paralyzed, but a quick glance revealed that the Southern California world around him was still the same. Furthermore, when the man smiled and handed him back his change, it was without a hint of New Yawk accent.

Perversely preferring his tube steak plain, Max disdained the ranked jars of colorful condiments and accepted the hot filled sandwich. Thanking the vendor, he turned to cross the street. As he raised the enbunned meat to his lips, he happened to glance down. His fingers froze.

The feverish frank was covered with tiny, glistening, millimeter-long cilia that wiggled with energetic internal animation. The casing glowed an electric hot pink. As he stared, a single tiny green eye opened in the middle of the meat, focused on him, and winked.

Gagging, he threw the abomination into the nearest trash can. Fighting to retain the contents of his stomach, he broke into a doubled-over run as he crossed the street. Behind him, the pushcart vendor stared in wonderment at the inexplicable actions of his now highly agitated customer.

Everything about his building looked familiar, even to the dog droppings in the hibiscus bushes out front. As he struggled to let himself in through the pedestrian entrance, he saw that his hand was shaking. Mentally, he found time to marvel at the phenomenon. As far back as he could remember, he had never been troubled by shaky hands.

So badly rattled, so panicked was he that he could not get the key in the lock. He had to stop and turn away from the steel door. Making a conscious effort to regulate his breathing, he stood on the concrete steps and stared out at the ocean, the sand, the cavorting, worry-free beachgoers. Children squealed with delight, L.A. ladies lay prone on the sand clad in narrow strips of brightly colored cloth as they worked silently on their melanomic tans, Frisbees and footballs soared through the faintly stained blue. The world around him looked, smelled, and tasted normal.

Maybe, just maybe, he told himself grimly, the genetically misshapen hot dog was the last of it—a final burst of broken laughter from the field. Maybe he truly was home *now*, the effect worn off, his life returned to him. Life, and a simple, normal, uncomplicated existence. Taking a deep breath, he turned back to the door. This time the key slid smoothly into the lock. The barrier opened to reveal a hallway painted dull white that blissfully smelled of nothing more exotic than concentrated pine disinfectant.

The elevator let him off on the top floor and he hurried toward the far end of the corridor as desperately as if in search of some long-lost sibling. The door to his apartment yielded with an achingly familiar click when he turned the key. He was, perhaps at last, home.

Everything was as he had left it, except that his big TV and stereo were still gone. The burglar and his two paras had not been figments of his imagination. But everything else was unchanged, from the forlorn bachelor contents of the refrigerator to the pleasantly mussed state of his bedroom. Checking out the latter, he saw that the small portable television was still standing by his bedside. That meant the thieves had not returned in his absence to clean out what they had overlooked on their first visit.

He could go in to the office without fear of encountering the slavering minions of Cthulhu, could go knowing that the office and the rest of the city would be there, could go out to a movie or a restaurant or call up friends knowing they were his friends and not some ever so slightly altered or addlepated paras. The appalling hot dog really had been the last of it, a final flickering flash of parallel otherworldliness.

The wave of emotion that washed over him as he stood there in the dust and solitude of his own bedroom was as painfully poignant as it was unexpected. The last time he had cried, really cried, had been at the funeral of a favorite uncle who had died tragically young. That had been two years ago. Sitting down on the foot of the king-sized bed that occupied most of his bedroom, his hands in his lap, he sobbed now. Silently and steadily, his shoulders heaving occasionally, he allowed all the emotion that had built up inside him over the past couple of days to spill out all at once. He cried until his eye sockets ached and his head hurt.

When it finally ceased, leaving him drained but sore, he got up and went into the bathroom. After making some sense of his face, he stripped down, luxuriated in the catharsis of a long hot shower, forced himself to shave and brush his teeth, prepared the coffeemaker to begin making coffee at the appointed wake-up hour, set the alarm timer on the TV, and crawled into bed.

He slept all through the rest of the day and into the night, soundly and dreamlessly, only to wake with the sun and the sound of the TV tuned to his favorite early-morning show. A glance at the clock showed that it was ten till five. Rising, he staggered into the kitchen and watched as the coffeemaker clicked on and began to burble. The nearly stale doughnut sitting alone and forlorn on a plate on the counter did not tempt him.

He found that his brain could once more focus on the minutiae of everyday life. One of those was the need to report the details of the burglary to his insurance agent. He savored the written presentation he intended to prepare. Anything that smacked of reality, even additional paperwork, was a welcome reminder that he was back where he belonged.

As he waited for the coffee to finish and contemplated what he might prepare to accompany it, he glanced at the TV. The five-o'clock news was just coming on. The morning of his world seemed normal enough. There was the usual reporter's grab bag of troubles and triumphs, economic and political news, weather that was worse everywhere else in the country, and soft-core human-interest stories. These last were the items that drew most of his attention, since they were the same ones he wanted to make his own business.

There was an interview with the glazed-eyed bomber of an abortion clinic in Massachusetts, whose beatific expression reflected the inner peace of the killer who knows for a certainty that he murders for God. This was followed by the story of a dog lost in Kansas who made its way back to its owner in Toledo, a report on the critically underfunded state of Long Beach city schools, an interview with a Santa Monica city bus driver retiring after an unprecedented forty-nine years cruising the same route, a couple of rapes and thefts, and lastly, a shoot-out at a popular nightspot in Venice Beach that had left a security guard, two unruly patrons, and one reporter dead. He perked up. The club was an exciting but unsavory one he had visited numerous times himself.

The channel four news anchor's voice was an educated accusation. A fight had broken out and the security guard had tried to intervene. As for the unlucky reporter, he had made an effort to try and diffuse the situation while simultaneously interviewing both of the eventual participants in the gun battle. Drugs were rumored to have been involved. As the report wound energetically toward a conclusion, the names of the deceased were given. Andrew Vashon, Efren Rodriguez, Dervon Crispas, Maxwell Parker . . .

No.

Coincidence. Too much of a coincidence, sure, but coincidence it had to be. Maddeningly, the report did not say whether the deceased Parker had been the hapless reporter, or the security guard, or one of the demised disputants. He wanted to reach into the set and grab the utterly self-possessed anchor, shake her out of her chipmunk drone, make her go back through her readout, and sift for the information he desperately needed.

It did not matter, he told himself. Coincidence it had to be. Since reality was back where it belonged, the story could not be referring to a murdered para of his. He was in his apartment, watching TV, considering what to eat for breakfast. Patently and irrevocably, he could not also be a dead man on a slab in some west-side morgue. Executing a small cliché could only confirm what he already knew. Reaching down with a hand, he pinched his leg.

And felt nothing.

He squeezed the skin again, harder—to no avail. Quietly frantic, he ran into the kitchen. The coffeemaker had finished its job and the half-full carafe awaited him, black and steaming. Reaching for the carafe, he wrapped his fingers around the handle and pulled it toward him, intending to spill some on his bare thigh. The fingers closed and pulled—but the carafe remained on the nightstand, unmoved and undisturbed. His fingers had passed cleanly through the plastic handle.

Looking down, he saw that he was but a pale shadow of his former self. Literally. Through the pallid outline of his thighs he could see the bed, and the floor. He held his hands up in front of his face and found that he could see through them, as well.

Again he tried to lift the carafe and failed. Putting one hand around it he thought he could feel a faint warmth, but that was all. Every time he tried to move the container, his fingers slid through it as though they were composed of ashen air.

That *was* him who had been killed at the nightclub, he realized dully. According to the news report he, Maxwell Parker, was right and truly dead. Only, in this world, he was also present. He was, as one might say, a mere ghost of himself.

It was heartbreaking. Everything else since the delirious hot dog had been so familiar, so achingly normal. He was home, back in his own world for sure. But only as an echo of himself. In his current discorporeal guise he could not even contact Boles to ask for help.

There was no point in staying in the apartment. Stumbling into the den, he headed for the door. Instead of yielding to his grasp, the knob slid through his fingers. Or rather, his fingers slid through the knob. Astonished, he stared at the door where his arm had penetrated up to the wrist. Presumably the rest of his ghostly fist was present on the other side, the fingers wriggling freely out in the hall. Experimentally, he leaned forward.

And found himself in the hallway, having passed without resistance through the solid door.

The ocean had always been his refuge, the sea his most understanding therapist. Stepping into the elevator, he tried to push the button that would take him down to the ground floor. As he did so, he found himself beginning to slip, falling slowly through the floor of the elevator. After a moment of panic, he relaxed. He was drifting, rather than plunging, down through the shaft. Not that it mattered. He was already dead anyway.

At the bottom, he climbed out and headed down the hall, striding effortlessly and painlessly through the solid steel door at the far end. Outside, the world was as orderly as the one within his apartment. The same children chased each other across the beach, the same tanned and mindless young men ran and roughhoused by the water's edge, the same sleek women roasted themselves in the Pacific sun.

He crossed the street and the parking lot beyond. As he trudged across the beach, gliding through sand that previously would have slowed him down, he paused once to bend and study the figure of a particularly attractive woman who was sitting on a beach lounge reading a magazine of more gloss than substance. Even when he knelt near enough to kiss her, she did not move. Her only reaction came when he actually pressed his mouth to hers. Frowning slightly, she rubbed the back of her hand several times against her lips, as if scratching a minor itch, before returning to her negligible reading. Needless to say, she did not notice his nakedness because she did not notice him at all.

Resigned at last to his anesthetized condition, he rose and continued on toward the water. What would happen if he kept going? he wondered. Surely a ghost could not drown. Would he float, or sink, and if he sank, could he walk all the way to China? Or at least, he thought, editing down an ambition unrealistic even for a ghost, to Catalina?

He paused at the edge of the foam-lipped, transparent surf. Children made ecstatic by sun and sea raced around and through him, as did serious-faced, inward-gazing joggers. Once, a Frisbee soared right through his head, causing him to flinch as it approached his eyes. There was no discomfort, no feeling whatsoever as it passed through his forehead and out the back of his expensive haircut. He was ignored by everyone, seen by no one. He was invisible, incorporeal, insubstantial. As they would have said in the South, day-ed. But not gone.

That's why he was surprised when the nude older man spoke to him. It was not the smiling senior citizen's bucknaked corpus that startled him. He was no more nude than Max himself. No, he was disconcerted because the oldster was not only looking directly at him, but also speaking to him. There was no mistaking it. Then he thought about it, his focus seemed to unpuddle, and he saw why, and understood.

The old man was a ghost, too.

"What happened to you, son?" The oldster's voice was appropriately ethereal and slightly shaky.

"I—I guess I died. I just watched a news report that informed me I was shot in a bungled drug deal."

The elder ghost shook his head sadly. "Bad business, that drug nonsense." He gazed wistfully inland. "I remember when this was a pleasant city to live in. Civilized, you know. People were nice to each other, even if everyone didn't have a house in the suburbs and a pool and two cars. That's because they expected to, someday." He returned his attention to the spectral Max.

"Lower expectations invariably lead to higher crime rates."

"But I wasn't there," Max tried to explain. "What I mean is, I wasn't there in this world. The real me didn't die."

The old ghost made clucking sounds with his tongue and shook his head knowingly. "That's what they all say."

"It's true!" Max found that no matter how loudly he strove to shout, the level of his speaking voice never changed. Death, he thought glumly. The ultimate censor. "Never mind. You wouldn't understand even if I took the time to try and explain it to you. I don't really understand it myself." He looked up the beach. "I would've thought there'd be more of you." He could not bring himself to say "us."

The old man sniffed and rubbed his nose. It was bulbous

and slightly warty. Despite the fact that he had clearly reached a ripe old age before passing on, he was in comparatively good shape, especially for one of the deceased.

"You are new to this business, aren't you, son?"

Max smiled wryly. "I haven't been dead for very long, if that's what you mean."

"Rookie. It shows. This is Limbo, son. The place where ghosts reside."

"I thought it was Santa Monica," Max joked. Nervously, he looked around for the ghost of himself that had died in the shoot-out at the club, but did not see him. Perhaps the shade of his shade was walking another section of beach.

The oldster did not crack a smile.

"Only those who die violently or unexpectedly or both, unsettled in mind and spirit, spend time here as ghosts. Those who perish of natural causes or with peace in their hearts pass on to the next level. Whatever that is. No ghost has ever returned to tell about it. But we know it's there."

Max was curious in spite of himself. "If no one's ever come back to elucidate, then how do you know there is a next level?"

The old man let out a sepulchral snort. "For the obvious reason that when ghosts disappear, they have to go somewhere." Raising a hand, he pointed out to sea. "There's Charlie. Hey, Charlie! Got a rookie here!" Out among the waves, a middle-aged male shadow body-surfed alongside healthy young board surfers oblivious of his presence.

"That's Charlie," the oldster added redundantly. "Got smacked upside the head with a board driven full force by a ten-foot wave. Bad juxtaposition of bone and fiberglass. He's been body-surfing ever since."

Max watched the other ghost's oceanic antics. "Doesn't sound like such a bad way to spend a piece of eternity to me."

The old man maintained his solemn expression. "He can't feel the water. It's kind of like making love to a shadow. Which you may also have the opportunity to do, depending on the length of your stay here."

"I'm not staying here." Max was firmer in his resolve than in his confidence. "I'll be moving on, to another parallel world. One in which I'll be alive. You can bet on it." He turned away. "Not that I much care anymore."

The senior eyed him speculatively. "Well now, that's certainly a different take on things. Parallel worlds, eh? And you reckon that in one of these so-called parallel worlds you're still alive, is that it?"

"In all of them. Or," Max corrected himself, "in most of them. That's been the case so far, anyway."

"Interesting. So tell me: You think that maybe I might still be alive in one or more of these parallel worlds, too?"

"It's possible," Max told him, without having a clue as to whether it was really possible or not.

His sage beach companion sighed profoundly. "I'd like to think it so. The attractions of Limbo wear thin in a hurry. It's temporary temporal immortality without any of the pleasures of reality. Scientist fella told me that, once. Course, he was dead, too." The oldster tapped his chest with an open palm. The expected hollow sound was absent. "Something about working with solid fuels. The experiment produced plenty of push. Unfortunately for him, a fair bit of it pushed right into his chest."

"What about you?" Max thought to ask. "How did you die?"

"It's not really considered polite to ask, son—but I reckon that since you're new, I can overlook it this time around. Besides, ghosts don't have a lot to talk about." He shrugged. "I got knocked down and mugged near the corner of Bundy and Pico. Right outside Nu-Way Chili Dogs. Not far from here."

"And that's what killed you?"

"Hell, no! I got up and chased the punk. In my day, people didn't get away with shit like that. Fifty pedestrians would've jumped him. But like I've been saying, times have changed. It was left up to me.

"So I ran the little prick down, I did. Been running marathons all my life, to keep in shape. Cornered the little bastard behind a furniture repair shop. That's when I saw he couldn't have been more than sixteen. Tired and sweaty and scared, he was. So I told him we'd forget it, and let's talk."

Max nodded thoughtfully. "How did he respond to that?"

"Shot me four times, the little bugger." The oldster tapped his torso. "Here and here, here, and here. Don't remember if I said anything after that. Don't even remember if I was angry, or sad, or a little bit mad. But I sure was dead." For the second time he sighed heavily. "Don't really matter. I was seventy-eight. Probably could've broke ninety, but it don't really matter. What matters is that poor, sorry-ass, gonna-die-before-he's-twenty kid, and the fact that I can't help him now."

They stood in silence for a while, watching the surfers and the gulls, the joggers and the sunbathers, chatting amiably about the absent inconsequentialities of life and remarking on the shocking indifference with which the living treated it. After a while, two young couples came walking down the beach toward them. They halted, expressions of supreme confusion on their attractive faces. The men were twins and the women likewise.

Seeing double again, Max thought. Except that he was dead, and the old man he had been talking with was dead, and with the sun and scenery shining through them, both of these unhappy couples were most assuredly dead.

"Maybe you can help us," one of the youthfully demised inquired hopefully. "We seem to have something of a problem here."

"I'll say you do." Somehow Max was not surprised. But then, at this point there was very little that was capable of surprising him. "When did you die?" he asked the nearest of the two couples.

The pair exchanged a limpid glance. "Nine-twenty this morning," the young woman replied softly. "I know because I remember checking the watch on the arm of my body as they were loading it into the ambulance."

Max turned to the other couple. "And you?"

"Nine-twenty-one," the man replied firmly as he glared at his double.

The reporter turned to the old man, who was looking on curiously. "See? It's just like I was telling you." He gestured at the couple on his left. "Sir, madam—meet your paras. Para ghosts, that is."

Apparently, he told himself resignedly, even ghosts could have paras. They never would have met, of course, if he did not transport the effect of the Boles Field with him wherever he went. The revelation opened up an entirely new field for metaphysical speculation.

One that his overloaded psyche wanted nothing to do with.

XI

"I don't understand." The pale young woman on his right was very pretty, Max decided. She must have made a beautiful corpse.

Teenagers cavorted in paroxysms of aimless delight while adults looked on tolerantly. Gulls swooped and snapped at errant french fries that tumbled like the softened feathers of Icarus from young fingers held too close to the sun. California girls sleek as the blond sea lions of south Australia strutted the boundary between sea, sky, and sand, inviting ogles and comparisons. In the midst of all this life, six ghosts discussed the transitory nature of life and existence.

"It's kind of hard to explain," Max began.

His elderly companion chipped in. "He's been trying to educate me about it, and it still don't make a whole lot of sense."

"In the real world, in my world," Max told them, "an amateur scientist invented a machine that generates a field that allows whoever is caught within that field to move between parallel worlds. Unfortunately, he had no idea how to turn it off, or negate the effects. This field travels with me, or maybe I travel within it as it moves around. I'm not sure which. All I know is that I've been jumping between parallel worlds faster than a politician switches their stance on entitlement cutbacks.

"At first I thought it was going to drive me crazy. Since I'm not crazy yet, I guess that's not going to happen." He offered a crooked smile. "I'm not sure I wouldn't prefer it that way." He indicated the seething, crowded beach scene.

"In this para, I'm dead, and a ghost. So is my friend here. So are you. But in your case, the Boles Field has snapped you into a para with me in which your para selves have also died. That's why there are two sets of you. One comprised of the real ghosts, the other of para ghosts. That's not to say that you're not both real. Or equally unreal. You are. You're just paras of each other."

The skeptical young man on the left looked at his diffident companion, then back at Max. "You're wrong. You are crazy."

Max smiled tolerantly. "Like I'm really going to accept an opinion on the matter from a ghost. Were you a psychiatrist when you were alive?"

"No." The youth's expression fell. "I drove a truck. Delivered snacks and sundries to convenience stores. But I had hopes. High hopes." He hugged his downcast companion. "We'd been married three weeks."

"That's right," agreed his male para. "Eighteen-wheeler on the Marina Freeway had a double blowout right in front of our car. It rolled, and we piled right into it."

The old man nodded understandingly. "You're lucky. You died before you had to see what you looked like at the time of death. There are some stragglers wandering around this city who weren't so lucky." He made a face. "They're convalescent—all ghosts are—but they're not real pretty to look at. Ambulatory ectoplasm can exist in some mighty strange shapes."

"We don't want to be dead." The young woman on the left eyed her perfect double uncertainly. "We were just starting our lives together. We had everything to look forward to."

"Sorry," the oldster informed them. "You have my sympathies, for whatever good the sympathies of the deceased may be. Bad luck."

Her husband stared at his duplicate. "If we really are more or less the same person, at least we'll all have someone to talk to while we're stuck here."

"That's right," his counterpart readily agreed. It's hard to spin-doctor death, but the young truck driver was trying his best. "I never did double-date while I was alive. It's strange to think that we're doing it now that we're dead."

Feeling a little better about themselves, the two couples resumed their walk down the beach, chatting animatedly, enjoying the scenery if not their situation. Occasionally, a child or two would run through them, pause as if encountering a strange smell, and then resume whatever play activity they had been engaged in. Children seemed more sensitive than adults to the presence of the departed, Max noted absently.

"This para provides the basis for some interesting speculation."

"How so, young fella?" The oldster watched a sand flea dig itself a hole at his feet. Under his right foot, to be exact.

"If ghosts exist, and they self-evidently do, and there are such things as para ghosts spending time in Limbo, does that mean there is a Heaven and a Hell? And if so, are there para Heavens and para Hells that likewise differ slightly from one another? Is there a para God, or just one Supreme Being who rules over not only the Universe, but an infinite number of para Universes? If so, can these hypothetical para Gods communicate with one another? After all, if they're all-powerful, they ought to be able to regulate a simple thing like the Boles Effect. Or are they unaware of one another's presence? Is there a higher authority or law governing how even God can exist that prevents him from moving between paras, or even knowing of their multiple existence?"

The oldster looked away to study the sea. "Give it a rest, young fella. My head's starting to hurt tryin' to follow you."

Max moved to stand next to him. Foam-flecked water rushed through their ankles. "How do you think mine feels?

Sometimes I really think it would be better if I just did go mad."

"Don't be so hard on yourself, young fella." The old man smiled up at him. "You're already dead, so your situation can't get any worse."

"You don't know what I've been through so far," Max told him. "Compared to some of it, being deceased isn't such a bad deal." He stared, then nodded up the beach. "Here comes a perfect example of what I'm talking about right now."

There were three sets of the aliens, all matching precisely, all chattering away in their click-cluck tongue. Three sets, and all of them as insubstantial as the two men who stood conversing on the sand.

"Now that's a new one on me," the oldster confessed. "What the devil are they?"

"Aliens," Max explained.

The senior shook his head slowly as he tracked their approach. "Heard about aliens all my life. Didn't think they existed. Certainly never expected to see one, much less half a dozen. And a bunch of 'em matching up."

"It's the Boles Effect." Looking down, Max watched fingerlings swim between his toes. Also through his toes. "There are para worlds where the aliens have landed and made contact with us. Not only made contact, but established formal relations. In one para they operate a big spaceport up in the hills above Malibu."

The oldster let out a derisive snort. "Folks up that way been seeing aliens for years."

"I know, but this isn't Hollywood hokum. In at least that one para, and probably others, they're really here. Pretty decent folks, actually. At least, the ones I met were."

He nodded at the approaching figures. They wore no elaborate robes of elegant otherworldly design this time. Like himself, the old man, and the forlorn newlyweds, the aliens likewise were stark naked. All three sets of them—one original, and two sets of paras. As always, it was impossible to tell the paras from their progenitors.

Para alien ghosts, he thought. At that moment he decided that the Cosmos *was* ruled by multiple Gods. There would have to be more than one just to keep it all straight. But then, who said that the Cosmos had to be organized? Even for someone who had gone through what he had already experienced, who had seen everything that he had seen, the concept of parallel Chaos was one he found beyond his ability to deal with. The Universe might be a little insane, but it was organized insanity.

Turning to their right, the aliens headed inland. Looking for a crashed ship, maybe, or whatever had been responsible for their demise.

He kicked absently at the sand. His foot passed repeatedly and effortlessly through the glistening grains, despite his most energetic efforts disturbing not a one. "I don't know if I can go on like this."

The old man grinned humorlessly. "What are you going to do about it? Kill yourself?"

"Look, it's not funny," the reporter responded more sharply than he intended. After all, the old specter was only trying to help.

"Sorry. A sense of humor is one thing you don't lose when you die. Well, some seem to, but me, I suspect they never had one when they were alive. You find out fast that those ghosts who don't appreciate a good laugh aren't worth hanging out with." He turned to leave.

Max looked up in surprise. "Hey, where are you going?"

The oldster glanced back over his shoulder. "You think I've got nothing better to do than haunt around here all day? Well, actually, that's pretty much the case. But I like to move around. I keep hoping that I'll find peace, if not contentment, and that I'll finally depart Limbo for whatever lies beyond. One thing's for sure: I'm not getting any peace from you."

Max called after him. "It's not my job to supply solace to spooks!"

"I got news for you, young fella. You ain't got a job no more. You ain't got a purpose to your existence, because you ain't got no existence. And there isn't a damn thing you can do about it. So you might as well chill out and lighten up." His irrepressible grin returned. "Mentally, I mean. Nature's already taken care of both for you physically."

The elderly beachcomber was right, of course. Max watched the old man's figure fade, literally fade, into the mystic golden light where sea and shore merged. Then he turned away, deep in thought.

The situation was not very encouraging. Even if he could make it up the coast back north to Trancas and find Boles, there was no way he could communicate his condition to the scientist's para in this world. Not that it was likely to matter. As far as he knew and could figure, the device itself worked only on the living.

The beauty of the day gave no indication of diminishing. Since there was nothing he could do to improve his plight, he decided that he might as well enjoy it. Few pleasures besides sight were left to the deceased, but while he could not feel the water, or taste it, or smell it, he could still ride the waves. The deceased surfer had shown that.

Just gossamer. That's me, he thought. *I am less than the breaking spume.* By the same token, he did not have to worry about going over the falls or choking on mouthfuls of brine. Since he was already dead, the biggest waves could not hurt him, nor could sharks, stingrays, broken beer cans, or any of the other less salubrious dwellers of the bay.

Wading out into the deeper water was easy. Instead of holding him back by pushing him toward the beach, the waves exerted only the slightest pressure while passing through him. Being back in the eternal sea buoyed him up and helped to banish any thoughts of trying to walk to China—or anyplace else. He allowed the waves to thrust him gently up and down, up and down, enjoying the movement even though it was otherwise devoid of any sensory input.

He caught one wave and, like a surf-driven gust of wind, rode it all the way into the beach, shooting right through a young girl paddling in circles on her boogie board. Gliding effortlessly back out, he caught a second breaker, and then a third. When the fourth one presented itself he did not hesitate. Where its size and sharp curl would have frightened him previously, now he lay back and let it lift him up, cloudward, and fling him down hard. He made no effort to avoid its pile-driving force as it slammed him toward the bottom, knowing that he would simply drift up and out through the sand as readily as the roiling waters would pass through him.

He came up coughing, sputtering, and soaking wet in the same clothes he had been wearing prior to finding himself a representative of the walking demised. Fighting for air, salt-stung eyes bulging under the churning pressure of the tumbling wave, he kicked hard and pushed himself forward until he broke the surface. Children ceased their playing momentarily to gape at him. Joggers slowed and stared as he dragged himself, gasping and choking, out of the water and up onto dry sand.

"You all right, mister?" The young, bronzed blond surfer who had just entered the water stopped paddling and turned toward him, rising out of the swells while keeping a firm grip on the wrist strap fastened to the front of his board.

Weighted down by his sodden attire and the several ounces of seawater that were sloshing around in the bottom of his lungs, Max struggled to rise. "I'm fine, I'm okay." He coughed again, regurgitated brine spilling from his lips, and forced himself to smile. "I'm an actor. I'm just rehearsing a part."

Not entirely convinced, but willing to accept the explanation, the youth turned and aimed his fiberglass chariot out to sea. It was not a rationale that would have been swallowed in Dubuque, but this was L.A.

"Yeah, right. Method drowning." He shook his head sadly. "Actors. You're all crazy." In seconds he was gone, shooting rocketlike through a breaking wave, intent on spending as much of his waking life as possible engaged in riding a flat slab of painted fiberglass back and forth, back and forth, over a single short stretch of ocean.

Once safely clear of the water, a dazed Max collapsed on the sand. Sitting up, he turned to face the sea so that he would not have to meet the stares of the curious. Salt stung his throat, acrid water clogged his lungs, the sun burned his eyes, his muscles ached, his wet clothes hung heavily from his skin, and he was starting to stink like old laundry. It was divine.

He was alive again—but in what para?

There was no sign of the old ghost, or the commiserating couples, or the bemused aliens. When a chill ran down his back, he looked around sharply, half expecting to see a transcendent, spectral figure making its way inland. But it was only the sea wind evaporating water from his saturated shirt.

They were still around, he knew. Not necessarily the diverse group of revenants he had conversed with, but others. They had always been there, always would be there. He had learned a great truth about the afterlife by momentarily becoming a part of it.

Not that anyone would believe him if he chose to try and share it in an article, of course. He, who had written story after story making fun of and debunking earnest believers in the hereafter, and in the existence of spectral beings, did not have the kind of byline that would engender respect for such subject matter. Having temporarily, or temporally, been one such phantom himself, he would no longer be able to write about such matters with quite the same skeptical, jaundiced eye.

In fact, he reflected, the dead were very much like me and thee, except that they did not take up space in lines waiting to get into the latest movie, or appear on TV talk shows to discuss their predicament, or vote in annual elections—except in Alabama. No, the deceased were regular folks whose company, based on what he had seen, was in many ways preferable to that of the living.

A second chill sparked a response in his lungs, and then in his sinuses, disclosing itself by means of a loud, sharp sneeze. *If I don't get out of these wet clothes,* he thought, *I'm liable to take a real, good, old-fashioned, unpleasant cold.* Then pneumonia might set in, he reflected, and he would die. Again.

Climbing to his feet, he turned and started off in the direction of his apartment building. Providentially, his wallet and keys were still in their respective pockets. Like many of his friends, he wore tight pants not only for appearance's sake but because it made life more difficult for the professional pickpockets who often infested the coastal beach communities on warm, crowded days such as this. Everything important in his wallet was either plastic or laminated, and he never carried much cash, so his temporary saltwater bath should not have done him any great harm. His only concern was that the car and apartment keys might corrode.

The joy and delight of finding himself among the living was tempered by the realization that, while his immediate situation had changed for the better, his own personal reality was in all likelihood still in a state of unpredictable flux. Unless something concrete proved the contrary, he was compelled to believe that he was still under the influence of the Boles Effect and thus still subject to its whims. The field continued to be a gigantic, imperceptible monkey on his back.

How could he plan for any kind of tomorrow, much less just live, without any way of knowing what tomorrow was going to be like? Certain paras were more or less similar and familiar, but others, such as the ones in which he found himself among visiting aliens, or walking the surface of a devastated planet, or conversing with the dead, left him feeling unsettled mentally as well as physically.

In many ways the near identical paras were even more disturbing than the radically different. Easy enough to know that the field was still operative and his life still in uncontrollable flux when the world was full of Elder Gods or utopian Eloi-like teens. Much harder when the only difference might lie in the design of a ketchup bottle or the subtle rearrangement of an unfamiliar constellation, or the water in the toilet flowing counterclockwise. If the latter, how could he tell for certain if he was in yet another para, or just in Perth?

As he left the dry, hot sand for the parking lot that separated Appian Way from the beach, he found himself watching the too-rapid passage of a heavy delivery truck with morbid interest. How easy it would be to step in front of the next oversized vehicle that came barreling along, its driver intent on his schedule and distracted by the beauty of sea and sky. An instant of disorientation, a few seconds of shocking pain, and it would all be over: no more soul-shattering confrontations to deal with, no more trying to figure out if he was back in his world or in some subtly different doppelgänger, no more having to deal with cultures that he would never have the opportunity to interact with for more than a day or two.

Of course, he might return for an indeterminate period of time as a ghost, but at least he would know that he was haunting the right world, his world. All it would take to put an end to his wanderings was a single step, a final closing of the eyes, one brief moment of sickening impact . . .

Unless he didn't die, but instead suffered only painful, crippling injuries. That would not be a way to ride out the rest of existence in his own world, much less while jumping between unpredictable multiples. But the temptation to give up, to throw in the towel, to bite the bullet, to rid himself of the ongoing cliché of a thoroughly unpredictable future, was tempting. Except . . .

He had never been a quitter. When his high-school English teacher had told him his spelling and grammar bordered on the atrocious, he had persevered. When his university professors insisted repeatedly that he had no talent for writing whatsoever, he had persevered. When interviewer after interviewer had told him that his work was colorful and catchy but had nothing to say, he had persevered.

No wonder he had been able to land a plum job at a nationally distributed tabloid.

He straightened a little. If he could handle being dead, he could survive anything. Already he had dealt with maleficent Elder Gods and enigmatic aliens. *Let* the Boles Effect continue to make origami of his reality. He would cope with whatever resulted.

People always needed, always wanted, to know what was happening around them. That had been a constant in every para he had visited. Wherever he was, there would be a market for his reportorial talents. He would make a life for himself even if that life changed without warning every day, or week, or month. A stable existence it might not be, possibly the most unstable in the entire history of humankind, but he would press on. After all, where there was life, there was hope, and in his case, perhaps an infinite number of hopes.

He would not give in. If Barrington Boles would continue to work on the problem, so would Max. Perhaps in another para, he thought optimistically, Boles had already solved the problem. Even now, a hundred para Maxes might be returning home from the inventor's hilltop lab secure in the knowledge that they would no more be roaming the prairies of parallelity.

Unless his Barrington Boles was the only one, out of all those millions of para Boleses, who had actually succeeded in making his device work. In which case it was up to Max to wait until he was certain he was back in that same world before he again confronted the inventor.

Reaching the far side of the parking lot, he climbed the short concrete stairway and paused on the sidewalk up top. Paused and waited, until there was no traffic in sight. Then he crossed carefully, fumbling in his sodden pocket for his slick, cold keys.

When they fit the lock to his building, and neither building nor lock metamorphosed into something unimaginable, he felt, however falsely, much encouraged.

It was a sensation that another long, hot shower greatly intensified. Amazing, he thought, what effect a simple civilized luxury like a hot shower can have on someone's emotions. As he showered, he forced himself to relax. The soap did not turn into something alive that scampered out of his hand, the water did not turn to acid, or tomato juice, and the fresh towel with which he dried himself retained the weft and softness of which its manufacturer boasted in an exclusive, overpriced mail-order catalog.

Making himself forget about work, he determined to spend the rest of the day puttering about the apartment performing relentlessly simple domestic tasks. Not even Boles knew what affected the Boles Effect. Who knew—perhaps a little positive mental reinforcement might have a dampening effect on its propensity to toss one around parallel worlds at random. With this in mind he climbed into a pair of shorts, a favorite old shirt, and considered how best to submerge himself for the rest of the day in the remorselessly commonplace.

With some trepidation, he shoved a frozen lasagna into the microwave and set temperature and time. Fifteen minutes later it was done: crisp, cheesy, and moist, without a suggestion of wriggling cilia or latent greenness. No gourmet meal was more enjoyed than the simple, weighty contents of that thin plastic pan. The beer that accompanied it stayed cold and the bubbles rose to the surface instead of descending or complaining out loud about their status as a transitory accessory to degustationic enjoyment.

Popcorn popped instead of turning into tiny flowers or brown pebbles or something equally unenticing. It accompanied an evening of TV-watching that was balm in its banality. He purposely chose to watch the most insipid programs available, each one reassuring in its inanity. He found comfort with Gilligan, surcease with the Skipper. Quiz shows, talk television, reruns of ancient situation comedies—all served to half convince him that the field with which he had become burdened at Boles's mansion had finally worn off.

But he remained cautious. He had been disappointed before, and he intended to be as prepared as possible should the stereo suddenly begin playing music by berserk lutists or if the furniture independently elected to rearrange itself. It was not easy. The comforting familiarity of his surroundings, the undisturbed deployment of personal effects within the apartment, the soothing stupidity of prime-time television, all combined to relax and encourage him.

Was he truly back home, in his achingly personal reality, instead of in some subversive para that was only waiting for him to relent mentally before it sprang some surreal, Lewis Carrollish ambush-in-waiting on him? For the thousandth time he remembered Boles describing how the Effect might dissipate of its own accord, without warning or sign. Was that what had happened? And if so, how could he be sure? He dared not let his guard down completely.

Morning might provide confirmation. Until then he could only live as if his life had never been turned upside down, as if the cosmos were still ruled by laws fixed and immutable. Only two men knew better: himself, and the brilliant but erratic Barrington Boles. Next time, he thought decisively, Boles could demonstrate his device while standing under the field-generating arch himself. Max would be happy to sit off to one side and throw the necessary switches.

Bed felt like a bower descended from Olympus. Naked, he

slid between the sheets and died. Figuratively, of course; but so rapidly and deeply did he fall into a state of motionless sleep than an unknowing onlooker might well have taken him for one of the deceased. It would not have fooled the deceased themselves, though. As he knew better than anyone, they were much more active than he was at the moment, and did not sleep.

XII

He awoke greatly refreshed in mind and spirit, threw an English muffin into the toaster oven, and showered with more pleasure than he had done anything in days. Toweling off, he sauntered into the kitchen and let his eyes drink in the simple view of other apartment buildings, the pier, and the Pacific beyond. It looked like another typical, fine Southern California day. He was anxious to get to the office. Cognizant of the peccadilloes of his chronologically challenged staff, Kryzewski made grudging allowances for habitual tardiness, but that did not mean a reporter could take days off without so much as calling in, much less filing a story or two.

Well, that would all be fixed by this evening, Max knew. He would catch up on back work and missed meetings to everyone's satisfaction. The toaster oven dinged, indicating that his muffin was ready. Removing it, he yawned and went to check the refrigerator to find some jam. Blackberry this morning, he decided. The fridge door opened easily.

And he fell in.

The polar bear rose with a startled snort as Max tumbled down its back. Behind him, a handful of startled Inuit shouted warnings. Cold shot through him like one of their barbed harpoons.

Struggling to his feet as soon as he hit the snow, he sized up the situation in an instant. The Inuit hunters had killed a walrus, which lay dead on the white field of the earth not ten feet from where he now stood. Its deep red blood stained a trail in the snow. The bear had caught the scent and, roaring and bellowing, had shown up to claim the booty. This forced the hunters to retreat until they could unpack a couple of rifles from the packs on the backs of their two sleds, rifles not being of much use in hunting walrus. Barely kept in restraint by their anxious owners, teams of sled dogs barked madly at the intruding bear.

Out of nowhere, Max had appeared, landing hard on the bear's back and rolling off. He now found himself, stark naked and beginning to feel the first effects of freezing, shivering between the agitated hunters and the monstrous ursine. The Inuit continued to shout loudly at him, and to beckon. He could not understand a word they were saying, but their expressions and gestures were unmistakable. What they were saying in Inuit was "Get the hell out of there, you dumb naked white man!"

Outraged at the interruption, not to mention the un-bridled temerity of the intrusive human, the bear reached down and grabbed Max before he could turn to run. He felt the unlimited strength of massive forelegs as he was raised off the ground by a pair of paws, each of which was larger than his head. Shifting his gaze, he saw yellowed teeth set in a black mouth, all framed by white fur that blended seamlessly into white sky and white ground. The teeth were several inches long and doubtless could penetrate the bone of his skull with very little effort. He screamed.

And sucked in a mouthful of water. Fresh, not salt. Not that it much mattered under the present circumstances. He could not breathe either one.

Kicking and gasping, he fought his way toward the light, his head coming up beneath an overhanging circular green mass that was floating on the surface. Wiping at his eyes to clear them, he peered cautiously at his surroundings and saw that he was treading water in some kind of lake or swamp. The water in which he found himself was tepid as an old bath, and the ambient air temperature anything but arctic. Though per-fectly breathable, the air around his head seemed incapable of holding any additional moisture. Humidity bordered on a hundred percent.

Strange cries and bellowings came from the surrounding

forest. Something immense went stomping through the trees off to his left. It looked, in its immense brown passing, like a brontosaurus. *No, that's not right,* he told himself. Indifferent paleontologists had gone and changed the name. But irregardless of nomenclature, it was certainly a dinosaur, and a sizable one at that.

Enormous batlike specters soared silently through the humid air, while vast groanings and sputterings echoed through the trees. He felt the water ripple behind him and turned sharply, but it was only a frog. If he had been sufficiently sensible, he would have laughed. Amidst the giants of a bygone age, the frog looked so homey and normal as it arranged itself on the huge lily pad beneath which Max had surfaced that he wanted to kiss it.

He did not. Not out of worry of contracting some mysterious amphibian poison but for fear it might turn into a prince, or princess, or God knew what. Tired of treading water, he headed for the shore opposite the one occupied by the foraging brontosaur. Undoubtedly there were dinosaurs there as well, perhaps even some of the famously carnivorous variety, but he could not hover next to the lily pad forever. His legs were beginning to ache.

The frog watched him go and said, clearly and in an appropriately deep and reverberant voice, "Good luck, Max."

It wasn't so much that the frog spoke perfect English as the fact that it knew his name. A para wherein frogs vocalized was one thing, personal contact another. He spun around in the water to confront bulbous eyes and warty face.

"How did you know my name?"

"Looked it up in the computer." Having no shoulders, the frog could not shrug, but it managed to convey the feeling nonetheless.

"Computer? What computer?" Since none of the conversation made any sense, Max felt perfectly at ease going with the same unbroken flow of intoxicated disbelief.

"Mine." So saying, the frog reached back under the brilliant white flower of the lily and removed a miniature laptop. This it proceeded to display to Max while tapping on the tiny keys with dark green, thickly webbed toes. "Yarp, you're Max, all right. Maxwell Parker, of Los Angeles. You work for a slimy tabloid—and I know my slime—called the *Investigator*, you spend more than you make, and you lust after a certain peroxided blonde name of Lisa Sanchez who works in the advertising department."

"How do you know all this?" A safe distance behind Max, something massive and toothy stalked the shoreline, growling under its breath like the mother of all pit bulls. Tired legs or no, he wisely elected to remain out in the deep water.

"Easy. It's all right here." Turning the tiny laptop so that Max could see better, the frog showed him the active-matrix screen. Squinting, he moved nearer for a closer look and quickly discovered just how active its matrix was.

Like the refrigerator, he fell into it.

It sucked him right in. Drifting aimlessly and beginning to lament the absence of clothes, he discovered that he was surrounded by a sea of tiny, sparkling crystals. They crowded close, pressing firmly against him, and he began kicking and shoving them aside. They resisted, though not painfully.

Pixels, he thought wildly. *I am in the screen, so these must be pixels.* Even as he scrutinized the notion and tried to rein in the thought, sure enough, the pixels turned into pixies. Perfect little folk fluttering like hummingbirds on wings of diaphanous luminescence, they swarmed about him, studying his helpless form intently, gesturing at various body parts and giggling uncontrollably.

"Get away, that's enough!" He swung wildly, but they were far too agile for his clumsy great arms and avoided his mad flailings easily.

For the second time in too short a while, he found himself surrounded by cold and wet. Looking up, he saw the prow of a boat bearing down on him. The pixies scattered, chittering nervously to themselves, as he found himself once more afloat. This time the water was salty, and much colder than the Jurassic swamp where he had encountered the frog. He tried to thrust his torso as far up out of the water as possible as he waved and shouted.

"Hey! Hey, over here!"

Someone on board must have heard, because the boat slowed and angled to miss him. Imagining sharks, he fought the periodic swells and the current as the sturdy craft slowed its approach. A flurry of hands reached over the gunwale to help him up. Acutely conscious of his nakedness, he allowed himself to be half helped, half hauled up onto the deck.

Wiry, well-dressed crewmen gaped at him and whispered among themselves as they regarded the eccentric castaway in their midst. No one offered him a towel or a blanket. He heard someone murmur, "Make way for the captain."

The seamen stepped aside to make room for a gnarly, weather-beaten individual not much older than Max himself and slightly shorter. Clad in basic, no-nonsense sailor's attire and cap, the captain had the most enormous forelegs and forearms Max had ever seen on a human being, yet his biceps though not his thighs were oddly emaciated by comparison. Nevertheless, he looked every inch the stalwart officer in command, and the respect in which the crew held him was evident in their expressions. A corncob pipe jutted like a permanent appendage from the left side of his mouth, while his jaw and left eye were locked in a permanent squint.

"Well now," the swarthy seadog muttered, "what have we got here?"

One of the crew spoke up. "He was just floatin' in the water off to starboard, Cap'n. Stark naked and yellin' fit to beat the band. We hove to and fished him out."

The captain came closer, studying Max intently with his one good eye. There wasn't a hint of malevolence in that gaze, and a shivering Max began to relax a little.

"Is that a fact? You don't look none too well, matey. Better get some food into you. Not to mention something to wear. I hopes you don't mind sailors' cotton. This ain't no floatin' Lord and Taylor." He smiled so engagingly that the last of Max's uncertainty vanished. Despite the immutable squint it was a smile that demanded one in return.

Turning toward the main above-decks cabin, the captain called out loudly. "Hey, Olive! We gots us a castaway up here! Put on some of that bonito we broughts in yesterday, and don't forgets the spinach!" He laughed then, a most exceptional and peculiar sort of high-pitched chuckle.

Max did not wait for him to introduce himself. The nature of the strangely uniform waves on which the uncomplicated boat rode; the oddly flat, threatening sky; the highly animated crew; it all struck him simultaneously. With a wild, despairing, maddened cry, he threw himself back over the side, much to the astonishment and dismay of the solicitous captain and crew.

Only to wake up sputtering, water running down his face and into the sheets. In his nightmare flailing he'd knocked over the glass of water he always kept on the end table next to the bed. The contents had landed on his face and spilled down his body. The empty glass lay on the sheets nearby.

He was in his apartment. It was morning again.

Breathing hard, he checked the clock radio on the table. The water had missed it, landing instead on him and in the bed. It was 7:20 A.M. on Wednesday morning. Date and month checked out. So did the landscape of his bedroom, and the pale blue sky outside the window, and the lightly tanned hue of his fingers and legs. He was neither hot nor cold and the air was neither freezing nor humid.

Throwing off the sodden sheets and blanket, he rushed into the den, only to find everything normal and as it should be. The view out the kitchen window revealed buildings, beach, ocean, wandering human figures: everything routine and ordinary.

Trying to slow his breathing, he slumped down on the den couch. Falling asleep in bed, he had dreamed of awakening and preparing breakfast. That much was more or less typical, but the other dreams had been something else. Several something elses. He had not just been dreaming, but para dreaming. When he was asleep, the Boles Effect had carried him into another, perhaps several other worlds. In these paras he had lain unconscious, dreaming away the same night. Reflecting his physical condition and locale, he had experienced a series of para dreams.

And what of the inhabitants of his dreams? Were they themselves paras acquired from someone else's dreams? If so, had he temporarily existed as a dream in someone else's sleep? In that event, it meant that not only was the cosmos composed of para realities, it was rife with para unrealities as well.

He had to believe he was sane, because it was the only option left to him.

Everything was as he had left it the night before. The

recyclable remnants of his lasagna still reposed exactly as he had deposited them in the bag reserved for plastic scraps. His empty beer bottle rested atop the rest of the glass in its bag. A check of the television in the bedroom revealed that it was still tuned to the same channel he had been watching before he had drifted off to sleep. His bath towel was where he had hung it, and his toothbrush still waited on the side of the sink to be put back in its holder.

He had enjoyed a conventional evening, fallen asleep, sped through a succession of para dreams, only to awaken once more in his own world. There were other possible explanations for what he had experienced, but that was the one that suited him, and since no one materialized to dispute it, he clung to it as tightly as a young orangutan holds to its mother.

Work, he reminded himself. He was going to go in to the office and catch up on work. And he would shock everyone by arriving early. As he readied himself, he reveled in the ordinariness of his actions and surroundings, everything from shaving to preparing and consuming the English muffin he had dreamed about. There was one bad moment when he had to open the refrigerator to find his blackberry jam, but the interior of the appliance held nothing more exotic than familiar food and drink. Now that he was awake, it was no longer a portal to preposterous polar dreams.

Restored to lucidity, he took pleasure in the simplest activities, from choosing what to wear in to the office to enjoying the percussive jangle of his keys when he snatched them off the dresser. Later, he decided, when he had caught up on meetings and on work, he would make his way back up the coast to once again confront Barrington Boles and inform him that the para effect that had been tormenting his former visitor had finally, to everyone's relief, worn off.

His car was waiting where last he had parked it. The electronic lock responded instantly to his key—his single key, he noted gratefully. No matching Mitch waited in the shadows with a second set of keys, no beautiful yet unaccountably disturbing Maxine waited in the front seat to contest him for ownership.

Enormously relieved, he backed out of his space and swung out through the open gate, making sure as always to close the electronic and steel barrier behind him.

The sun continued to shine and the environment outside the Aurora remained stable as he headed up the coast toward Wilshire. Because of heavier traffic, the roundabout route he had chosen would take him a little longer than his usual itinerary, but he felt as if he had earned the additional touring time. A few clouds drifted lazily over the mountains, teasing the earth with hints of rain that would not arrive until winter.

Switching on the radio, he hit the preset for one of the all-news channels. It was time he caught up, he told himself, on what was happening in *his* world. He even enjoyed listening to the sigalerts, knowing that unlike so many of the unfortunate commuters who metastasized the freeway system, he lived near enough to work to be able to stick to the surface streets. He was immune to the problems the majority of L.A. drivers suffered through daily and could listen to them with an indifferent ear.

The voice of the announcer was soothing and oddly familiar. It puzzled him that he was unable to immediately identify it, since he thought he knew most of the news stations' anchors by name. Part of his job was knowing the competition, even if it happened to reside in a different medium. You never knew, he reflected, when a major radio or television station might need a writer/reporter with his particular abilities. It was not a call he was waiting for, but he knew he would be ready if it came.

The voice droned on, reciting the usual litany of early-morning disasters that plagued motorists around the metropolis. As soon as the traffic report was completed, another reader took over for his predecessor. Max frowned slightly as he listened. It sounded as if the same man was doing both reports. That was uncommon, but not unheard of. Or maybe there was something wrong with his audio system.

Not that it mattered. He turned up Wilshire, regretfully leaving the ocean behind for the balance of another day, and cruised east toward Lincoln. People were out walking, enjoying the weather, intent on errands or relaxation or work. The prominent billboard on the north side of Wilshire one block past Lincoln caught his eye, as it had been doing on a predictable basis the past week. Currently it was advertising a certain brand of Finnish vodka. He looked forward to the billboard, because it featured a full-length portrait of an up-and-coming young European actress clad in a white fur bikini that displayed her as mostly up-and-coming. The vodka, whose brand name he could never remember, was incidental to the presentation.

His jaw dropped, his eyes bulged, he nearly rear-ended the car in front of him, and it was all he could do to keep from bursting out in uncontrollable sobs. Because the actress had—suitably made up, younger, and cinematically modified—a familiar face.

His face.

He shut his eyes and opened them again. The curvaceous figure, the prominent, thrusting bottle of faux-frosted spirits, the blatantly enticing logo—nothing had changed from his first sight of the sign. The starlet still had his face, though most definitely not his shape.

Having run out of patience, the driver of the car behind him leaned heavily on his horn. Stunned, Max fumbled with his right foot for the accelerator, pushed down too hard when he finally found it, and shot forward, almost ramming the car in front of him for the second time in less than a minute. Fighting to get ahold of himself, he pulled over into the right-hand lane to let those behind him pass. He kept moving, but as slowly as possible.

Bafflement changed to disbelief, then to fear, and finally to agonized resignation as he drove on. As he had discovered on too many previous occasions, there was no getting around the reality of unreality. He was too aware of it when it happened to disown it.

In spite of a most relaxing, deceivingly ordinary morning, he was still not home, not back in his original world, but in yet another para. The Boles Field continued to work its mischief on reality, its effects as powerful as ever. Not that this world wasn't his. It most decidedly was, in a way he could never have imagined.

Actually, when you thought about it, he ruminated tiredly, there was nothing here for him to fear. Beyond the obvious fact that he was still slip-sliding between parallel worlds, he ought to be reasonably safe in this one. There were no Elder Gods or dinosaurs tromping about, no ghosts within view, no evidence of Armageddon or rampant diseases. He really should feel right at home.

Because not only the starlet on the billboard, but everyone on the streets, and in the cars, and in what buildings and businesses he could see into, looked exactly like Maxwell Parker.

Staying in the right-hand lane, he continued to drive up Wilshire as slowly as possible without provoking an incident. It was not only the adults who looked like him, the men and the women. The kids looked like him as well, as did the old people. Scrutinizing the streets, he saw himself as an old man with a beard, as a toddler with a rattle, as a nattily dressed street musician, and as a tired pushcart vendor huckstering twenty, count-'em twenty, varieties of hot bagels.

Where a narrow alley met the sidewalk he was a rheumy-eyed bum loosely clutching a nearly empty bottle of cheap wine. In the copy shop against which the bum lay he was the entire busy staff of young people bustling about serving assorted impatient versions of himself. Max Parker drove a city bus; he was also all of its passengers. Max Parker in long hair constituted the entire population of a beauty salon. Max Parker drove Hondas and Fords, low-rider Chevys and Harleys, messenger bikes and scooters. One especially prosperous and hefty Max Parker even went cruising majestically past in a Mercedes 800SL.

At every intersection there were pedestrian Max Parkers waiting for the light to change, and exhibitionist Max Parkers standing in the front windows of small restaurants tossing pizza, and more Max Parkers carrying bags full of groceries or pushing carts or dragging protesting infants in and out of Ralph's. A matronly Max majestically bestrode a landscaped section of sidewalk, led eastward by a duet of dachshunds. Smiling, grinning, imploring Max Parkers beamed down from every billboard, every window ad, every soot-stained photo decorating the side of a bus.

At last his dreams of great success had been realized, Max reflected numbly, and in a way he could not have imagined. Truly, Max Parker was everywhere and known to everyone. Not only did he dominate the world, he *was* the world. He knew this for a fact, because included among the matrons and pizza tossers and bus drivers and schoolchildren and shoppers and nameless pedestrians he had passed were suitable examples of Korean Max Parkers, Vietnamese Max Parkers, black Max Parkers, Hispanic and Native American and Jewish Max Parkers. It was Max Parker omnipotent, Max Parker omnipresent, Max Parker omni. He had conquered the world by becoming it.

So it was hardly surprising that no one gave him a second glance when he pulled into the garage beneath the *Investigator* building and climbed slowly out of his car. Why should they? The garage attendant was a young Pakistani Max Parker and the two women who passed him as they headed toward the street were younger female versions of himself.

They might all have his face, but surely they had different names, he thought as he slowly wended his way toward the elevator. Otherwise chaos would reign alongside uniformity.

Thankfully, he was alone in the elevator, and was therefore for the duration of the ride spared the necessity of conversing amiably with himself.

But once he was back out on his familiar floor, every face he encountered was his own. Bodies differed in size, shape, and sex, as did voices, but male or female there was no mistaking the endless parade of Max Parker pusses that stared blankly past him, smiled in greeting, or marched on by, submerged in private Parkerish reveries of their own.

His cubicle appeared undisturbed, exactly as he had left

it—in another para, he reminded himself. For several long moments he did nothing but stare silently at the achingly familiar computer station, the cut-out cartoons, the pictures pinned to the interior of the motile wall partitions, and the rest of the debris of his working life. Then he went for a walk.

Passing by a number of the other cubicles and workstations brought him face-to-face with individuals whose bodies and voices he recognized, but whose faces he knew all too well. As for their inner selves, their distinctive personalities, the hidden whatevers that defined them as individuals, except for minor variations, all that was gone, subsumed in the overwhelming Parkerness of the population. Oh, there were differences, but they were the differences that arose from a dilution of a Sam or Dave or Milly or Nanci with Essense of Max. They were individuals with one underlying unifying linking commonality: all were, in addition to being the selves that he knew from other worlds, part Max.

He knew he ought to have been flattered by the fate that had dictated the makeup of this world, but a certain nagging discomfort continued to trouble him. Certainly casual conversation was facilitated, since he often knew exactly what those he encountered were about to say. These predictions were correct about half the time: the Max half. None of those he chanced to speak with identified themselves as Mitch or Maxine, for which he was grateful. Jumping through parallel worlds was difficult enough to cope with without having several of them merge into one another.

Having nothing else to do but wait for the next paradigm shift, he returned to his cubicle and resumed work. He was glad he was not a photojournalist. Working without images allowed him to concentrate on the story at hand. He would leave it to the editor to sort out and identify the appropriate Maxes he was now describing in his notes.

From time to time, friends stopped by to chat or discuss upcoming projects. Some he was able to recognize by their distinctive voices, others he had to accept on trust. The diversity in Maxness was truly astonishing.

As the day wore on and he went to lunch with several of himselves it struck him that if he had to be stuck in another reality, this one might not be the equal of the gentrified utopia he had visited earlier, but it had definite unbeatable attractions of its own. For example, he rarely had to explain what he meant or say anything twice. Those around him understood intuitively. Everyone enjoyed much the same food, films, music, and politics. It all made for the most easygoing, relaxed, friendly conversation imaginable.

After the initial novelty wore off, it was also unutterably boring. Maybe homogenized milk was good for you, but a steady diet of the stuff would make anyone yearn for the comparative sharpness of two-percent acidophilus.

Max, who had always thought himself clever and witty and entertaining, was now made forcibly aware of how boring he could be. Not to mention self-centered, obnoxious, overbearing, and downright rude. It wasn't a pretty picture, particularly when he was forced to acknowledge his inadequacies several times in the space of a single conversation. Every bad habit he possessed was mirrored in every one of his lunch companions. Unlike him, they took no notice of their painfully obvious shortcomings.

Maybe I'm not quite the journalistic genius, imminent Pulitzer Prize winner, and GQ-model-in-waiting I thought I was, he found himself thinking.

Boles! Surrounded and overwhelmed by himself, he had forgotten about the inventor. There was no reason to suspect that he would look like Boles instead of Max. That didn't matter. What *did* matter was whether he thought like Max—or like himself. If this world proved to be his final destination, Max suspected that the local Boles would not be one capable of terminating the field and allowing him to return home—not even if he was ninety percent Boles and ten percent Parker. Max knew himself well enough to know that that ten percent would surely be fatal to any scientific enterprise.

Though he could handle the computer at work, at home Max had trouble determining which end of the videotape to insert into the machine. In short, his scientific knowledge was not of a kind and quality likely to facilitate breakthroughs in the time-space continuum. Or any other kind of space, including the one between his ears.

Well as it began, lunch rapidly degenerated into the usual bickering and argument over matters trivial and inconsequential that Max was prone to. Multiplied by half a dozen takes on himself, it quickly became unbearable. Excusing himself from the table, he wandered outside, ostensibly for some fresh air but really to get away from a superfluity of himself. In that regard, stepping outside was not all that much of an improvement.

Because no matter where he went or where he looked, he was still surrounded by Maxes. They filled the streets, drove the delivery vans, operated the businesses, occupied carriages, cars, and handicapped grocery carts, overwhelming him with their sheer Maxness. How they stood so many of one another he could not imagine. In less than a day he had already reached the point of barely being able to stand himself.

Back off, calm down, chill, he told himself. He could handle it. It just took some getting used to, that was all. As he prepared to go back into the restaurant and rejoin himself, he caught sight of the several vending newspaper racks lined up near the entrance. In addition to the feature news stories of the day, there were several articles accompanied by photos. Unfortunately, the *Investigator* was not among the papers displayed for sale.

Bending, he tried to read through the scarred and battered plastic cases. Sure enough, there was a slightly blurred color photo of himself, darker and slightly more hirsute but otherwise quite recognizable, loudly promoting his eminence as the murderous conquering warlord of some small, unfortunate African country Max could not place geographically. Below this story was another showing a slim him being led off to jail after being convicting of multiple counts of child molestation. On another rack, in another paper, he saw a short, stocky, undeniably belligerent redaction of himself on the stand in a local court accused of embezzling more than a million dollars from an outraged west-side charity.

On the front page of the *Sporting News* it was revealed that he had also scored three touchdowns in last week's pro game, only to be arrested later that same week on charges of conspiracy to distribute a quantity of banned substances. In the next vending case he was near the bottom of the page, grinning from ear to earring as he resigned his position as shock jock for a Chicago talk-radio station, only to announce that he was accepting a new position in Atlanta at a considerably higher salary. Socially diminished agents and much gratuitous profanity seemed to be involved.

A hand tapped him on the shoulder. Turning, he found himself looking back into his face: lined, grubby with the filth of the habitually unwashed, fragrant with ancillary aromas dubious in origin, and blank of eye.

" 'Scuse me, mistah. Spare some change so's I can get something to eat?"

Digging blindly into his pocket, Max fumbled with his wallet until he found a bill. Without even bothering to check the denomination he thrust it at the looming panhandler, a distorted, disturbing vision of himself at his least appealing.

"Here, take this."

Smacking his lips in a manner suggesting that the meal he now saw looming before him like a vision of the grail itself was to be of the liquid rather than the solid variety, the bum (an archaic but still efficacious term, Max thought abstractedly) shambled off clutching the bill before his eyes. He did not offer so much as a thank-you in return.

The absence of common courtesy did not matter to Max, who by this time had had just about enough of himself.

"That's it! I resign from myself! I concede, I give up!" He shouted it at the sky, drawing some uncertain stares from passing himselves. They quickened their pace when he dropped his gaze to glare at them—even though it was a familiar glare.

All the good that was in the world, he was responsible for, he knew. Also all the evil, and all the mediocrity, and every level of mendacity and moronity and goodness in between. Over all this he had no control. Only the knowledge that in his own, absent world he was the one and true Max Parker kept him from going mad.

But how did he *know* that he was the true Max, he found himself wondering? Why should it not be one of his friends waiting for him in the restaurant, or someone still back at the office, or one of the dozens of motivating Maxes hurrying to and fro along the sidewalks? Did they not have equal assurance of their own reality, of their own individual uniqueness? Perhaps he was after all no more than a para Max deluding himself into thinking that he was the true Max, and the real Max was out there on the streets somewhere, or at this very moment up at Trancas conversing with Barrington Boles. Could the real Max be subject to para delusions? Or were his paras the same ones and the original Max delusional?

Einstein was right, he decided. God did not play dice with the universe. Instead, it was set up as a kind of cosmic Las Vegas, where anything was possible and, if you hit the right combination of numbers, or ideas, or concepts, even probable. Yahweh not only played dice with the universe, but also roulette, baccarat, keno, and for all Max knew, reservation bingo.

As for he, him, himself, Max, he had crapped out.

About many things he was ignorant, and others self-deluded, but he knew with certainty that he did not have the type of mind required to deal rationally and sensibly with abstractions of such breadth and scope. All he knew for sure was that he was tired, and bored, and worn out from trying to make sense of the insensible. All he could do was what he had done when cast into previous para worlds: try and ride it out.

At least, he thought, this time he would not be forced to do so in the company of strangers. Though by now he would have found a real stranger, anyone patently different from himself, preferable to yet another insufferable version of Maxwell Parker.

With a sigh that seemed to encompass not merely a single breath but entire worlds, he headed back inside the restaurant to rejoin himself.

He made it through the rest of lunch by saying as little as possible and leaving it to the other multiples of himself to carry the conversation. Being him, this they had no trouble in doing. Instead of entertaining or enlightening him, the conversation only made him inescapably aware of what a puerile and self-centered conversationalist he often was.

He was relieved when the dishes were removed and it was time to pay the check. Naturally, every version of himself tried to stick every other version of himself with it. He ended up paying it himself. And why not? Wasn't he paying for himself, several times over?

He allowed the others to walk on ahead, keeping to a deliberately slow pace so as to be able to avoid participating in their conversation. Back at the *Investigator* building, morose and unhappy, he found a message on his voice mail requesting that he report to his boss.

Might as well, he told himself. Anything that hinted of non-Maxness was a welcome diversion from the lukewarm pit of himness in which he found himself inextricably trapped.

Hoping against hope to find his old boss waiting for him, he was once again disappointed. The man who sat behind the desk in what should have been Kryzewski's office possessed the same physical and vocal characteristics as the curmudgeonly old editor with whom Max had worked for over a year, but the face that looked up over the pile of printouts was just another distorted replication of Max Parker. Defeated and discouraged by the twin demons of Uncaring Fate and Barrington Boles, Max took an indifferent seat in the chair opposite this latest, puffy-faced, gruff version of himself.

"How're you doing, Max?" the seamed, elder mirror of himself inquired.

"As well as can be expected under the circumstances." *There*, he thought. *An honest answer.*

Parker Boss looked at him uncertainly, but both his personality and position allowed little if any time for in-depth probing of his employees' state of mind. Since anything by way of reply short of "I just found out I have a terminal disease" or "I need an advance on next month's salary" qualified as satisfactory, he shrugged off the reporter's conspicuous lassitude and pressed on.

"Got a live one for you."

Max perked up. Working on a story, even in a para that was not his, might help keep him from dwelling on his unfortunate situation. He knew it couldn't be healthy to flinch inwardly every time he encountered a face that looked like his. If he didn't do something soon, the flinch would take over the rest of him.

"Saucerologists?" The UFOnuts were always good for a line or two, and the photo department loved them. It gave them the opportunity to put together some really inventive mock-ups in the computer. "Bigfoot? A turnip in the shape of Elvis's head?"

"Better." Max's enthusiastic response pleased the Kryzewski substitute. An interested and happy employee was a productive employee. "Here's the particulars." He slid a sheet of paper across the desk. Max pocketed it absently. "You ought to be able to get a full page out of this one. Maybe a page and a half."

"Pictures?"

"It's not that kind of story. Maybe we'll be able to get something later, but I doubt it. The guy's too serious. Don't worry. Not your responsibility. Photolab will throw something usable together."

"Yeah, they always seem to." Max rose and headed for the door.

"Oh, and Parker?"

"Yes, sir?" Max paused, his fingers on the door handle.

"Talk to accounting when you get a chance. If you've got

some vacation time coming I think you should take it. You don't look well. I think some time off would do you good. Recharge the batteries, that sort of thing. Go on a trip, do some traveling. Get out of L.A. for a while."

Max smiled thinly. "I'll look into it, sir, but I'm not really in the mood to go touring. Sometimes I think that's all I do." Leaving the editor to wonder what he meant by that, Max swung open the door and exited the office.

His mind awhirl, he took a cursory glance at the info sheet he had been handed and marked the address in his memory as he made his way out of the building. Maxes of both genders in various stages of youth or advancing decomposition hailed him as he departed.

He continued to ponder his situation as he pulled out of the underground garage and headed for Pico. That would be the fastest and simplest route to the address he had been given. There was so much on his mind, there were so many things he was trying to deal with simultaneously, that it did not occur to him that the address was that of his own building until he pulled up outside the gated garage.

Frowning uncertainly, he checked the tip sheet. Nineteen hundred Appian Way. Sure enough, that was his address, his building. He let his gaze crawl farther down the paper.

"Interview a Mr. Parker—funny coincidence, ain't it?—in apartment 3F. Parker claims to have participated in an experiment put together by some rich nitwit up north of Malibu. I know it sounds like your standard mad-scientist scenario, but I think that if you can put your usual witty spin on it you might be able to do some good storytelling.

"Seems this crazy claims to have built a machine that can access parallel worlds, and this Parker, who insists he's a stringer for, of all things, the *Investigator*, actually let himself be used as a guinea pig in its first tryout. Now he says he's being tormented by dreams of other worlds, and he wants to tell his story. The interviewer on the phonebank who took his call asked him why, if he's a stringer for us, he didn't write up the story himself, but he says that since yesterday he's been plagued with visions of himself slipping in and out of reality and until they go away he's afraid to leave his apartment. As if his apartment's any more real than the rest of the world. Can you beat that?

"There might be a nice little yarn here. See what you can get out of him. But watch yourself. I got the ol' gut feeling this one could be violent."

He wouldn't be violent, Max knew as he let the paper slip from his limp fingers. He knew the man would not be violent because Maxwell Parker was not a violent man. Ignoring the cars that were forced to slow on the narrow hill street and then go around him, he let his gaze rise to the top floor of the building. His building.

The Kryzewski-Parker had sent him out to interview himself.

Only, this Max Parker did not differ in age, or ethnic

background, or gender. This was a Max Parker who claimed to be a writer for the *Investigator*, who lived in Max Parker's building, and who was even now waiting for Max Parker in Max Parker's apartment. Inevitably, he found himself wondering just who was the real Max Parker: himself, or the anguished individual waiting upstairs?

What if it was the one waiting upstairs?

Then I'd just be a para, he thought with icy calm. *And the Max upstairs is the one who should be going back to the real world.* Trouble was, they were all real worlds.

That way lies madness, he assured himself. *I know who I am. I'm me, and he's him, and all these other Maxes are themselves.* But that was not quite the case. None of the other multiple Maxes except Mitch had claimed to be writers for the *Investigator*, he reminded himself, nor did they live in his apartment.

What would happen when he confronted the man upstairs? Would one of them disappear, canceled out by the reality of the other? Or would one of them finally flee to the peaceful land of the insane? Or would they both? Or was he crazy already?

Parallel worlds and Barrington Boles, and a space-time continuum that's full of holes, he sang silently to himself. In the midst of them all, why not a world populated by nothing but Maxwell Parkers, ad hominem, ad infinitum? And if you take blueberries and paint them red, they taste more like cranberries than rhubarb does.

He could sit in his car until reality or death overtook

him, or he could keep moving, keep living. He chose to keep moving.

Unsurprisingly, the garage gate yielded to his key-ring remote. Another Aurora was parked in his space and he slid his own into one of the two empty slots reserved for guests of tenants. In spite of everything he had been through, there was something surpassing strange about having to park in the guest space in his own building. Locking the car, he marched grim-faced toward the elevator.

There's nothing here to fear, he told himself. *You're just paying a little visit on you, much as a Max named Mitch once did. Maybe you can even help the poor guy. After all, you're probably responsible for at least several of his bad dreams.*

On second thought, maybe his unexpected appearance would not be so salutary after all. But then, since everyone in this world looked more or less like Max Parker, why should the appearance of yet one more startle another?

Before he could change his mind and back out, he found himself confronting an all-too-familiar door. It was 3F, the entrance to his apartment down to the scratches in the paint near the bottom where Mr. Kraus's dog had attempted to claw its way in. Thumbing the bell, he waited for a response, half hoping none would be forthcoming.

He heard the security chain rattle in its holder, and the door opened.

The man standing there was him, all right. Not a close copy, this time, or one distorted by a different haircut or

darker complexion or excess avoirdupois, but as exact a duplicate as could be imagined. Only the expression was different.
Where he was anxious and resigned, the Maxwell Parker
standing in the portal looked harried and apprehensive, as if
he had not slept in a long time.

That was understandable, Max thought, if the poor
schmuck's dreams were in any way shape or form mirroring
Max's multiple realities.

The man jumped slightly as soon as he got a good look at
his visitor. "Christ, I know that everybody looks more or less
like everybody—that's the natural state of the world—but I've
never met anyone before who looked so much like me!"

"You don't know the half of it, bud. Or the multiplicity.
Can I come in?" He felt like a prize fool asking for permission
to enter his own apartment, except that it was not his apartment. It belonged to *this* Max Parker, and he had no intention
of being hauled off to the Lincoln Street jail by blue-clad
clones of himself for forcibly violating the privacy of another
version of him.

"Yeah. Yeah, sure you can come in." His other self stepped
aside. "You're from the paper, aren't you? They called and said
they might send someone out. Can I get you a drink? I've
got . . ."

"Two six-packs of Hinano, a half-empty liter of diet RC,
and a couple of bottles of flavored iced tea. I know." Pushing
past the dumbfounded copy of himself, he headed for the
kitchen.

With an expression that was a mixture of astonishment and confusion, his other self trailed behind. "That's exactly right. I'll be damned. How'd you know that?" His tone turned suspicious. "The paper have somebody check out my place while I was at work? That's breaking and entering."

"Not if the manager lets them in, but don't sweat it. It never happened. I can assure you that nobody's been spending time in this apartment except Maxwell Parker."

Max fumbled in the fridge until he found a chilled tea. Popping the vacuum seal, he sat down at the table and took a long, cold swallow. Then he looked over the tabletop at his troubled but curious self.

"Then how did you know what . . . ?" the local M. Parker started to ask. Gesturing grandly with the tea bottle, Max cut him off.

"Why don't you tell me a little about these dreams of yours."

The other Max hesitated, as if trying to make up his mind whether to respond genially to the extraordinary intrusion or call the cops. After a moment or two, he decided to cooperate. Max knew he would. If there was one set of reactions he could predict, it was his own. Helping himself to a beer from the door of the fridge, the other Max sat down in the chair opposite. There he sat and gazed across the table in abiding wonder at the perfect, and perfectly at home, archetype of himself.

"You promise you won't laugh? I thought the girl I spoke to at the paper was going to laugh."

"Believe me," Max told him somberly, "you are looking at the last person in the world who'd laugh at you."

"Okay, then." Feeling a little more comfortable in the presence of, what was after all, himself, the Maxwell Parker of this particular para started in. "This is going to sound crazy, and it's thrice wacko, because I'm usually interviewing the weirdos, not setting myself up as one."

"I know," Max told him gently.

His counterpart looked at him uncertainly, but continued. "I keep seeing myself in this other life, or other world, or other someplace. Everything's normal there. I'm still a writer, still single, still living here at the beach. Only, there's this wild, wealthy inventor character there named Boles. Barrington Boles." Max nodded and held out his recorder, numb and unresponsive. Mistaking his glazed expression for a sign of interest, the other Max became more voluble.

"So my editor gives me a tip that this Boles character might be good for a story because he claims to have built something that's sort of like a gate between parallel worlds. What he calls paras, for short. His idea is that everyplace and everything has lots of paras. So I go out there, and he's not at all like what I expect."

"You mean he's sensible, and seems sane," Max supplied quietly.

His double nodded slowly. "Yeah. Yeah, that's it exactly. Anyway, it's clear right away that he has plenty of money, but in spite of appearances I'm still not sure about the sense part.

He takes me downstairs, and the place is fitted out like a new ride at Universal Studios. He tells me that I'm real lucky, because I'm going to be present for this room-sized gadget's first full run-through. So while he's busy lighting the place up like Times Square on New Year's Eve, I decide to take a little stroll and check everything out. And like a fool, I find myself stepping under this flickering arch." He smiled wanly, a smile Max knew all too well.

"The result is that I end up being the guinea pig for the guy's initial tryout." He laughed hollowly. "I mean, can you imagine anybody being that stupid?"

"Actually, I can." Max looked away.

"Yeah, well, you must know dumber people than me. Anyway, I don't really feel a thing, but it turns out that I come out of this crazy contraption well and truly zapped, you know? But I don't know anything's wrong until I'm asleep."

"What happens then?" Max prompted him.

His counterpart hesitated, but having decided to tell all, could hardly find a decent excuse not to continue. "It's hard to describe. I think what's happening is that in my dreams I keep seeing myself slipping between these paras he alluded to. Each dream takes me to a different one, and I'm telling you, they're so goddamn real you can practically smell them." He leaned back and crossed his arms, gazing out at the placid Pacific.

"But I know they're not real, that they're only dreams." He leaned forward and lowered his voice significantly. "Want to know how I know?"

"I'd be very interested," Max assured him dryly.

The other Max stared unblinkingly into his visitor's eyes. "Because they're too fantastic. Dream worlds come out of and are based on our own personal realities. They're not like the inventions of some crackpot novelist out to sell fragments of his imagination for a few bucks. And these dream paras, well, even the least of them is just too extreme to be believed." He sat back in his chair.

"Now, if they made some sense, bore any relation to the real world, I might really be worried. But as it is, I think they're pretty harmless. They just ruin my sleep. What I'm thinking, and the reason I called your paper, is that the vividness of them might be worth sharing." He winked. "You know what I mean?"

"Why don't you write about them yourself?" Max inquired apathetically. "Don't you work for a weekly tabloid newspaper?"

"Got some background on me, did you?" The other Max grinned. "That's para for the course." His expression twisted. "Sorry. Bad joke. But I thought you'd understand. I have this strange feeling we share a lot in common besides looks."

"Yeah. Yeah, I'd have to agree with that."

"I work for the *National Enquirer*." The other Max stated it proudly, as though it was significant of something.

Max looked dubious. "Never heard of it."

His other self frowned. "Come on, man. Don't put me on. The *Enquirer* has the largest circulation of any tabloid in the country."

"I'm telling you the truth." The tiny green light that indicated the status of the batteries in Max's recorder had gone to red, but he did not bother to stop and change them. This interview was not going anywhere anyhow. Even if it was, he could fake whatever else his counterpart might choose to say.

Everything the local Max had said about Barrington and parallelities and the effects of the Boles Field rang true—but what was this *Enquirer* nonsense?

Before he could think of a follow-up query that would not make him sound like a complete lunatic, the other Max was shaking a knowing finger at him. "I get it. You're testing me."

"Testing you?" The bewilderment in Max's voice was genuine.

"Sure. To see if I'm crazy." He grinned understandingly. "Hey, if I was in your position, I'd do the same thing. But I think you could have come up with something a little more subtle. Imagine another tabloid reporter claiming never having heard of the *Enquirer*! Stick to that line and you'll have me wondering if you're the crazy one."

Enquirer, Enquirer. Could there be a large but highly localized scandal sheet by that name somewhere back East, or maybe overseas? Max racked his memory and drew only blanks. Since he knew he was not insane, the only conclusion he could come to was that the publication in question had to be a para tabloid paper in this parallel world.

Careful now, he warned himself. *Tread cautiously or you're liable to lose your perspective here. This guy is the para Max, you're the genuine one. The first Max, the Max prime. Focus on that and whatever happens, don't lose sight of it.*

"It doesn't matter," he told his double finally.

"I thought it wouldn't." The other Max chuckled. " 'Never heard of the *National Enquirer*.' Yeah, sure. Anyway, you see why I can't write this up myself. Can't file a report on my own dreams. We're supposed to go *outside* for our stories. No way my editor would buy anything so personal. But you could do it, and we can both make a couple of bucks." Content with this explanation, he waited for a response. When none was forthcoming from his dull-visaged visitor, he tried to encourage him.

"How about it? I know it's a wild story, even for your typical tabloid dream yarn, but we can polish it to the point where it's acceptable. Hell, I can even do the rough draft for you. Or you can listen to me ramble and do your own thing from the transcription. None of your readers need to know what I do for a living." He continued enthusiastically.

"I'm telling you, when you hear about some of the places I've been in my sleep lately you'll be glad you don't have the same kind of dreams. It's been pretty damn unsettling. I figure getting it out, telling it to somebody else, could be good therapy for me. Because I'll tell you, sometimes they feel so authentic, sometimes I'm so *right there*, that I wake up in a cold sweat from the reality of it." He took a long swig of his beer.

"You want to know what the most unsettling thing about them is?"

"No, what's the most unsettling thing about them?" *I'm*

the real one, Max kept assuring himself, over and over. *I'm the original*. Not this joker, with his virtual dreams and imaginary newspaper.

His counterpart's voice softened. "The way they linger in the memory. By the time I've been up a few hours the following morning, I usually have trouble remembering the details of a dream. Not with these. They stick around like they've been epoxied to my brain. I can tell you details of the dream I had *last week*. For me, that's unreal." A sudden concern made him twitch slightly.

"Hey, you don't think there really is a nut named Boles running around town with some kind of generator or ray that makes people have violent, unforgettable dreams, do you?"

"Ordinarily, I'd say not a chance." Max pushed back his chair and rose from the table. "I don't think you have to worry about anything like that. In fact, I can pretty much guarantee it. What you're describing doesn't sound like the kind of apparatus that would be very portable. For one thing, it'd have to be permanently locked down somewhere so it could draw on a continuous source of power."

"I hadn't thought of that." The double nodded admiringly. "You're a bright guy, Max. Not to mention good-looking." He grinned. "How come you're still working for a second-rate rag like the *Investigator*?"

"It suits me" was all Max could think of to say to his double. "I have to go now."

The other Max looked distressed. "But we're just getting started. I think we could establish a real good working relationship here." As Max headed for the door his anxious counterpart followed, persistent and maybe a little hurt. "What about my dreams?"

"I told you—write them up yourself."

"And I told you why I can't do that." His double was clearly baffled. Everything had been going so well. Almost from the start he had felt that his visitor understood him better than any other journalist he had ever met, even those he had worked with for months at a time on the *Enquirer*.

Max was anxious to be out of there, to get away from the apartment that looked, felt, and smelled like his, but was not. His impatience was reflected in his reply. "Then find somebody else to write your story. I can't do it." Like the doorknob at the bottom of the rabbit hole in *Alice*, the one attached to his front door seemed to be willfully resisting his efforts to turn it.

His bewildered counterpart pleaded with him. "Don't run out on me like this, Max. I mean, I know we just met, but dammit, I feel like I know you already."

Just as Max was about to scream, the stubborn door finally yielded. Turning, he favored his other self with a look of such anguish that his double flinched.

"You don't want to know me. At this point, I'm not sure that I want to know me." A lopsided grin cracked his face.

"It's not necessary anyway. Everybody else you know here knows me already."

With that he exited quickly, deliberately pulling the door shut behind him and leaving his other self standing alone in their apartment, mystified and more than a little wounded.

Instinctively, he stumbled down the hallway, heading for the elevator because there was nowhere else to go. The elevator could take him to the garage, or to the other floors, but neither it nor anything else under his control could carry him home. Home. But wasn't he already home? Wasn't this his building, his address, his Santa Monica?

It was, and it was not. This apartment, like this world, belonged not to him but to his other. His para other. Unless, of course, the Max Parker he had just left behind was the real Max Parker, the first Max Parker, Maxwell Parker fundamental, and he himself was nothing more than a figment of the other Parker's dreaming. Even now, the other Parker might actually be lying asleep in his bed, dreaming that he had just been awake talking to a duplicate of himself about turning his strange dreams of parallel worlds into a series of stories for a competing tabloid. Soon, tomorrow, this evening, he was liable to wake up, startled awake by the depth and color and richness of still another in an endless succession of dreams of infinite parallelities.

In which case he, the Max Parker staggering down the hall even now, would cease to exist except as a memory in the mind of his newly awakened self.

Tripping on the same loose piece of carpet he and his neighbors on the top floor had been besieging the landlord to fix for the past several months, he stumbled sideways. His left leg banged into the wall and pain shot through his knee. Wincing, he halted and grabbed the injured joint. If he was nothing more than a dream, and a dreaming parallelity at that, then the sleeping Max Parker was capable of more detailed and vivid reveries than Max had ever imagined.

I am not a dream, he told himself angrily. Straightening, he worked his fingers up his body. There was nothing dreamlike about the throbbing pain in his knee, or the mushy feel of his underexercised belly, or his damp mouth and sensitive eyes. No, goddamn it! If anyone was a dream it was the Max he had just finished speaking with. A para Max. Just like this was a para world.

I'm the real one, he reassured himself furiously. *All these worlds, all these paras, revolve around* me.

In the garage, he passed a young couple he recognized but did not know. They lived in the building, and might easily have been residents of the same floor, but, man and woman both, they looked like him. As he made his way back to the Aurora, his Aurora, a late-model Lincoln drove in and parked. A well-groomed older man emerged who might have been Walter Konigsberg, the retired engineer who lived on the second floor. Might have been, except that he looked like a well-weathered, time-aged, slightly Teutonic version of Max Parker.

The first thing Max did upon sliding behind the wheel of

his comfortable, familiar automobile was to lock all the doors. It was as if he could seal out the madness that had engulfed him simply by keeping the clear power windows closed against the outside.

Sitting motionless in the car allowed him to gather his thoughts as well as his wind, but it was far from satisfying. Without a clear notion of where he was going or what he was going to do when he got there, he started the engine and backed out of his assigned parking space. Better to be doing something, anything, he thought, than meditating morosely while waiting for the cosmos to rescue him from the onrushing approach of insanity.

How many paras were there? An infinite number for every individual? Or was the incomprehensible, too, ruled by strictures and laws he could not imagine? In addition to the paras where aliens commuted to Earth and the minions of Cthulhu ruled and civilization had been devastated or utopianized or just ever so slightly bent, besides the paras where ghosts and para ghosts and para alien ghosts walked the Earth and where the most perfect mate for himself was himself, was there one like this one for every man, woman, and child? A para existing for and inhabited solely and entirely by themselves? It nearly beggared the question of how many inconceivable paras existed that he had not yet visited.

Imagine if you will for a moment, he instructed himself, *a reality inhabited entirely by paras of Barry Manilow.* For the first time all that day, or all that para day, he managed a smile. Not a para smile, but one that could lay claim to reality. Feeling a little better, he thumbed the built-in garage-door opener and pulled out onto the steep side street that intersected Ocean Avenue. On the way up, he waved to a derelict resting in a bed he had fashioned from the flower bushes across the street. Looking back at him, the homeless man responded with a cheerful if none too steady wave. Para or not, the expression on the dirty, battered face was honest.

More honest than the physics of my life, Max reflected. *There's a whole lotta cheatin' goin' on there. Give me a para smile over a real glare any day.*

An unexpected euphoria filled his mind and thoughts. No matter what the universe around him chose to do, he was still him, still Maxwell Parker. Nothing could change that. Not the presence of grisly, ravenous carnivores or unnatural quadruplet beauties or even a world populated entirely by several billion versions of himself.

I am me, he decided, *because nobody else is. Nobody else can be me.* To paraphrase a well-known saying: No matter where I am, there I is. As a writer he hated to resort to paraphrasing, but that was as much a part of him as the fine car and beach apartment and as yet unrealized ambitions. Cobbled together, lumped as a whole, they combined to make up the one, the only, the original Max Parker.

It was a good feeling to be once more assured of himself.

Why *not* an infinitude of possible paras? Why *not* one for everybody, in addition to the infinite multiplicity of shared worlds? Let us have a para just for the kindly Konigsberg, and for the recently married lovebirds he had encountered in the garage. A perpetually grumpy one for the irascible Kryzewski, and one of voluptuous innocence for the curvaceous Omaha sisters. One for Alanis Morisette, in which thoughtful lyrics ruled, and another for the committed disciples of dear, departed Havergal Brian and his music too overwhelming for the curmudgeonly conservative cognoscenti, a para in which thirty-two symphonies ruled and "Prometheus Unbound" had not been lost.

Worlds enough for everyone, and time. Paras uncountable as the stars in the sky, paras enough to make a pinch of all the sands on all the beaches of the world. Paras unbounding, so that anything that could be imagined was possible; paras sufficient to make the unimagined a reality.

Quadrillions upon quadrillions of paras, piled upon and beneath and side by side one another in a macrocosmic volume wherein a single universe was but a pinprick.

Not for the first time was it all too much for his mind to cope with, too much even for a legion of para Einsteins to come to grips with. For that matter, imagine a world inhabited by nothing but para Einsteins, he thought. What a world that must be! Genius truly triumphant—or else a world filled with millions of multiple versions of real dreamers endlessly dreaming their dreams of other universes while nobody did the cooking or the cleaning or the washing-up. It would be a disheveled, badly dressed world, to boot.

He did not need Utopia. The threat of disease and brush-fire wars and too much poverty existing side by side with the super-rich and inane television programming and homogenized fast food and carjackings he could handle. But he could no longer deal with a Fate that indulged in repeated hijackings of reality. His reality. Hell and dammit, the novelty had worn off. He had to do something.

The first consisting of forcing himself to think in simpler terms. *One para at a time*, he ordered himself. *Focus on the here and now and don't try to make sense of the distant and tomorrow. Minute by minute does the trick. Next, find something to focus on. Something to rivet the mind, limit the scope of perception to what can be immediately comprehended.*

As it turned out, that was less difficult to do than at first it seemed.

Boles.

XIV

Staring grim-faced over the wheel, he roared up the access street and out onto Ocean Avenue, ignoring the angry bleats of drivers he cut off and those who were forced to slam on their brakes to avoid crashing into him. The Aurora sped down onto the Pacific Coast Highway, accelerating as it turned northward and elbowing aside lesser vehicles. Max was the recipient of murderous stares from other drivers that he single-mindedly ignored. Having already dealt with monstrous tentacled shapes from other worlds, subtle variations on Armageddon, blighted scenes of terrestrial destruction, aliens, ghosts, and assorted other para phenomena, he was not about to be disturbed or even distracted by the comical, angry gestures of bellicose commuters on their way home from work.

By now the patience of his editor was likely to have run out, but Max did not care. His job no longer mattered to him. Nothing mattered except terminating the Boles Effect and getting himself snapped back to his own para line. If that was even possible now, he found himself wondering. Like a ship whose engine had died at sea, he was adrift, floating across parallel worlds, riding a crest one moment and plunging into apocalyptic troughs the next. His greatest fear was that he might have drifted too far to find his way back, even if the Effect suddenly evanesced. He only hoped that if that was the case and he found himself permanently attached to a para different from his own, it would be one that was more or less benign.

Either way, he fully intended to survive. He had learned how to do that much, anyway.

As if determined to discourage him, the field in which he was unwillingly embedded showed signs of strengthening. The world around him seemed to shift and flow even as he drove up the coast, reality melting and coalescing like some great cosmic pudding in which he was the sole, lonely raisin.

The ocean vanished, to be replaced by a heaving mass of pale pink flesh from which massive, lugubrious bubbles slowly rose and burst. Each time one erupted, a burst of discordant music filled the air. People and animals still lined the beach, gazing contentedly out to where the sea had been. Cats listened intently to the pulsating pink chorus side by side with humans, and bears and coatimundis shared aural space with sunning sheep and monkeys dressed in shorts, vests, and wraparound sunglasses. Jaw set, lips tight, Max kept his eyes on the road and drove on.

The crumbling sandstone cliffs of the Palisades, familiar to him from hundreds of trips up the coast, had vanished. In their place a long stone wall stretched from north to south as far as the eye could see, the endless rampart interrupted only by occasional towers and redoubts. He was no longer in the Aurora but on the back of a chariot drawn by three white horses, whipped along by a charioteer while he sat, petrified and disoriented, on the seat behind.

From the direction of the sea rose the commingled howling of half a million throats. Rushing toward the wall in an unbroken line a half mile wide came the Golden Horde, thundering over the desert that had previously been the sea on foot and on horseback.

Their terrifying battle cry was met by a roar of thunderous defiance from the tens of thousands of armored defenders who lined the crest of the immense wall. A hail of arrows and heavy spears began to fly from the parapets to fall with devastating effect on the berserking attackers. The martial pealing of drums and bugle-like horns rose above the shrieks and cries and humanoid bellowing.

Abruptly and without warning, the rattling chariot vanished and he was back in the enclosed metal womb of the Aurora. As he grabbed frantically for the steering wheel, one bronze-tipped spear grazed the passenger's side of the sedan's windshield, crazing the glass. Mouth set, Max didn't even wince. Ignoring the fact that he was driving down the rapidly shrinking divide between two onrushing, opposing armies of monstrous size and murderous intent, he continued to barrel up the wide dirt road that the Pacific Coast Highway had become.

The Golden Horde winked out of existence, the impossible Great Wall of Santa Monica disappeared as cleanly as if deleted from a computer screen. He was back on paved road, the friendly dark surface marred by familiar cracks and potholes and white striping. It didn't matter. He paid it no more attention than if it had transformed into one of the rings of Saturn and he was cruising along toward distant Triton at seventy miles per. His thoughts were focused not on place but on one man. Barrington Boles was the single coherent entity around which his existence now orbited, and it was to Barrington Boles that he was fleeing as fast as heavy horsepower could carry him.

He couldn't even kill the son of a bitch, Max thought bluntly, because he might end up killing the right son of a bitch. But it was a pleasing thought, and the protracted contemplation of assorted forms of homicide helped to pass the time as he continued up the coast.

Perhaps the worst of it was that, if he survived physically and mentally, the likelihood of extracting a story from his experiences was much reduced. Readers of tabloids like the *Investigator* were usually confused by any science more complicated than that necessary to explain the workings of a cheese grater. As a consequence, even adventurous editors tended to shy away from stories about the space program or new developments in computers or even mass consumer electronics—

unless they involved kidnapping aliens or secret government plots or new ways to lose weight, or Elvis.

Leaving Santa Monica and L.A. proper behind, he began winding his way along the base of the mountains, speeding past sun-bronzed surfers and flabby families and students from UCLA playing hooky. Much to his relief, none of them looked the least like him. The sky did not turn red, or purple, or polka-dot. The road did not metamorphose into the back of a giant, writhing snake. No little men, green or otherwise, materialized in the seat next to him, and no alien spaceships disgorged the bemused citizens of other worlds onto the increasingly rocky beach. With his window down, the damp rushing air that poured into the car smelled of salt and sea and rock and festering hydrocarbons. It stank, in fact, of reality.

He would not let himself believe, would not allow himself to accept. He had been burned by a chortling cosmos too many times already.

But the guard at the gated compound was one he remembered, and who in turn recognized him, waving him through with a sprightly California good-afternoon. Iceplant defined the limits of large yards, gluing the uncertain hillsides together with clutches of spiky, defiant greenery. He saw nothing more outré than a wandering poodle with a punk coiffure.

Boles's manse was exactly as he remembered it. A gardener was just leaving, the bed of his battered, dented pickup filled to capacity with bush and tree trimmings. He waved as

the emotionally exhausted Max pulled into the circular driveway and parked, not even bothering to take his keys.

As before, Boles answered his own door. It looked like
Boles, sounded like Boles, acted and talked like Boles. The
overriding and all-important question was—was it the correct
Boles? Was this the right reality, or one sufficiently subtly different to permit the existence of a Boles who did not have a
clue as to how his addlepated work had distorted the true nature of the universe?

"Hi," Boles said jauntily. "It's not Tuesday yet."

Silently, Max thanked whatever god or gods was looking
over him at that moment. "I won't last till Tuesday." Without
waiting for an invitation, he stepped past the older man and
into the house.

His expression becoming one of honest concern, Boles
shut the door and followed the reporter into the front room.
"You don't look so good, Max. This has been hard on you,
hasn't it?"

"HARD?" Max counted to three—he did not have patience enough to wait till ten—and forced himself to stay
calm. "Hard. Look at me, Boles. Since the last time we met
I've been slipping in and out of parallel worlds like lead shot
through Jell-O. I barely know who I am anymore, much less
where I am." Pacing the room, he extended his arms in a posture of helpless supplication.

"Take right now, this moment, for instance. How do I

know this is my world and not some para? How do I know that you're my Barrington Boles? How can you be sure that I'm not some para Max Parker? How can anybody be sure of anything?"

The inventor made soothing noises. "Take it easy."

"Yeah, sure; take it easy." Moody and depressed, Max threw himself down onto the couch, bouncing a couple of times as he landed. "Easy for you to say. It doesn't matter to you what I am because you know for sure that this is your world. You possess a certainty that's denied to me." He looked up, his gaze desperate and searching.

"It's amazing the things we take for granted, Barrington. The reality of the world around us, the stability, the knowledge that what we go to bed with tonight will in all probability be there when we wake up in the morning. You lose that and it doesn't matter how successful you are or how rich or how healthy. Lose your reality and everything starts to come loose, to fall apart. Even if it's a better reality than the one you're used to, and I visited one or two of those, you never manage to quite fit in." He grabbed a handful of mixed nuts from a glass dish on the coffee table and began munching them nervously.

"Let me tell you something, Barry. Shifting realities and parallel worlds suck. I just thought that, as an anticipative scientist, you ought to know that."

Boles did his best to commiserate. "I'm not sure how to quantify that observation as empirical data, but it's nice to have the opinion of someone who's been there."

Unmollified, Max fidgeted on the couch, too edgy to sit still. "Been there, done that. Been lots of wheres, done plenty of things. And I'm sick of it, Boles. Sick and tired of it. I want my own world back, my own para. I want to get up in my own bed, by myself, and drive to work, and write amusing stories about mildly outrageous incidents in the lives of ordinary citizens without becoming an outrageous incident myself." He leaned forward and his tone turned dead earnest.

"Give me back my reality, Barrington. I want it back. I need it back. Take the Boles Effect and bury it someplace quiet where it won't be found. It's dangerous. It's destabilizing. It makes a man inclined to do violent, unpleasant things to inventors they hardly know who monkey around with the fabric of the universe without a clear vision of what they're getting other people into."

The two men stared into each other's eyes for a long moment. Then Boles announced quietly, "I've been working on the problem."

"You found a way to kill the field," Max shot back instantly.

"Well, I'm not sure." The inventor rubbed at his chin. "I haven't been sure about quite a lot since I started this project—but then, you already know that. But I've been working on it."

"Great," Max muttered, his hands working against one another. "I'm losing my mind, and you're 'working on it.' "

The inventor was eyeing him thoughtfully. "I wonder if

you *are* in the right para? I mean, I *know* that I'm the right Barrington Boles, but I wonder if you're the right Maxwell Parker. Just as you said, you could be another Max entirely who just happened to wander into this para by mistake. If so, and I help you and everything works, that means I might be marooning the real Max Parker in some other para forever."

"Screw the other Max Parkers!" The reporter's tone was choleric. "If you don't do something to end this for me then you'll have at least one angry maniac on your hands for sure. *That's* something you don't have to speculate on."

Boles dug tiredly at his eyes and spoke thoughtfully. "You *talk* like the Max Parker I know, anyway."

The reporter laughed hollowly. "Wouldn't all the different mes talk alike?"

"Not necessarily. If the paras you say you've been slipping and sliding between are so different, the Max Parkers that inhabit them might speak and act differently as well. The differences would be subtle, but they would be real." He continued to concentrate speculatively on his visitor.

After a little of this Max began to grow uneasy. "What are you staring at?"

"I told you. I'm trying to decide if you're the real Max Parker, the original."

Max found himself nodding slowly. "That's exactly what I'd expect the original Barrington Boles to say. One who was familiar with the success of his machine. The other Boleses I met were familiar with the theory but hadn't succeeded in making the device work."

"Fascinating. I wish I could meet some of my paras."

"Don't get me wrong, Barrington. It's pretty damn interesting to be able to sit down and have a conversation with yourself, but it's no way to live. No matter what para you find yourself in, you're always better off in the one that you belong to. I found that out." He rose from the couch. "You said that you've been working on the problem."

Boles nodded. "Personally, I think it's premature to try using the equipment to negate the effect, but if you're that desperate . . ."

"Barry, I'm beyond desperate. I'm going out of my mind. As if going out of my reality wasn't bad enough. If you think there's a chance, even a small chance, of doing anything, then for God's sake let's take a shot at it. No matter what happens, it can't be any worse than what I'm going through now."

Boles took a deep breath and nodded. "Come downstairs."

The reporter trailed his host through the house, the locked metal door, and down to the equipment-saturated cellar. His first view of the subterranean chamber crammed full of unruly electronics left him limp with relief—relief that was short-lived when he reminded himself that if this was the wrong para, none of it would work.

Boles busied himself at the control console. "You need to stand over . . ."

"I know where to stand." An impatient Max did not hesitate to interrupt the inventor. "I was right here when it happened, remember? A guinea pig may not know much, but he doesn't forget the door to his cage."

"It was not my intention to imply ignorance."

Max calmed himself. "Hey, forget it. I'm just a little on edge, you know? When you're whacking through multiple realities like a hockey puck on a breakaway, it tends to make you a little jumpy."

"I know."

"No you don't. Nobody knows but me." Standing beneath the ominous arch, waiting for it to crackle to unsettling life, he somehow managed to smile and sing softly at the same time. "Nobody knows the parallelities I've seen, nobody knows but Jesus." He swallowed. "I wonder how many para messiahs there are? One for each Rapture?"

Boles didn't comment. He was too busy throwing switches.

Rapidly, the room came to life. Max remembered the colorful lights, the actinic flashes, and how he thought they would add spice to his story. He laughed bitterly, privately. Some story.

"What I've done," Boles was saying, "is recalibrate the oscillating input to the paradigm generator in order to . . ."

"Save it," Max snapped. "Do what you have to do. Fry me, toast me, burn all the hair off my head if you want—but get rid of this goddamn field that's stuck to me like a leech. Free me, Barrington. Let me live a normal life again. That's all I'm asking."

"That's what I'm trying to do." Peering over the crest of the console, Boles's hands hung poised above unseen controls. "You sure you're ready for this?"

Waiting beneath the soaring, intricately cabled arch, Max turned to face the inventor. "Barry, after what I've been through the past couple of days, I'm ready for Armageddon itself." He was silent a moment, then added hastily, "Provided it's the appropriate one, and not a para Armageddon, of course."

Boles did not reply, but his hands dropped. Something hummed loudly enough to lead Max to believe that he could feel the individual molecules of air in which he was enveloped begin to vibrate. He waited for his teeth to start to chatter, for his head to become light, for a sense of unease and nausea to slip over him.

He felt nothing. A mild sense of well-being left him feeling as if he had just downed a nice glass of chardonnay. He tried to remember what it had felt like before, the first time he had occupied the experimental position of honor in Barrington Boles's folly, but found he could not. He had been too preoccupied back then, too involved with the ramifications of a potential story to reflect on the possibility that the damn thing might actually do something, much less work.

His hair did not stand on end, he was not compelled to

utter any nonverbal vocal commentary, and the hoary-haired shade of Elsa Lanchester was not waiting to greet him when Boles finally shut the machine down.

Max took a deep breath and stepped out from beneath the arch. The meaningful glow of lights and telltales was fading around him, powering down, as if Dad had just switched off the Christmas tree. Santa was nowhere in sight.

He felt no different. The underground chamber, so fraught with vaguely unsettling suggestions of amateur science run amok, looked no different. Boles himself, gazing anxiously across from behind the cobbled-together console, was his same composed, engaging, country-club-cum-hippie self.

"Well?" the would-be inverter of universes finally asked after Max had just stood there for several moments.

The left corner of the reporter's mouth curled upward. "It was good for me. Was it good for you?" He took a couple of hesitant steps toward his host. "I hardly felt a thing. You sure it was on?"

Boles nodded. "Everything was working, if that's what you mean. Whether it worked as it was supposed to remains to be seen. I don't feel any different myself." He gestured around him. "How about your surroundings? Does anything look any altered to you? Modified, shifted, unnatural?"

"This whole dump looks unnatural, if that's what you're getting at. By which I guess I'm saying that it looks the same. So do you. Believe me, I was ready for anything. For this place to turn into a pit of fire and brimstone and you to grow horns and a tail." His gaze narrowed. "Come to think of it, I don't know that I ever really noticed the resemblance before."

"How droll. I'm hardly an evil person, Max. Only one who is interested in pushing back the boundaries of knowledge."

Max started for the stairs. "From now on you can use somebody else's life to push with. I'm resigning as chief boundaries pusher, as of now. Provided you've put everything back the way it was meant to be, of course. Cured the ether, as it was."

"You're sure you feel all right?" A concerned Boles trailed his guest closely, watching his every move.

"I won't be all right until I wake up in my own bed, in my own apartment, without any multiplied paras offering me orange juice or alien creatures crawling through my closet. I won't be all right until I spend a whole day under a brown smoggy sky, working with friends who look like themselves instead of like me, eating food that lies as peacefully on my plate as it does in my stomach." He looked unblinkingly back at the scientist. "Then, and only then, will I be all right."

"You're bitter." Boles followed the other man up the stairs. "You should be proud. You're a pioneer of instability, Max. A voyager on the farthest fringes of theoretical physics. A trailblazer in the realm of the possible."

"I'd rather do the Pirates of the Caribbean, thanks. And as far as instability is concerned, I'll take the occasional earthquake." At the top of the stairs he opened the heavy door and stepped through.

The rest of Boles's house looked the same, as did the world

outside. Still, he refused to accept what he saw as so. Reality had played him false before. Among all men only he, and to a certain extent Boles, knew how it could twist and knot and contort and flow like bad karma. In the whole history of humankind only he, Max Parker, knew for a certainty that the cosmos was actually composed of silly putty.

It made him perception-shy. What you saw, he knew, was not always what you got. But the silvered sheen of the nearby Pacific, the intermittent overflight of patrolling gulls, the calm atmosphere within the great house, were encouraging if not yet entirely reassuring.

"How do we know?" he asked Boles as he stared out the sweeping picture window at the lazy, hazy Southern California panorama. "How can I be sure that you've put everything right, that I'm back where I belong not just for a few minutes but permanently?"

"The field distortion isn't like malaria," Boles assured him. "Either you're stuck with it, or you're not. It's present, or it's absent. And if the calculations were correct and I did my job right, it's gone. Permanently. You should be back, Max. You should be home. But there's only one person in the universe who can know that for a certitude, and that's you." The inventor was uncharacteristically subdued, his tone solemn.

Max turned to face him. "And how am I supposed to know that? I want to hear what you're telling me, Barrington. I want to believe. Christ, but I want to believe! But I've been ambushed too many times these past few days. I'm reality-shy."

"Go home," Boles advised him. "Go back to work. Go to a movie, have some popcorn, lose yourself in another kind of unreality. I've done all that I can. I can't even tell you for absolute certain if I'm the Barrington Boles you needed to find to help you. I hope I am." By way of farewell he offered up one final, engaging, aging-beach-boy smile. "I'm truly sorry for all the trouble. Until I can find a way to moderate and control the field a good deal better I don't think I'll be playing at parallel-worlding for quite some time."

Max agreed, readily and vigorously. "At least next time try to give the poor schmuck you stick under the wedding arch some idea of what he's letting himself in for."

"How could I do that?" Boles followed him to the front door. "I don't have any idea. You're the only one with any real notion of what slipping between parallelities means. You're the only one who's done it, Max. Only you and I and a few dreaming mathematicians know that there's a great deal more to the cosmos than there appears to be, and only you know it firsthand." Standing to one side, he held the door open for his guest. Beyond, lotus land beckoned.

"Write it down, Max. Write it all down. Not as some snide tabloid story but in the form of a journal. Record everything you experienced while you were living within the field. You owe it to science, and to mankind, and to future generations of quantum mechanics."

"Forget it." Max's position was unshakable. "I don't even want to think about it, much less relive it. If you did your job and I'm well and truly back where I belong, then the last thing I want to do is spend time rehashing the nightmare."

"I'll pay you."

"Deal. As soon as I've got my life back in order, and I'm sure that it's my life I've got back, I'll send you a contract. Standard exclusive North American rights work-for-hire."

His smile widening, Boles followed him outside. "Whatever you're comfortable with, Max, but this won't be for publication. Not for the foreseeable future, anyway. It'll just be between me and you. Like everything else that's happened."

Max shrugged as he climbed back into his car. "Suit yourself. You pay for the words, the words are yours." He pulled the door shut.

"You may want these particular words back someday," Boles called out to him.

"Not these words!" Max shouted back through the window.

He could see Boles in the rearview mirror, standing in the circular drive, watching as his guinea-pig guest departed. With luck, the reporter thought, it would be the last time he would ever have to set eyes on the brilliant but undisciplined Barrington Boles. The man, his inventions, and his scattershot intentions would be out of his life forever.

The drive back down the coast looked, felt, and smelled normal. The Golden Horde had left no evidence of its passing. Death and destruction had been replaced by thriving chaparral and elaborate landscaping. Crows and buzzards glided effortlessly through the sky, no longer in competition with rejuvenated condors. He found that of all the parallelities he had encountered, the only one he missed was the majestic sight of the soaring raptors over the coastal mountains.

Seeking surcease in normalcy, he grew more and more hopeful the nearer he drew to the city. Maybe this really was it. Maybe Boles, for a change, had known what he was doing.

Certainly nothing appeared abnormal or out of place as he approached Santa Monica. Even the friendly bum was still lying in his flower bed, ready to greet him as he neared the garage. *Have to slip the sorry old son of a bitch a twenty*, a grateful Max thought.

For the first time in recent memory, his apartment felt like home again. His big TV and stereo were still missing, but at this point he would have been delighted to see even the burglar again—provided he came skulking in by himself and not in the company of compatible doubles or triples, of course.

When he called in to the office and tendered an excuse for his extended absence that sounded lame even to himself, Kryzewski responded by heaping on him a wonderfully scurrilous assortment of calumny. Max positively reveled in the choice collection of expletives. Not only was he truly back home, but his work environment promised to be exactly as he had last left it—frantic, frenetic, grudgingly appreciative, and fondly abusive.

At long last able to relax, he luxuriated in the performance of simple, basic daily activities. He made coffee. He warmed a cheese Danish in the microwave. He ate, and listened to the all-news channel on the radio, and watched people—ordinary, out-of-shape, happy Angeleno-type people—enjoy the beach and the polluted bay.

Home he was, and so being, he could finally take time to reflect. For such memories Boles would have paid him, and paid him well, but they were his memories, Max told himself. His nightmares. He had suffered them, survived them, and if he desired to keep them private, then by God they would remain his and his alone.

Parallelities, he mused as he watched the day's quotient of surfers illegally shoot the pilings of the main pier. Parallel worlds, parallel people, parallel ghosts. He found that he was able to smile. *Parallel mes. What an unstable soup we exist in, tiny motes bobbing back and forth convinced that our universe is a stable, knowable place.* With reality offering so many options, how to tell what was your world and what not? No one knew otherwise except himself, and to a certain extent Barrington Boles, and perhaps the occasional insightful madman.

He felt no nostalgia for any of the paras he had visited, not even for the true Utopian vision-version of Los Angeles. That was somebody else's para, not his. He would take the smog, and street crime, and burglaries, and bad television, and banal popular music, and inept politicians—take the whole uneven, irrational, imperfect mishmash of a world, and be happy in it. Because it was *his*.

Let the other Max Parkers be as happy as they could be in

their own para worlds, he thought. Leave him just this one and he would from now on forever be content with his lot. In another para he might be a Nobel Prize winner, or a movie star, or a president, or even a character in another writer's para tale of para worlds. No need for any of that for him.

Holding the coffee in one hand, he walked over to the window and looked out at the brightly lit panorama visible from his apartment. Sea, sky, beach, the children cavorting on the sand, the trim and tanned volleyball players battling at the net—all was as it should be. He was home at last.

A small mirror hung over the sink and he turned to it, noting with confidence that he, too, looked exactly as he should, from tousled hair to contented smile. Through grease splatters and water stains his reflection smiled back. Then it frowned uncertainly.

The only trouble was, he was still smiling.

**Read on for a special sneak preview of Alan
Dean Foster's forthcoming hardcover
chronicling the birth of the Commonwealth . . .
coming to a bookstore near you in
Summer 1999!**

Dozens of invited guests were arrayed in the traditional circle
in the garden where Wuuzelansem was to be recycled. The cere-
mony had already gone on too long. Much longer than the humble
dead poet would have liked. Had he been able to, Des reflected
amusedly, the master would long since have excused himself from
his own sepulture.

Wandering through the crowd as the sonorous liturgy wound
down, Des was surprised to espy Broudwelunced and Niowinhomek, two former colleagues. Both had gone on to successful
careers, Broud in government and Nio with the military, which
was always in need of energetic, invigorating poets. Des wa-
vered, his habitual penchant for privacy finally giving way to the
inherent thranx proclivity for the company of others. Wandering
over, he was privately pleased to find that they both recognized
him immediately.

"Des!" Niowinhomek bent forward and practically wrapped
her antennae around his. The shock of familiarity was more
soothing than Des would have cared to admit.

"A shame, this." Broud gestured with a foothand in the direction of the dais. "He will be missed."

" 'Rolling toward land, the wave ponds on the beach and con-
templates its fate. Evaporation become destruction.' " Nio was
quoting from the master's fourth collection, Des knew. His friends
might have been surprised to know that the brooding, apparently
indifferent Desvendapur could recite by rote everything Wuuzelansem had ever composed, including the extensive, famously
uncompleted Jorkk fragments. But he was not in the mood.

"But what of you, Des?" As he spoke, Broud's truhands
bobbed in a manner designed to indicate friendliness that bordered on affection. Why this should be so Des could not imagine.
While attending class he had been no more considerate of his
fellow students' feelings than anyone else's. It puzzled and even
unnerved him a little.

"Not mated, are you?" Nio observed. "I have plans to be, within the six-month."

"No," Desvendapur replied. "I am not mated." Who would want to mate with me? he mused. An unremarkable poet languishing in an undistinguished job leading a life of untrammeled conventionality.

"I don't think it's such a shame," he went on. "He had a notable career, he left behind a few stanzas that may well outlast him, and now he no longer is faced with the daily agony of having always to be original. It was good to see you both again." Dropping his foothands to the ground to return to a six-legged stance, he started to turn to go. The initial delight he had felt at once again encountering old friends was already wearing off.

"Wait!" Niowinhomek restrained him with a dip and weave of both antennae—though why she should want to he could not imagine. Most females found his presence irksome. Even his pheromones were deficient, he was convinced. Searching for a source of conversation that might hold him, she remembered one recently discussed at work. "What do you think about the rumors?"

Turning back, he gestured to indicate a lack of comprehension. Suddenly he wanted only to get away, to flee, from memories as much as from former friends. "What rumors?"

"The stories from the Geswixt," she persisted. "The hearsay."

"Chrrk, that!" Broud chimed in with an exclamatory stridulation. "You're talking about the new Project, aren't you?"

"New Project?" Only indifferently interested, Des's irritation nevertheless deepened. "What new Project?"

"You haven't heard." Nio's antennae whipped and weaved, suggesting restrained excitement. "No, living this far from Geswixt I see that it's possible you wouldn't." Stepping closer, she lowered her voice. Des almost backed away. What sort of nonsense was this?

"You can't get near the place," she whispered, her four mouthparts moving supplely against one another. "The whole area is fenced off."

"That's right." With a truhand and opposing foothand Broud confirmed her avowal. "With as little fanfare and announcement as possible, an entire district has been closed to casual travel. It's said that there are even regular aerial patrols to shut off the airspace. Right out to orbital."

Mildly intrigued, Des was moved to comment. "Sounds to me like somebody wants to hide something."

Using four hands and all sixteen digits, Nio insinuated agreement. "A new biochemical facility doing radical research. That's the official explanation. But some of us have been hearing other stories. Stories that, in the fourteen years they've been propagated, have become harder and harder to dismiss."

"I take it they don't have anything to do with biochemical research." Des desperately wanted to go, to flee surroundings become suddenly oppressive.

Broud implied concord but left it to his companion to continue with the explanation. "Maybe a little, but if so and if the stories are true then such research is peripheral to the central purpose of the Geswixt facility."

"Which is to do what?" Des inquired impatiently.

She glanced briefly at Broudwelunced before replying. "To watch over the aliens and nurture a growing relationship with them."

"Aliens?" Des was taken aback. This was not what he had expected. "What sort of aliens? The Quillp?" That race of tall, elegant, but enigmatic creatures who refused to ally themselves with either thranx or AAnn had long been known to the thranx. And there were others. But they were well and widely known to the general populace. Why should they be part of some mysterious, secretive "Project"?

"Not the Quillp," Nio was telling him. "Something even stranger." She edged closer, so that their antennae threatened to touch. "The intelligent mammals."

This time, Des had to pause before replying.

"You mean the humans? That's an absurd notion. That project was shifted in its entirety years ago to Hivehom, where the government could monitor it more closely. There are no humans left on Willow-Wane. No wonder it's the basis for rumor and speculation only."

Nio was clearly pleased at having taken the notoriously unflappable Desvendapur aback. "Bipedal, bisexual, tailless, alien mammals," she added for good measure. "Humans. The rumor has it that not only are they still around, they're being allowed to set up a colony. Right here on Willow-Wane. That's why the Council is keeping it quiet. That's why they were moved from the original Project site near Paszex to the isolated country around Geswixt."

He responded with a low whistle of incredulity. Mammals were small, furry creatures that flourished in deep rainforest. They were soft, fleshy, sometimes slimy things that wore their skeletons on the inside of their bodies. The idea that some might have developed intelligence was hardly to be credited. And bipedal? A biped without a tail to balance itself would be inherently unstable, a biomechanical impossibility. One might as well expect the delicate hizhoz to fly in space. But the humans were real enough. Reports on them appeared periodically. Formal contact was proceeding at a measured, studied pace, allowing each species ample time to get used to the notion of the fundamentally different other.

All such contact was still ceremonial and restricted, officially limited to one Project facility on Hivehom and a humanoid counterpart on Centaurus Five. The idea that a race as bizarre as the humans might be granted permission to establish permanent habitation on a thranx world was outlandish. Des said as much to his friends.

Nio refused to be dissuaded. "Nevertheless, that is what the rumors say."

"Which is why they are rumors, and why stories imaginative travelers tell so often differ from the truth." For the second time he started to turn away. "It was good to see you both."

"Des," Nio began, "I—we both have thought about you often, and wondered if, well—if there is ever anything either of us can do for you, if you ever need any help of any kind . . ."

Des stopped, turning so suddenly that Nio's antennae flicked back over her head, out of potential harm's way. It was an ancient reflex, one she was unable to arrest.

Preparing to leave, Des had been struck by a thought pregnant with possibility. Tentative, restricted contacts between humankind and the thranx had been taking place for a number of years now. There were not supposed to be any humans on his world. Not since the Project, begun on Willow-Wane, had been shifted to Hivehom. But—what if it were true? What if such outrageous, fantastic creatures were engaged in building, not a simple research station, but an actual colony right here, on one of the thranx's own colony worlds? The promise, just possibly, of the inspiration his muse and life had thus far been lacking?

"Broud," he said sharply, "you work for the government."

"Yes." The other young male wondered what had happened to

313

transform his former colleague's manner so dramatically. "I am a third-level soother for a communications processing division."

"Near this Geswixt. Excellent." Desvendapur's thoughts were churning. "You just offered me help. I accept." Now it was his turn to lean forward, as the members of the commemorative funeral crowd began to disperse. "I am experiencing a sudden desire to change my living circumstances and go to work on a different part of the planet. You will recommend me to your superiors, in your best High Thranx, for work in the Geswixt area."

"You ascribe to me powers I don't possess," his age-counterpart replied. "Firstly, I don't live as near this Geswixt as you seem to think. Neither does Nio." He glanced at the female for support and she gestured encouragingly. "Rumors may alert and influence, but they weigh little and travel easily. Also, as I told you, I am only a third-level soother. Any recommendations I might make will be treated by my superiors with less than immediate attention." Antennae dipped curiously forward. "Why do you want to uproot your life, shift tunnels, and move nearer Geswixt?"

"Uproot my life? I am unmated, and you know how little family remains to me."

His friends shifted uncomfortably. Broud was beginning to wish Des had never come over to talk with them. They should have ignored him. But Nio had insisted. It was too late now. To simply turn away and leave would have been an unforgivable breach of courtesy.

"As for the reason, I should think that's obvious," Des continued. "I want to be nearer to these bizarre aliens—if there is any basis to these rumors and if there actually are any still living on Willow-Wane."

Nio was watching him uneasily. "What for, Des?"

"So I can compose about them."